The Colour of Death

Warwickshire County Council

7·11·13			
26·11·13			
7·12·13			
29·4·14			
BED 1/17·			
30/4/21			

This item is to be returned or renewed before the latest date above. It may be borrowed for a further period if not in demand. **To renew your books:**

- **Phone the 24/7 Renewal Line 01926 499273 or**
- **Visit www.warwickshire.gov.uk/libraries**

Discover • Imagine • Learn • *with libraries*

Warwickshire County Council

Working for Warwickshire

The Colour of Death

Frances Lloyd

ROBERT HALE · LONDON

ISBN 978-0-7090-9283-4

Robert Hale Limited
Clerkenwell House
Clerkenwell Green
London EC1R 0HT

www.halebooks.com

2 4 6 8 10 9 7 5 3 1

Typeset in 10.25/13.25pt Sabon
Printed by the MPG Books Group in the UK

AUTHOR'S NOTE

Shetland is rich in the wild, dramatic beauty of her rugged islands, but the setting for this novel, Doomdochry, off the north coast of Unst, will not be found among them. The haunted castle, the appalling events which took place there and all the characters in the story, living or dead, are entirely fictitious, existing only in that psychological bomb-site, the imagination of the crime novelist.

Frances Lloyd

PROLOGUE

DOOMDOCHRY CASTLE – SHETLAND
DECEMBER 1490

Her small, pale hands ceased their hopeless clawing as his cruel grip squeezed the last breath from her throat. And thus the foul deed was done. In a frenzy of jealous rage, Alistair MacAlister, Earl of Doomdochry, had strangled his beautiful young wife. Slowly, he released his grasp and watched in horror as her lifeless body slid to the ground, her bright green skirts spread upon the snow like a patch of new spring grass.

The Earl had followed Lady Jean to an avenue beyond the castle where she was accustomed to take her afternoon walk. Unable to trust her, he was certain that this was the trysting place where she met her lover. He had no proof of her infidelity, just a burning, intolerable suspicion made stronger by her piteous denials. She had proclaimed her innocence even as she drew her last breath. Now her eyes, once emerald green and smiling, stared up at him in sorrow and bewilderment and in that dreadful moment, his boiling fury turned to panic. Lady Jean's family was rich and powerful; her dowry had been substantial. Under the certainty of heaven, they would call him to answer with his life for this evil deed. Her body must be hidden where it would never be found. He glanced furtively about him then swiftly gathered up his wife's limp corpse concealed beneath her velvet cloak, and hastened back to the castle.

The tower bedchamber had been in ruins since a bloody clan battle destroyed the roof and part of one wall, rendering the room unsafe and exposed to the elements. Now, no one in the castle ventured there. The very place, thought MacAlister, where Lady Jean's body might remain undiscovered for all time. The rotting floorboards came up with ease

7

but the space beneath proved full of stones and rubble with room only for the top half of the corpse. The Earl was desperate. Unable to endure the silent reproach in her sad, unseeing eyes, he drew the heavy broadsword intended for the slaying of his wife's lover, and with one stroke, cleaved her body in two.

Late that night, under cover of darkness, MacAlister bore the gruesome bundle containing his wife's lower half, still clad in her green, gore-spattered skirts, to the family burial ground. He prayed silently as he dug, forming no words. Lady Jean had died unshriven. What if she had, indeed, been blameless, as she claimed? Could he have misinterpreted innocent actions? As a wife, she had given her love freely and looked for nothing in return. How could he explain her sudden absence without deadly retribution? As long as her body remained hidden, he could claim that she had run off with her lover, violating the blessed sanctity of her marriage vows. To men who would pass judgement, he would represent himself as the victim; a cuckolded husband abandoned by a faithless wife and charged with rearing their wee, motherless son alone.

And thus it was. But still he lived in terror for he knew that in God's hands, vengeance was certain. However long delayed, however strangely manifested, the reckoning was sure to come.

CHAPTER ONE

DOOMDOCHRY CASTLE – SHETLAND
MIDNIGHT, DECEMBER 10th, 2010

Doomdochry Castle rose up six storeys high, stark and menacing against the night sky. It was a gaunt monstrosity of a building, set on an isolated outcrop above the waves of a savage Shetland coastline. A harsh December wind gusted around its battlements and moaned in and out of the arrow-slit windows. The massive keep, stained by the nests of seabirds, was the tallest of six great square towers, its stone crenellations blackened and crumbling like rows of decaying teeth. On the wall-walk behind the parapet, two figures struggled in the moonlight.

The girl screamed and clawed at the man's face with small, helpless hands. He grabbed her roughly and yanked up the sleeve of her tunic, exposing her skinny, white arm. Despite her pitiful pleading, he neither felt nor showed compassion. She was a pathetic bag of bones: a flimsy creature who drifted naively through life in a trance-like state, but not for much longer. She had become a nuisance, a liability, and therefore, she had to be eliminated. He pulled off the braided leather belt encircling her waist and twisted it tightly around her arm to bring up a vein. Then he jabbed the needle into the crook of her elbow and drove home the plunger.

Slowly, her pale face became flushed and her breathing, laboured. For some moments, he held her fast as the huge dose of heroin took effect. Then he released his grasp and watched impassively as her limp body slumped to the stone floor. Casually, he lit a cigarette and stared out into the cold, black night. Every twenty seconds, two bursts of white light from the Muckle Flugga lighthouse bounced off the distant waters of the murky Burra Firth. Snow started to fall again, seeping through his jacket and chilling his bones. He shivered and took a long swig of whisky from his hip flask. What a bloody awful place! Stubbing out his cigarette on the castle wall, he put the dog-end carefully in his pocket then bent to feel for the girl's pulse. Surprisingly, he found one, albeit very weak. She was stronger than she looked and he couldn't afford to take a chance. He leaned over the crumbling parapet; it was a drop of over eighty feet to the ground. How easy it would be for a silly young girl to sneak up here for a fix and misjudge the dose in the dark. And it was entirely believable that she might then lose consciousness and overbalance. He took the syringe, wiped it on his handkerchief and carefully wrapped the girl's fingers around it. Then he slipped it into the pocket of her tunic, replaced the belt and wrapped her woollen shawl around her. Effortlessly, he lifted her in his arms and held her over the edge of the parapet. Suddenly, her eyes snapped open, emerald green and beseeching. For a heartbeat he suspended her there; then he smiled.

'Goodbye, Astrid.' He watched her plummet into the pitch-black void.

Snow muffled the thud as she hit the ground, her neck and most of her bones shattered. Her bright green shawl fluttered down after her and spread upon the snow like a patch of new spring grass.

CHAPTER TWO

The woman on the bed wore a peephole bra and sex-shop knickers that barely covered her dark bush of pubic hair. Lacy suspenders held up black, fishnet stockings. She lay on her back, empty eyes staring at the ceiling, arms and legs flung sideways. Blood oozed from a deep gash across her throat and congealed in her bottle-blonde hair, now matted and sticky. On the bedside table, a red lamp, spattered with vomit, cast a warm glow over the blood-soaked sheets.

Detective Sergeant 'Bugsy' Malone of Scotland Yard's Murder Investigation Team was no stranger to violent death but his stomach churned. It was the sickly, slaughterhouse smell more than anything. He stuffed his half-eaten bacon roll into the pocket of his grubby over-coat and flattened himself against the wall as the SOCO officers surged in. They flocked around the body, picking it over like a convergence of white-coated vultures. There was nothing more Malone could do till his boss arrived, so he decided to leave the team to their grisly task and go outside for a breath of fresh nicotine.

The lift that served the tower block stank like a urinal. For the second time that day, Malone tried to hold his breath while it juddered down twenty floors to the ground. Outside in the clean air of a frosty December afternoon, the snow was just beginning to fall. He turned up his collar, lit a fag and inhaled deeply, watching the traffic streaming around the gyratory system. The old Elephant was changing, like a lot of South London. He had silently applauded when they started to demolish the grim, tower block estates. Tenants were being re-housed in swanky modern flats with burglar alarms and CCTV. Years ago, he'd pounded the beat here as a rookie constable. The job was simple back then: he nicked the crooks who broke the law. He helped to keep the streets clean and safe and was bloody proud to do it. That was all in the bad old days, though, before he learned that counselling was the answer when some toe-rag punched you in the face and that the real solution to crime on the streets was a lecture in sociology. Well, that kind of thinking hadn't done much to protect the poor cow in the flat upstairs, had it? When they caught the bastard who did it, the courts would probably fine him ten quid and make him pick up litter for a week. Sometimes he felt he was banging his head against a brick wall of human rights that stopped coppers from putting any bugger at all behind bars. Behind him, Detective Inspector Jack Dawes's voice cut short his pondering.

'Perfect weather for a murder, Bugsy. What have we got?'

Malone spun on his heel and pinched out his half-smoked cigarette. 'Afternoon, guv. It's a tom with her throat cut. Very nasty.'

Dawes shivered. 'Aren't they all? Who found her?'

'Dunno. It was an anonymous tip off. Someone called 999 from that telephone box on the corner to report a dead body in the top-floor flat then hung up.' He jabbed a thumb towards the kiosk where a SOCO lady was flicking over the receiver with her fingerprint brush, more in hope than expectation. There were enough prints to keep her busy for months. 'When the area car got here a few minutes later, the door to the flat was wide open. Now here's the interesting bit. Guess who they found in the bedroom, standing over the body with a whacking great knife in his grimy little mitt?'

'Surprise me.'

'Lenny Lennox.'

'Not Lenny *I-know-my-rights* Lennox?'

'The very same. He was white as a sheet and he'd spewed up all over the bedside lamp.'

'Where is he now?'

'In a cell down the nick, waiting to be questioned. I arrested him on suspicion and a couple of uniform lads took him away in handcuffs. I can't see him topping a tom, though, can you? Pinching her handbag maybe, but not slitting her throat. It's not his style.'

'So what was he doing there?'

'Bugger only knows. He was gibbering when we lifted him.'

'OK. We'll leave him to calm down and question him in the morning. Let's go take a look at the body.'

This was harder than it sounded: the ancient lift, protesting at its unaccustomed workload – firstly carrying a posse of policemen, then the SOCO team and their equipment – had demonstrated its indignation by breaking down. Fortunately, there was no one in it at the time. According to the constable guarding the doors, the contract engineers had been called, but they were already fixing the lift in an office block on the other side of town so they might be some time. The stairs were filthy; flaking walls covered in obscene graffiti and a stench even worse than the lift. By the time the two detectives reached the tenth floor, they were wheezing and clinging to the handrail for support.

'What do we know about the victim?' gasped Dawes, glad of a rest.

Lungs burning, Malone reached into his pocket for his notebook. 'Her name's Karen Baxter, a.k.a. Angel. She was what they call a sex worker in modern lingo. Angel's her professional name. Neighbours suspected she was on the game but said she was pleasant and discreet so nobody complained. Mind you, most of them are probably up to something naughty so they wouldn't want the police sniffing around.'

'Any form?'

'Not for soliciting. We gave her a tug a while back for smoking a joint in one of the local clubs, but she was let off with a caution because she didn't have enough gear on her to be dealing.' Bugsy trousered his notebook. 'Big Ron's here and SOCO are all over the scene like a rash.'

'Right. Let's get up there while there's still something left to see.' Jack started to climb again, stepping wide to avoid the places where residents had either urinated, vomited or both. He braced himself for a sight that threatened to be even more repugnant.

Doctor Veronica Hardacre, a pathologist of some distinction, bent over the bed and gently probed the gaping wound across the dead woman's throat with a podgy, latex-clad forefinger. Known as 'Big Ron' behind her back, Dr Hardacre was a formidable figure, strong and muscular with bristling black eyebrows and a moustache to match. She greeted the arrival of DI Dawes with a tepid smile and the caustic sarcasm she reserved for all policemen.

'Good afternoon, Inspector Dawes. Good of you to join us. I trust we haven't interrupted anything important, like your tea. Is the lift working? No, I can tell from Sergeant Malone's advanced state of dyspnoea that it is not.'

'Afternoon, Doctor.' Jack liked Big Ron. She was the best in the business, knowledgeable, meticulous and an absolute virago as an expert witness in court. He had watched her run circles around some smart-arse defence lawyer who thought he could get a vicious criminal acquitted by discrediting the pathologist's evidence. 'Nice to see you, too. Pity we only meet over a body. What do we know about this one?'

'She's dead.' Big Ron measured the wound then directed the SOCO photographer to take close-ups from various angles. She returned to Jack. 'It was a clean slash to the throat from right to left. Death occurred less than an hour ago. I can't tell you a great deal more until after the post mortem.'

'Could it have been suicide?'

'Unlikely,' she said, cautiously. 'A right-handed person would logically slash from left to right; also, there's only one wound. Suicides very often make some initial, tentative cuts before the fatal one. And she has extensive defence injuries so she knew what was coming and fought back. My guess is that your murderer knelt on her chest, grabbed her hair in his left hand to hold her head still, then … zip!' She made a slashing motion. 'He slit her throat with a large, very sharp knife held in his right hand; almost certainly the one the police found when they arrived at the scene but I'll let you know for certain after forensics have finished with it. If you look closely, you can see small areas of her scalp where the hair was torn out as she struggled.' Dr Hardacre pointed to some red spatters staining the floral wallpaper. 'And considerable amounts of blood spurted from the wound and splashed up the wall.'

'And on the killer?' suggested Malone. When they found Lenny Lennox, he had very little blood on him; just his hand from the knife he was holding and his tatty trainers, where he'd slipped in a puddle of it.

'The killer would have been smothered in gore,' affirmed Big Ron. 'Certainly on his right arm and probably all over his chest and face as well.'

'There's blood in the bathroom waste-pipe,' offered a helpful chap from Forensics, 'so he probably washed it off before he left.'

'Yeah but what about his clothes?' asked Bugsy. 'He couldn't go out still wearing them, they'd have been covered in blood.'

'Not if he took them off before he killed her.' Jack's eyes travelled round the room taking in the pile of adult magazines and DVDs, a cardboard carton labelled "50 ribbed condoms – assorted colours" and inside the open wardrobe, a variety of bizarre outfits. All the obvious trappings of a tart's profession. Maybe it was simply a bit of "business" that went badly wrong. 'Any indications of a violent sexual assault, Doctor?'

'I'll know more about that after the autopsy but there are no obvious signs of forced penetration and she's still wearing her knickers, such as they are. Rapists don't normally stop to put them back on the victim afterwards. Obviously I expect to find evidence of frequent sexual activity; it was her job. Prostitution is a risky occupation at the best of times, but no young woman deserves to end up like this. Make sure you get the bastard, Inspector.'

'How d'you know she was right-handed, Doc?' Bugsy asked.

Dr Hardacre gave him a withering look. 'You're the detective, Sergeant Malone. Observe the clues. The bedside table, with alarm clock, tissue box and table lamp, are on the right side of the bed. If you check the hand basin in the bathroom, her toothbrush, soap and other washing paraphernalia are also on the right. And the muscles in her right arm are more developed than her left.'

It was dark by the time they'd finished and the engineers had got the lift working again. The mortuary men had taken the body away and most of the blood-stained items had been removed, but the abattoir smell still lingered. Outside, a uniformed copper stamping his feet against the cold, guarded the crime scene. Snow fell steadily in big flakes and by morning, everything would be covered in a festive blanket of white and traffic would grind to a halt because, although it was nearly Christmas and bitterly cold, snow always took everyone by surprise.

On the way to their cars, Jack and Bugsy shared what they knew so far, or more accurately what they didn't know. That particular block of flats was next on the demolition programme so no CCTV. Enquiries of neighbours had revealed nothing helpful about Karen Baxter. Nobody saw anything; nobody heard anything. There was no sign of a forced entry so whoever it was either had a key or she let him in. The carving knife, honed to a razor's edge, had come from a set in the kitchen. It was doubtful whether forensics would produce any real clues to the killer's identity; it was, after all, a prostitute's workplace and no doubt crawling with the fingerprints, DNA and unsavoury detritus of a succession of men, any one of whom could be the murderer. Their only real lead was Lenny Lennox.

CHAPTER THREE

DECEMBER 13TH

It was barely 9 a.m. and already, the stuffy interview room reeked of fried onions and stale sweat. The onion smell came from Malone's greasy hot dog; the sweat oozed from Lenny Lennox, who was in the hot seat and had been for the last two hours. Malone swallowed the last of his breakfast and wiped ketchup off his mouth with the end of his tie.

'Come on, Lenny. You don't want to be a smelly, insignificant little arsehole all your life, do you? I expect you've got a perfectly plausible explanation for being in that dead tart's bedroom with the murder weapon in your hand. Why don't you share it with us? It must be at least a week since we listened to a load of old bollocks from a suspect. Isn't that right, Inspector?'

'Right, Sergeant.' DI Dawes, clean-shaven and immaculate despite having been on duty since 6 a.m., studied Lennox's file without glancing up. Lenny had more form than a Derby winner; burglary, petty theft, possession of stolen goods, even dipping pockets when times were hard, but never violence.

'Oi!' Lennox wagged a grimy forefinger under Jack's nose to get his attention. 'You going to just sit there and let 'im speak to me like that? I know my rights. You 'ave to give me a cup o' tea, some breakfast and access to the duty solicitor.' He sat back in his chair and crossed his arms with as much bravado as he could muster. Lenny knew the drill all right. An underweight, pasty-faced little man in his late forties, he'd spent nearly half his life in prison. Whatever crime he committed, he nearly always got caught. He'd even been sent down for jobs he hadn't done but, philosophically he regarded it as one of the more unfortunate consequences of his profession. Right now, though, he was scared. He'd never been nicked for anything as heavy as murder and it was looking bad. He licked his lips nervously. 'I've told you all I'm going to. I ain't saying nothing else till I get a brief.'

They'd taken Lenny's clothes and blood-stained trainers away for forensic examination and given him a disposable coverall. His shifty little eyes peered out from inside the hood like a malevolent goblin. The dirty clothes may have gone, but the filth embedded in his skin and under his fingernails was permanent, as was the stink.

Malone leant downwind, balancing his chair on two legs, a precarious exercise for a man of his proportions. Over the years, his predilection for fast food and beer had increased his girth to an impressive, if unhealthy, rotundity.

'Lenny, you've told us sod all, so far. Do yourself a favour and come clean.' He wrinkled his nose. 'It'll make a nice change. Why did you knife that prostitute?'

Lenny appealed to Jack. 'How many more times, Mr Dawes? I never touched her, straight up. I'd never harm Angel. She was good to me. Gave me a hot meal and somewhere to sleep when I was down on me luck. Why would I want to kill her?'

'Maybe you were after a freebie and she didn't fancy it,' said Bugsy. 'So when you couldn't stick your dick into her, you stuck a knife in her throat instead, to teach her a lesson.'

Lennox sighed. 'For Gawd's sake, Mr Malone, I 'aven't been able to get it up since I started drinking cheap booze for breakfast. And I could never slit anyone's throat. All that blood.' He shuddered. 'Made me spew.'

Jack leaned towards him. 'OK Lenny, let's suppose we're feeling generous and we believe you. Tell us what you were doing in her flat.'

'She asked me to go there,' he said in desperation. 'She phoned Honest Harry Hoxton, the bookie, where I was 'aving my usual flutter and said she needed to see me, urgent.'

'Haven't you got a mobile?' asked Malone.

Lenny scowled, witheringly. 'Yeah, I left it in the glove box of me Ferrari, didn't I?'

'OK so how did she know where to find you?'

'She knows … I mean, she knew because I'm always in the bookie's at that time of day. You can check with Harry, he took the message.'

'Oh, we will, Lenny, you can bet on it. So what happened when you got to her flat?'

'Nothin'. The door was wide open so I went in, calling out her name. Then I saw her on the bed, covered in blood with her throat … well, you saw her, Mr Dawes, it was 'orrible.'

Malone eyeballed him. 'So if you didn't do it, how come you were holding the murder weapon when we found you? The lab boys say that the only fingerprints on it were yours. Come on, Lenny, it isn't looking good.'

Lennox was really rattled now, looking desperately from one inquisitor to the other. 'I don't know, do I? Whoever killed her must have wiped it or maybe he wore gloves. I saw the knife lying on the floor and I just picked it up without thinking, like you do. ' His mouth was dry and he licked his lips again. 'Can I 'ave a fag?'

Bugsy pointed to the "no smoking" sign and sighed heavily. 'We're wasting our time here, guv. He's not only a slimy sod, he's a lying bastard as well. Why don't we charge the little scrote with murder and have done with it?'

Lennox panicked then. In his experience, charges had a nasty habit of sticking whether he was guilty or not. 'No, wait a minute. What about a deal, Mr Dawes? I might know something useful.'

'Forget it, Lenny. I don't do deals with killers.'

'I keep telling you … I never killed no one! At least listen.'

'All right but make it quick.' Bugsy chucked him a fag and ignoring the no smoking sign, stuck one in his own mouth. Lenny took a long, grateful drag and blew out a stream of smoke.

'It was yesterday morning, about eleven. Angel was in the Blue Ray Club where I do a bit of cleaning and collecting glasses...'

'... and dipping the customers' wallets,' finished Bugsy, scathingly.

Lenny ignored him. 'She wasn't with a punter so I went across to blag a few quid off her; I had a dead cert in the three-thirty.'

'There's some point to all this I hope?' said Jack.

'Her mobile rang and she answered it. She listened for a bit then she suddenly started howling, tears running down her face. Then she turned all white and spiteful and got real pissed off with someone. I heard her say, "I'll get you for this, you bastard. I know you did it and I can prove it," then she switched off her phone, grabbed her coat and ran out.'

'Is that it?'

'It's enough, isn't it? She was real upset. That's why I went straight to her flat when she called. I thought she might be in trouble. Stands to reason whoever she was talking to got there first and shut her up. All you've got to do is find her phone, trace the caller and you've got your killer.'

'And you couldn't possibly guess who it might be?'

Lenny fidgeted uncomfortably. 'Have a heart, Mr Dawes. You know what it's like out there. Whether I guessed right or wrong, I'd still be a dead man. All I'm saying is, it weren't me. Can I go now?'

They put him back in his cell but it was obvious he wasn't going to tell them anything more, however much they leaned on him.

Jack stroked his chin thoughtfully. 'Big Ron says the killer's right handed. Which hand was Lenny holding the knife in when the uniform lads found him?'

'His left,' said Bugsy, already there. 'The same hand he used to catch the fag I chucked him.'

'Let him go.'

Because of the weather, DI Dawes delayed his initial briefing in the Incident Room until noon but, even so, it was sparsely attended. It had snowed steadily for nearly twenty-four hours and several of the Murder Investigation Team were still crawling into work through snarled up traffic. There were gruesome photographs on the white-board of the dead woman's body and surrounding areas soaked with blood. There was also a mug shot of Lenny Lennox looking typically guilty and scrofulous. Sergeant Malone gave them the information they had so far.

'OK, folks, we've got a dead tom, Karen Baxter alias Angel, aged around thirty-five. The post mortem carried out this morning by Dr Hardacre confirms that her throat was cut at approximately 2p.m. by a right-handed person using the carving knife from the kitchen. She died very soon after. No sign of a sexual assault or drugs in her system, but there were old tracks on her arms so she was a user at some time. The autopsy report showed that she'd given birth some years ago, but we didn't find any photos or evidence of a kid among her stuff so she probably put it into care or had it adopted. Defence wounds indicate the poor cow fought for her life but unfortunately, there was nothing useful like flesh under her fingernails or clumps of body hair in her teeth. They found shed-loads of DNA; on her body, the bed and all over the room. Forensics are sifting through it but don't hold your breath. Half the male population of South London have probably been there.'

Bugsy's stomach growled audibly. He pulled half a pork pie from his pocket, bit a large chunk out of it and chewed around the words. 'An anonymous caller reported finding her body at 2.15 and before you ask, the emergency switchboard operator couldn't be sure if the voice was male or female even after listening to the recording. At 2.25, our suspect, Lenny Lennox, was apprehended at the scene holding the bloody knife. Forensics found only one set of dabs on it ... his. He claims Angel phoned him at the bookmaker's across the road from her flat saying she needed to see him urgently. Now, pay attention to this bit. Harry Hoxton, the bookie, confirms that a woman called at 2.20 exactly. He remembers because the race at Kempton had just started. He gave Lennox the message and Lenny says he left straight away but she was dead when he got there.' Malone looked around the room. 'Any bright ideas?'

'If the carving knife belonged to the dead woman, why didn't it have her prints on it as well?' shouted someone at the back.

'And wouldn't Lennox have had more blood on his clothes if he'd cut her throat, Sarge?'

'Isn't it more likely that the killer was a dissatisfied customer?' asked a world-weary refugee from Vice. 'Maybe he'd paid her but she wouldn't do what he wanted and he lost his temper; there are some sick bastards out there.'

'Hang on a minute.' DC Julie Molesworth was one of the rising stars of MIT, bright and eager to impress. 'The 999 call reporting the murder was logged at 2.15, five minutes *before* Harry Hoxton got the alleged call from the victim at 2.20. Either someone got the times wrong or it wasn't Angel who phoned him; she was already dead.'

Malone looked at DI Dawes. 'What do you reckon, guv?'

'I reckon DC Molesworth just eliminated our only suspect, Sergeant. Not that I think Lennox was ever a credible candidate for murder; someone's deliberately put him in the frame. I've let him go because we've nothing solid to hold him on, although I believe he knows more than he's telling us.' The inspector uncrossed his long legs from where he was perched on the edge of a desk and strode to the front of the room. 'Nothing appears to have been stolen and there were plenty of things for a thief to nick, not least the five grand in 500 euro notes that we found under a pepperoni pizza in her freezer. But SOCO never found Angel's mobile phone so we must assume the killer took it with him to stop us checking her calls. We need a more comprehensive understanding of the dead woman. Does she have any family? Particularly a next of kin, who will need to be notified and who may know what happened to her child. Where did she spend her time when she wasn't working? Who were her close friends? Did she have any regulars with a record of ABH? She let the murderer in so she either knew him or was expecting him. And if we believe Lenny's story about the phone call she took the morning she was killed, she knew something about the caller that was dangerous enough to get her killed.'

Bugsy stood up. 'OK folks, you heard the Inspector. We need answers. Let's get off our arses and get cracking. The meter's running.'

CHAPTER FOUR

DECEMBER 15TH

In his lavish, oak-panelled office a few doors down from the Incident Room, Detective Chief Superintendent George Garwood put down the phone and rubbed his hands together gleefully. A suspicious death and a swine flu epidemic; two very fortuitous pieces of luck. Not so lucky for the unfortunate victims, of course, but it couldn't have come at a better time for Garwood. Next week, the Deputy Assistant Commissioner was due to pay his customary Christmas visit. Ostensibly, it was to wish his officers the compliments of the season and generally gee up the Command for another year. This time, however, Garwood needed to make a particularly dynamic impression, as he would be under the spotlight. There was a promotion exercise looming in the New Year and the DAC was on the board. This visit was by way of an unofficial appraisal of his leadership and organizational skills.

The Murder Investigation Team was one of the specialized homicide squads of the London Metropolitan Police Service and formed part of Scotland Yard's Serious Crime Group. The Commands were split geographically, each unit being led by a Detective Chief Superintendent. Once he had gained command of his unit, Garwood had taken pains to bring its success to the right people's attention. But for him, this job was only a springboard. The DCS was a career man, determined to rise to the top of his chosen profession. Garwood intended to become Assistant Commissioner. But one wrong move, one glimpse of him in a bad light, and his dream could be shattered. He had seen it happen to other senior policemen but it was not going to happen to him.

He settled himself comfortably on the throne-like chair behind his oversized, status symbol of a desk. At the other end of the room, there were two easy chairs and a coffee table where he would soon be entertaining the DAC with a dram or two of single malt and some mince pies obtained by his wife, Cynthia, from "Coriander's Cuisine". In fact, all their Christmas entertaining was catered for by this company, which co-incidentally was run by Corrie Dawes, Cynthia's old school chum and the wife of DI Jack Dawes.

Despite being his superior in rank, Garwood invariably felt Dawes had him at a disadvantage; that he was discreetly mocking him behind his back. It was nothing specific; nothing that would warrant a reprimand. The man couldn't be accused of insubordination or dumb insolence, but he had a quiet air of authority that made Garwood uneasy. It irritated him that the inspector was always in control, impeccably dressed and enjoyed total loyalty and respect from his team whilst apparently having no aspirations beyond the rank of DI. This made him something of a political liability in Garwood's book.

The success of the MIT was well documented with a sound record of arrests and convictions. But Garwood did not want the DAC to go away with the impression that most of it was down to Inspector Dawes, even though his track record proved this to be the case. It was imperative, therefore, to get him out of the way, right out of the area, before next week's visit and now the perfect solution had dropped into his lap. The sooner he set the wheels in motion, the better. He picked up the phone and asked Miss Braithwaite, his secretary, to find the Detective Inspector and send him in. He needed to speak to Dawes right away.

Icy snowflakes spattered the windows of the Incident Room. The team were sharing the results of thirty-six hours' legwork, much of it in freezing weather, before deciding their next move. Having established beyond reasonable doubt that Angel was not murdered for sexual motives or as part of a robbery, they were left with the assumption that someone simply wanted her dead. They began brainstorming ideas.

'The murder may not have been pre-meditated because the killer didn't take a knife with him; he used the one in the flat.'

'Who was the woman pretending to be Angel who phoned the bookie's and lured Lenny up to the flat and into the frame? And are we even sure it was a woman?' Malone drew an arrow from Lennox's photo on the whiteboard and ended it with a question mark.

DC Julie Molesworth consulted her notebook. 'I checked with Honest Harry. He says it was definitely a woman, but no one he knew and he'd never met Karen Baxter so he wouldn't recognize her voice. He thought the caller had a slight accent, but he couldn't identify it. Reckons it might have been Irish. She was only on for a few moments and he was busy, he was sure about the time, though ... 2.20 p.m.'

A thin, solemn-looking DC put up his hand. 'Was the call made from Angel's phone or just a phone containing her SIM card, Sarge?'

'We're checking the records with the bookmaker's phone company but it's like looking for a needle in a haystack because we don't know Angel's number and the killer nicked her phone.'

'Let's assume our killer's a woman. She could have made the 999 call from the phone box *before* she went up to the flat and did the murder, then used Angel's mobile to summon Lenny.'

'Too dodgy,' said Jack. 'She couldn't be sure how long the area car would take to get there. If it hadn't been for the snow and the slow traffic, and if they hadn't been on the other side of town, they could have caught her in the act. She wouldn't dare risk it.'

'And what if the lift had broken down while she was inside wearing bloodstained clothes?' asked someone. 'It would also mean she went there intending to kill Angel, but without a weapon.'

Bugsy put down his third jam doughnut and spoke through sugary lips. 'How about this for a scenario? The killer's another tom who's losing serious business to Angel or maybe they fancy the same bloke: that covers both money and love motives. Anyway, she decides to warn her off. She rings her at the Blue Ray Club and threatens her but gets a mouthful back so she goes round to her flat to sort her out and Angel tells her to sod off. The second tart grabs the knife in a hissy fit and slits her throat. That's around 2 p.m. Now she's got to think fast. She takes off her bloody clothes and puts them in a plastic carrier bag she finds in the kitchen, washes herself in the bathroom, then puts on some of Angel's gear. She nicks Angel's mobile phone so we can't trace her from the call she made to her at the Blue Ray Club. Then she has this blinding idea. She goes down to the phone box, rings 999 and reports finding a body. That's logged at 2.15. Then she uses Angel's phone to ring the bookie's and put Lenny in the frame for when the cops turn up.'

It went quiet while they chewed this over for snags then the questions started.

'Lenny says he overheard Angel say, "I'll get you for this, you bastard". Would she call another woman a bastard? Wouldn't she call her a cow or a bitch?'

'Good point,' said Jack. 'It's not impossible but it's unlikely.'

'I can accept that an angry tart might stick a knife in someone but cutting her throat from ear to ear? I don't believe a woman could be that vicious.'

'You haven't met my mother-in-law,' muttered a DC to a cackle of laughter.

'So what more have we learned about the victim?' asked Jack.

'Not much I'm afraid, sir,' replied DC Molesworth. 'She may have been public in her working life but she was virtually anonymous in private. Even her flat seemed impersonal, hardly anything of herself in it at all, just the sleazy paraphernalia of her job. Her handbag contained a hairbrush, make-up, condoms, just what you'd expect. There was a tenner and some change in her purse; no credit cards, driving licence or till receipts. She spent most of her free time in the Blue Ray Club and didn't have any close friends. We spoke to other prostitutes who worked the same patch and they said they rarely saw her on the streets and they didn't know who her regulars were. There was no apparent animosity towards her and they never heard her mention having a kid. We found a couple of her business cards on tables in the club, but the number on them was her landline. She seems to have kept her mobile for private calls rather than punters. As I said, there was nothing in her flat that you wouldn't expect to find there except, of course, for the five grand in euros in the freezer. We haven't yet established where that came from. Ninety per cent of 500 euro notes are in the hands of criminals, mainly because you can fit twenty grand's worth in a fag packet which makes it easier to launder. You can just stick it in your pocket out of sight. On the other hand, it could have been her savings, and she'd converted it to go on holiday. But do prostitutes earn that kind of money?'

'Thinking of changing careers, Julie?' called someone brave. DC Molesworth was a good officer to have on your side in a disturbance but not the sort you'd want to cross if you valued your gonads.

'No fear,' she retorted. 'I might have to do it with some sad, ugly sod like you.'

'Who owns the Blue Ray Club?' asked Jack. 'Anything useful there?'

'I covered that, sir.' There was a whiff of antiseptic as a young, acne-ridden detective jumped to his feet. 'It belongs to a bloke named Ray Hadleigh. He's Mr Clean, not even a speeding ticket and very co-operative, very keen to help. He's just had his business licences renewed, no problems other than allegations of heavy-handed behaviour by some of his security staff. There was one incident when they caught a couple of lads doing drugs in the gents and roughed them up a bit. One of the lads broke his arm falling against the urinal. No charges brought, though. This one is Hadleigh's fourth club in a very successful chain; there are three more around the city, all called Blue Ray – and pretty decent as clubs go. The name has nothing to do with high-density optical discs, incidentally. It's because Hadleigh's trademark is a blue Armani dinner jacket. He always wears one, apparently. And all his clubs have flashing blue neon lights outside in the shape of a jacket. Blue – Ray, you see. Quite clever, really.'

'Yes, OK, son, we get the picture. Rich geezer, sprauncy suit. Anything else?' Bugsy asked.

'He's divorced but not short of lady friends. According to his staff, he practically has to beat them off with a stick, but Angel wasn't one of them, not really his type. Hadleigh said he only knew her by sight. She used to come into the club occasionally for a drink, and then they wouldn't see her again for several days. He suspected she was a sex worker but turned a blind eye as long as she didn't solicit customers in his club. She was quiet, decorative and looked a bit depressed according to him so when he heard she'd been found with her throat cut, he assumed it was suicide. When we told him it was a murder inquiry, he was genuinely shocked and said he couldn't think why anyone would want her dead although obviously in her occupation, there was always the risk of meeting a psycho.

'Hadleigh might be right,' said Jack. 'This could just be a random killing by a nutter with a grudge against prostitutes, but I don't think so. We need to widen our inquiries. Someone wanted Angel out of the way; there must be somebody out there who knows something about her. Did she have a bank account?'

'Not that we've been able to trace. Of course, she could have had one in a different name.'

'Keep looking. If she was receiving regular payments from someone, she might have been doing a bit of blackmail on the side. Try local doctors, hospital records, the chemist where she bought her condoms, the supermarket where she got her food. And lean on the Department for Work and Pensions to trace a national insurance number and previous addresses. If they bang on about data protection, emphasize that it's a murder inquiry. Angel's phone could tell us a lot if only we could find it. Chances are the killer ditched it fast after making the call to Honest Harry, maybe along with the blood-stained clothes. Let's widen the search.' He drew a bigger circle around the Borough of Southwark on the white board then stood up. 'Sergeant Malone, you're with me. We'll give the Blue Ray Club another spin. If Angel spent most of her spare time there, someone must remember something.' A phone rang. Bugsy answered it.

'It's Beryl, DCS Garwood's secretary, guv. He wants to see you straight away.'

The light outside Garwood's hallowed portal was green so Jack rapped impatiently on the door and walked straight in. What did the pompous old windbag want now? This murder was a particularly brutal one and the first few days were crucial. He couldn't afford to waste time listening to Garwood rambling on about Home Office statistics or the Christmas overtime roster.

'You wanted to see me, sir?'

'Yes, Jack. Sit down.' Garwood's smile flickered on and off like the lights on his extravagant Christmas tree in the corner. 'I've got a job for you.'

Jack was baffled. What was the old fool talking about? He'd briefed Garwood about the murder investigation right at the start and he must know that the team now needed to focus on it without any distractions until they caught the killer. 'With respect, sir, you will recall that I'm heading up the murdered prostitute case and so far, we've very little to go on. I really need the team to concentrate all their resources until we get a lead.'

Garwood took off his glasses and polished them at some length. Then he gave Jack the carefully practised glare that meant he would brook no argument.

'I received a telephone call this morning from Detective Chief Superintendent Cameron of the Northern Constabulary in Scotland. Charlie and I trained together, more years ago than I care to remember.'

Jack groaned inwardly. Here we go. Another trip down the yellow brick road to Hendon with Garwood and his munchkin cronies. He looked pointedly at his watch but the DCS droned on.

'After we graduated, I stayed with the Metropolitan Police and Charlie returned to the Highlands but we have remained good friends. Mrs Garwood and I go up there quite often for the salmon fishing and a round of golf. But I'll come to the point....'

About bloody time, thought Jack.

'Charlie's team has been hit by a particular nasty outbreak of swine flu. Hardly an officer left standing, apparently. To make matters worse, the Northern Constabulary has responsibility for the largest geographical area in the United Kingdom, equivalent to the size of Belgium. Conversely, it's one of the smallest in terms of officers, hence DCS Cameron's current problem.'

'What exactly is the problem, sir?'

Garwood assumed a suitably grave expression. 'There has been a suspicious death in rather unusual circumstances. The Highlands of Scotland boast a magnificent heritage of ancient castles, many of them in ruins but some still inhabited and open to the public. It seems a young woman was found dead, having fallen from one of the towers. All DCS Cameron's senior detectives have succumbed to the flu virus and are too ill to continue with the investigation, so I'm sending you to assist for as long as necessary. You're leaving tomorrow morning.'

'Tomorrow morning?' yelped Jack before he could stop himself.

Garwood smiled. 'You know what you always say, Jack. The first forty-eight hours after a suspicious death are the most critical. This one occurred some five days ago, so the sooner you get started the better. You'll have some catching up to do.'

'But sir, I doubt if the Northern Constabulary will appreciate an inspector from the Met tramping all over their patch. Wouldn't it be more tactful to ask another Scottish Constabulary to help?'

Garwood slammed his fist down on the desk. 'Dammit, man, they're dropping like flies up there. Even their pathologist has gone down with flu and you'd expect a doctor to have some degree of resistance.'

'But what about the murder I'm investigating here?'

'DI Drake is taking over. You can brief him before you leave. He's an excellent officer with a talent for picking things up very quickly.'

No he isn't, thought Jack. DI Drake is a lazy git with a talent for sodding things up very quickly. 'Well, thank you for the opportunity, sir, but I'd rather carry on here, if you don't mind. I'm sure DI Drake would welcome a trip to the Scottish Highlands and ...'

Garwood stiffened, barely concealing his temper. 'This isn't a request, DI Dawes,' he said coldly, 'it's an order. I'm reassigning you and that's an end of it.' He gestured in the direction of his secretary's office. 'Miss Braithwaite has arranged your flight to Inverness first thing tomorrow morning. You'll be met at the airport. Pick up your ticket on the way out.' And he added as an inspired afterthought, 'You can take DS Malone with you for back-up.' He didn't want Malone slouching about the station in his scruffy clothes, stinking of fried food and leaving a pile of dog-ends in the porch. 'That will be all,' he barked, and to indicate that the audience was at an end, he whipped the cap off his pen, snatched a file from his in-tray and began to scrawl on it.

That showed the supercilious bugger who's boss, thought Garwood, after Jack had closed the door behind him. And he'd got rid of that fat, malodorous Sergeant, at the same time. Now he could relax and concentrate on impressing the DAC. He'd make a point of explaining, in a modest way, that although his unit was cost-effectively lean in terms of manpower, he had selflessly seconded two of his best officers to help a colleague in need in another constabulary. That should look good on his appraisal report. Smugly, he reached for a mince pie from the secret stash he kept in his desk drawer.

Back in the Incident Room, Jack shared the news that the murder investigation now belonged to DI Donald Drake. There were groans from the team and Bugsy's response was typically forthright.

'Flamin' Nora, guv! Not Ducky Drake! Tell me you're joking.' Sergeant Malone's opinion of Detective Inspector Drake was shared by everyone in the station except Garwood, who thought the sun shone from the seat of his shiny-arsed trousers. Most policemen acquired nicknames from a play on their real names. "Jack" Dawes' first name was actually Rupert and "Bugsy" Malone had been christened Michael. In the case of Donald "Ducky" Drake, anyone who didn't know him assumed it was due to the obvious Disney connection. In fact, it was his unerring ability to duck whenever anything unpleasant or arduous came his way. Any cock-ups on his watch – and there were plenty – always seemed to occur when he was off sick, on leave or looking the other way. He was impossible to contact in an emergency, *"I must have been in a radio black-spot"* and he had a reputation for making quick, ill-considered arrests, *"All the evidence pointed to the paperboy"*. It was generally considered that he had reached the rank of DI by a mixture of bravado, brown-nosing and bullshit.

'The team's well pissed off, guv,' Bugsy told Jack as they made their way to Drake's office to brief him. 'You know Ducky, he's a chancer. He cuts corners, plants evidence, nicks the wrong bloke then blames his team. Do you really have to take this case in Scotland?'

'Yep. I've been reassigned to help one of Garwood's old cronies. And here's the bit you really don't want to hear. You're coming with me.'

Bugsy thought about this for a moment and decided that on balance, he had by far the best deal. He liked and respected DI Dawes. Jack had a reputation for scrupulous policing, giving credit where it was due and taking full responsibility even when things went tits-up. The complete opposite of Ducky Drake who fannied about the station in a brown leather jacket like some born-again Bergerac pretending to be "one of the boys" but making sure he left the pub before it was his round.

'Och aye, guv,' quipped Bugsy, cheerily. 'You tak' the high road and I'll tak' the low road and between the two of us, we'll have this Scotch case cracked in a week. Or maybe we'll crack a case of Scotch in a week … either way, it'll all be over by Christmas.'

Jack smiled bleakly. 'When have I heard that before?'

DI Drake was sitting in his office with his feet up on the desk, talking on the phone. He ended the conversation abruptly and motioned them to chairs.

'What can I do for you, gentlemen?'

'Won't keep you long, Donald,' said Jack. 'We're leaving for Inverness first thing in the morning so I thought I'd brief you on the Karen Baxter murder as you're taking it over. I've brought the file and Sergeant Malone will update you on anything new. There isn't much to go on, I'm afraid.'

'The Jobcentre found something after a lot of searching,' began Bugsy. 'Apparently she had a proper job once, in a theatre, assistant stage manager or props or something similar. But then she left and dropped off the national insurance radar. Same with the tax people. The last address they had for her was in a block of flats that's since been demolished, so we don't know much about her before she became a tom.'

Drake looked puzzled. 'We don't need to, do we? We already know who killed her.'

'Sorry?' Jack was puzzled now.

'Lenny Lennox. The Chief Super briefed me this morning.'

Jack was exasperated. Was the man a complete incompetent? 'Lenny didn't do it, Donald. For a start, if you read the file, you'll see that the pathology report says the killer's right-handed and Lenny's left-handed.'

Drake laughed. 'More like red-handed. As I understand it, he had blood all over 'em. He used his right hand to put you off the scent then swapped the knife back to his left afterwards. Didn't fool me, though.'

'But what about opportunity, motive, evidence – things like that?' asked Malone.

Drake scoffed. 'That old stuff. No wonder it takes you lot so long to get a result. All right, if you want to be picky, Lennox had the opportunity because he was in the bookies across the road. Could've nipped out at any time without anyone noticing. Angel knew him and would have let him in without any argument. Plenty of evidence from his dabs all over the knife.'

'And motive?'

'He was a thieving little slime-ball. He found out about the five grand she had stashed away and went round intending to pinch it. She wouldn't tell him where it was hidden so he slit her throat.'

'What would have been the point of that? She couldn't tell him where it was after she was dead, could she?'

'I don't know, Sergeant,' said Drake, becoming impatient. 'Maybe he's got a nasty temper. Maybe you nicked him before he'd finished searching. I don't care. It's good enough for me. I've issued a warrant for his arrest and I'm going to charge him with murder.'

'But, sir, what about the phone calls and the discrepancies in the timing…?'

Jack put a restraining hand on Bugsy's arm. They were clearly wasting their time. Drake had already decided he was going to get a quick, easy result. He stood up and made for the door.

'Suit yourself, Donald. It's your case now.'

'That's right, Jack. Off you go and enjoy your little holiday in the frozen north. Don't worry about me, I'll have everything stitched up nicely before you can say "och aye the noo". Good luck with the skiing, Malone. Break a leg!'

As they walked away down the corridor, Bugsy sighed. 'He's going to sod it up, guv. I just know it. Garwood's nuts, putting him in charge.'

Jack agreed. 'I know that but we'll be six hundred miles away when it goes balls-up, so it'll be Garwood who has to sort it out.'

*

Ten days to Christmas on a bitter December afternoon, a few minutes past four o'clock. Corrie Dawes was icing her twenty-fifth Christmas cake of the season ready to box it up with the rest of the seasonal food and load into the 'Coriander's Cuisine' van for delivery to her customers next morning. Through the window of the warm kitchen, the grey day had aged prematurely into black night and a grim wind was swirling the snow into drifts. Jack would be home soon. She had a hot whisky toddy and warm mince pies waiting for him.

When he'd phoned to tell her Garwood was sending him to Scotland at twenty-four hours' notice and just before Christmas, she'd had half a mind to tell Cynthia that the catering she was doing for the Garwood's extravagant Christmas entertaining was cancelled forthwith. But Jack said that was plain daft. Business is business and the excellent reputation for quality and reliability that she had worked so hard to build must be preserved at all costs. One of the many things she loved about him was that he never assumed his job was more important than hers. For a very brief moment, she'd considered going with him to Scotland but Christmas and New Year were her busiest times. And despite financial pressures, people weren't cutting back on their celebrations and the Christmas goodies that went with it. The only constraint on her company making a record seasonal profit was the potential difficulty with deliveries if the snow continued. Mind you, it was probably nothing compared to where Jack was going. A key turned in the lock and Jack appeared at the kitchen door, carrying a bulging briefcase in one hand and a shovel in the other. His hair was frosted with snowflakes and his wonky nose was Rudolph-red.

'Jack, you look frozen.' Corrie passed him a mug of hot toddy.

'The car slid sideways into that bank of snow at the end of the lane and I had to dig myself out. I think my toes have dropped off.'

'I'll look out for them when I wash your socks. Speaking of socks, how many pairs are you likely to need? Do you know how long you'll be gone?'

'Not a clue. As long as it takes, I guess.' Jack drained his mug and munched a mince pie. 'I know nothing about the case other than it involves a young woman who died after falling from the tower of a castle somewhere in the Scottish Highlands. I guess there's a chance it could be accidental or even suicide in which case, I'll be home in a couple of days. On the other hand, the Procurator Fiscal has ordered a full police investigation so there must be some reason to suspect that her death may have been the result of a criminal act. DCS Cameron will be waiting to brief me when I get to Inverness. He's one of Garwood's chums so I expect he's a pompous old sod, too.'

'Not necessarily. Cynthia Garwood phoned me earlier today to order extra canapés for their Christmas Eve drinks party; it seems George has invited most of the senior officers in the Met, plus their WAGs. Anyway, according to Cynthia, Charlie Cameron is a real character. When I asked what he looked like, she giggled and said you'd be surprised. It'll be a laugh, she said.'

Jack shrugged. 'Did she, indeed? That might well be the case when she and George are fishing on the banks of the Spey and the ghillie is dishing out the champagne and smoked salmon sandwiches, but if this turns out to be a murder enquiry, I doubt if Bugsy and I will be doing much laughing.'

'What about your murdered prostitute case? Who's going to carry on with that?'

'Donald Drake.'

'Not Ducky Drake! He'll sod it up, he always does.'

'That's exactly what Bugsy said.'

CHAPTER FIVE

DECEMBER 16TH

Nine o'clock the following morning, DC Molesworth drove DI Dawes and DS Malone to Gatwick through conditions that Bugsy likened to one of those Christmas globes that kids shake to make a snowstorm. The advice from Traffic Division was not to travel unless the journey was absolutely necessary. Jack had suggested to DCS Garwood that it wasn't but he insisted it was, so they joined a sluggish convoy of traffic crawling across London towards the airport. Most travellers were flying out to join relatives for Christmas; others were simply in search of some sun. Not many were going on business. Jack sat in the back of the car studying a map of the area covered by the Northern Constabulary and the crime statistics. Bugsy sat up front, chatting to Julie.

'Have you ever been up north, Sarge?'

Bugsy thought about it. 'I had a girlfriend in Barnet, once.'

She laughed. 'No, not north of the river. I mean the far north ... Scotland.'

'Nope, but the Inspector has, haven't you, guv?'

'Mostly Glasgow on rugby tours when I was young and fit,' said Jack.

'Yeah, but we're not going to Glasgow, are we?' observed Bugsy, gloomily. 'We're going up the arse-end of nowhere.'

Jack looked up from his papers. 'It says here that Inverness is Europe's fastest growing city, forecast to grow by another forty per cent over the next two decades. I don't call that the arse-end of nowhere. What about Loch Ness and all those malt whisky distilleries? Then there's skiing in the Cairngorms.'

'I daresay you're right, guv, but funnily enough, I've never fancied skidding down a mountain on two planks of wood, knocking down trees with my face. Does it say what the pubs are like?'

'No, we'll check that out when we get there.' Jack caught DC Molesworth's eye in the mirror. 'Julie, you're still working on the Baxter murder, aren't you?'

She pulled a wry face. 'Yes, sir.'

'Do you think you could ring Sergeant Malone occasionally and keep him up to date on any progress? Obviously, DI Drake's in charge now but having started the case, I'd still like to know the outcome.'

'Certainly, sir.' Julie smiled. She felt much happier knowing that DI Dawes still had a couple of fingers on the reins, even from a distance.

The weather caused long delays at Gatwick and they eventually took off some four hours later than scheduled. But worse conditions awaited them. At five o'clock that afternoon, their plane was the last to skitter down the icy Inverness runway before the airport was closed. The snow was over a foot deep and the leaden sky promised lots more to come.

Outside the airport, a police car was waiting to take them to the Northern Constabulary headquarters. As the hordes of travellers streamed out into the snow, the driver stepped forward, waving a large placard on which was printed "DI Doors" in big red letters. Jack smiled at the spelling. It looked like a sign nicked from B&Q but it was easy to spot, as was the constable holding it aloft. Even without the multi-layers of chunky clothes, DC Maggie Mellis would have been hard to miss. She was just over five feet tall and almost spherical, with short spiky hair from which large ears protruded and a nose that looked like it had been broken at least once. Her plump cheeks were rosy with cold and her breath came in clouds as she bounced forward to greet them.

'Compliments from DCS Cameron, sir, and welcome to the Highlands. I'm DC Mellis and I've been assigned to mind you.'

'Thanks, DC Mellis,' Jack nodded towards Bugsy. 'This is Detective Sergeant Malone. Do you think you could mind him, too?'

Bugsy shook her beefy hand and winced. In the time it took him to separate his fingers, she had hurled their bags into the boot and opened the rear door for Jack.

Bugsy climbed in the front. 'You've managed to avoid the flu, then?'

'Och aye,' she said, squashing her large bottom into the driving seat and slamming the door with some force. She gunned the engine, spun the steering wheel and surged forward into the traffic, squinting through the gathering gloom as the wipers cleared a hole through the snow-splattered windscreen.

'How many officers are still well enough to work on this investigation, DC Mellis?'

'Well, sir, DCS Cameron is fine but most o' the men are peely-wally. One wee sneeze and they're awa' to their beds, greetin' for girlie things, like vaccines and paracetamol.'

Bugsy frowned. 'So what you're saying, love, is that apart from the Chief Super, it's mainly you, me and Inspector Dawes.'

'Aye, Sergeant.' DC Mellis beamed happily. 'It's a real treat for me, a suspicious death. If I'm lucky, it'll turn out to be a murder.' She rolled the word with morbid Celtic relish then went quiet, concentrating on the road in the appalling driving conditions. Soon, they reached the roundabout where the A96 joins the A9, but instead of heading south towards the Old Perth Road and the Northern Constabulary Police HQ, DC Mellis took the northern exit across the Kessock Bridge. Bugsy, whose unerring sense of direction had been honed by a lifetime of getting lost in London, screwed up his eyes to focus on the signposts through the mesmerizing snowflakes.

'Just a minute, Constable. You sure we're going the right way? I thought we should have turned off back there.'

'Aye, Sergeant, and so we would if we'd been going to Inverness.'

'And aren't we?' asked Jack. 'I assumed that's where we'd be meeting Chief Superintendent Cameron.'

'To save time, I was told to take you a wee bitty closer to the place where the body was found, sir. The Chief Super will meet us there.'

The snowflakes became thicker as they headed north and after a good hour's driving, Maggie finally stopped at a small police station on the coast, slewing the car sideways to fetch up neatly in front of the main entrance. Here, strong winds drove the snow almost horizontal so it was teeth-gritting work to grab their bags from the car and push themselves up the steps and through the glass door into the building. They plunged inside, glad of the shelter, leaving DC Mellis to park the car.

The desk sergeant tossed two paracetamol into his mouth and flushed them down with a shuddering swallow of cold, scummy tea. So far, all he had was a blinding headache and a runny nose. He envied the lucky devils that had gone down with full-blown flu and were tucked up in their nice warm beds, leaving mugs like him who could still stand, to do extra shifts. He'd been on duty since half-past nine, nobody to help him and no canteen so he was drinking the last dregs from his thermos. He looked up as Jack and Bugsy burst in bringing an icy blast and a good deal of snow with them.

'Afternoon, Sergeant.' Bugsy pulled out his badge. 'DI Dawes and DS Malone from the Metropolitan Police Murder Investigation Team. We're here to see DCS Cameron.' He shivered. 'Blimey, mate, it's bleedin' cold in 'ere. It was warmer outside in the snow.'

Och fine, thought Sergeant Ingram wearily. Two smart-arse Londoners up here on a wee jaunt to show us chookters how it's done. He bet their expenses amounted to more than his salary. He sneezed juicily. 'The heating's no' working. But ye'll be fine in Charlie Cameron's office. It's like the Costa del Sol in there.' He clicked open the security door and sneezed again. 'On ye go, gentlemen.' Jack and Bugsy edged past him and seeing the look on the sergeant's face, Bugsy commented in a hoarse whisper:

'We're like a dose of piles to the coppers up here, guv. Unwanted, a bugger to get rid of and a pain in the arse most of the time.'

The door bearing Detective Chief Superintendent Cameron's name-plate was ajar so they went straight in. The warmth that hit them came from a three-kilowatt heater, whirring away in the corner. A petite redhead in her forties was searching for something in one of the filing cabinets. She was smartly dressed in a navy business suit, crisp white blouse and furry snow boots. As they entered, she looked up and smiled pleasantly. This must be Cameron's secretary, thought Bugsy. Quite tasty for her age. He shoved a chair across to DI Dawes and flopped into one himself.

'Afternoon, love. I like the boots ... very sexy. Any chance of a couple of teas and some bacon rolls from your canteen? We haven't eaten since we left Gatwick and I'm bloody famished.'

While he was speaking, DC Mellis had walked in behind them and her relentlessly cheery face suddenly filled with alarm. She opened her mouth, desperate to say something, but the redhead, still smiling, silenced her with a look and addressed the visitors.

'Welcome, gentlemen, and thank you for coming to bail us out. I'm very pleased to see you.' She moved from the filing cabinet to a side table where there was tea-making equipment and a plate of cling-filmed sandwiches. She switched on the electric kettle and grinned at DC Mellis. 'It's all right, Maggie, you can stop gasping like a goldfish and help me make the tea. I'm bloody famished too.'

'I'm sorry ...' began Jack, hesitantly, 'but I was told to report to DCS Charlie Cameron and ...'

'That's me, Inspector.' It went very quiet.

'But you're a woman,' blurted Bugsy.

'Well spotted, Sergeant. I can see not much gets past you.' She grinned at Jack. 'Obviously George Garwood didn't tell you that Charlie is short for Charlotte. He always was a devious old bugger. I daresay he wanted us to start off on the wrong foot.'

Now Jack understood what Cynthia Garwood meant when she said he'd get a surprise.

DS Malone stood up, stiff and embarrassed. 'I apologize, ma'am. I didn't mean any disrespect.'

'None taken, Sergeant, and for Christ's sake don't call me ma'am. It makes me feel like the Queen.'

Relieved, Bugsy sat down again and took two sandwiches from the plate DCS Cameron offered him. Maggie Mellis passed around steaming mugs of tea and what could have been an awkward moment soon passed.

'The flu epidemic has hit us pretty hard, Jack,' said Charlie. 'I've pulled in every available officer and they're doing their best to cope but some of them are beginning to develop early signs of the virus. Poor old Sandy on the front desk should really be away to his bed.' She looked at her watch. 'I'll give you the brief background to this suspicious death which has come at the worst possible time, of course. Then, in the morning, you'll want to see the body and the place where she was found. There may be something to investigate, there may not, in which case you'll be back home by Christmas, but I've an uncomfortable feeling about this one. Call it intuition, if you like.'

What is it with women and intuition? wondered Jack. Corrie was always going on about hers. To hear her talk, she was only a séance short of psychic. She said Jack had no intuition at all, which was why she felt compelled to 'help' with his cases, despite his protestations and often at the risk of real personal danger. Well, not even Corrie could interfere in this one, he thought with satisfaction. Not from six hundred miles away.

'In any event,' continued Charlie, 'the Fiscal felt the same. He has the right to determine whether the body should be left where the death occurred or have it removed while he makes enquiries. In this case, he decided to remove it to the mortuary here and instructed that two pathologists should carry out the autopsy. The Fiscal's deputy was present to observe.'

DCS Cameron spread some forensic photographs of the dead girl on the desk in front of them. 'Her name's Astrid and she was eighteen years old. Very sad.' She pushed a file across to Jack. 'You'll want to study the pathologists' reports. Poor old Doctor Snoddy just managed to complete his part before the flu struck and he keeled over on his own autopsy slab. The other pathologist, Jenny MacLeod, is still on her feet and she'll answer any questions you may have. The basic facts are that Astrid was found with most of her bones broken at the foot of Doomdochry Castle having apparently fallen from the tower. She had a massive amount of heroin in her blood and an empty syringe in her pocket. As for her background, we know virtually nothing about her and there's nothing on record. The body was found by Mr Fraser Grant, the factor who manages the Doomdochry estate, and he knew her only by sight. He recognized her as one of the members of a commune, situated near the castle.'

Jack studied the photos. The dead girl looked no more than twelve, her delicate face as vague and bewildered in death as it most probably was in life. Now he'd seen her, Jack knew he had to find out whether there had been foul play; whether anyone else had been responsible for her death. There were many questions he wanted to ask but now was not the time and the DCS wasn't the person with the answers.

'It's getting late and this snow looks set for the night. I don't want to delay your journey home, Chief Superintendent. Perhaps DC Mellis wouldn't mind taking Sergeant Malone and me to our digs, then we can get started properly in the morning. After we've seen the body, we'll drive to Doomdochry Castle and examine the scene of the incident if it isn't totally obscured by the snow. Then maybe we could question Mr Grant and find some of the dead girl's friends and relatives.'

Charlie Cameron and Maggie Mellis exchanged glances.

'Ah,' said Charlie. 'That's obviously something else that George Garwood didn't tell you. You can't drive to Doomdochry, Jack, because it's on the Isle of Unst, near Herma Ness and the Muckle Flugga lighthouse. It's on the northernmost tip of the Shetland Islands.'

'The Shetlands!' exclaimed Bugsy. 'But that's bloody miles away, excuse my language. It's somewhere out in the flippin' Atlantic, isn't it? Either that or the North Sea.'

Jack fumed silently. Damn Garwood. No wonder he hadn't briefed them properly. There would have been every good reason for such a journey to be non-essential in this weather. No matter, they were here now and there was an investigation to be carried out and as soon as possible. 'My sergeant is prone to exaggeration, Charlie, but he has a point. Wouldn't it have been quicker to stay in Inverness and fly from there?'

She nodded. 'I thought of that, Jack, but the airport closed just after your plane landed, due to the snow. There's a ferry that runs from Aberdeen to Lerwick, but it takes around thirteen hours and I'm not at all sure it operates in this kind of weather. Then you'd have to get from Lerwick up to Doomdochry. So I've decided the quickest way is to fly you out by helicopter, which is why I asked Maggie to bring you up here, close to the heliport.'

A cold chill ran down Bugsy's spine. He'd only flown in a helicopter once before and was convinced that the pit of his stomach was still somewhere over Biggin Hill. He wasn't keen to repeat the experience.

Jack's brow furrowed. 'I believe I read somewhere that the Northern Constabulary doesn't have full-time police aviation cover.'

Charlie nodded. 'You're right, Jack, we don't. We hire in commercial support when we need it and in my judgement, we need it now. The body was discovered over five days ago and the longer we wait, the colder the trail will get and the less chance we'll have of finding out what really happened. When it comes to violent crimes, Shetland is one of the safest communities anywhere in the UK. Most of the time, the worst offences we have to deal with are alcohol and drug abuse, petty vandalism and traffic related incidents. At the same time, we have to be alert to the possibilities of drug trafficking and money laundering, due to our proximity to Norway and other Scandinavian countries. As for suspicious deaths, though, they're practically unheard of, so this one has come as something of a shock and I need to be sure it's investigated thoroughly.'

She stood up, indicating that it was time to get moving. 'The heliport is close by; get a good night's sleep and Maggie will drive you there tomorrow morning.' She spotted Sergeant Malone's worried face. 'Don't worry, Sergeant, you'll be perfectly safe. I know the pilot who flies the helicopter quite well and he's very experienced and totally reliable. Maggie was born on Unst and she has details of where you're staying in Doomdochry and you have the file with the information we hold so far. I appreciate it's difficult picking up an investigation part way through, so take as long as you consider necessary, keep me in the loop and let me know if you need anything ... as long as it isn't manpower. Good luck, gentlemen and try not to catch the flu.'

DC Mellis dropped DI Dawes and DS Malone at the Gordon Arms where they were to spend the night, promising to return early next morning to escort them first to the mortuary, then the heliport for the flight to Doomdochry Castle. She sped off home, wheels spinning in the snow.

The public bar was noisy and festive. Bunches of holly and mistletoe had been nailed to the oak beams and a Christmas tree, festooned with tinsel and baubles, flashed erratically in the corner, upstaging the ancient fruit machine. Jack and Bugsy sat at a table close to the crackling log fire. Having eaten a very substantial supper of mince and tatties, which appeared to be the chef's signature dish, they decided they'd earned a pint before retiring. Jack was thumbing through the background notes that DCS Cameron had given him.

Bugsy looked around him appreciatively. A couple of blokes were knocking out ceilidh music on an accordion and fiddle, setting people's feet tapping. Elsewhere, customers were simply having a drink and a blether and generally enjoying the friendly atmosphere. This was Bugsy's idea of a proper hostelry. Not like some of the poncey London pubs, full of techno-nerds drinking lager out the bottle and *Tweeting* on their *Blackberries*. He'd have been happy to stay here for Christmas but tomorrow they were leaving for Doomdochry. Even the name sounded depressing. Gloomily, he fingernailed a speck of roasted peanut from his beer-froth.

'What did I tell you, guv? We're going to spend Christmas up the arse-end of nowhere. And what's the betting we'll find that this Astrid is a smack head who was out of her mind on heroin and thought she could fly, so she schlepped off to the nearest ruined castle, climbed up the tower and chucked herself off. End of investigation.'

Jack looked up. 'She didn't look like a smack head in her photo; she looked like a fragile, frightened child. But you could be right, it may turn out to be suicide or even an accident. Incidentally, you're wrong about the castle, it isn't ruined. Not entirely, anyway. Take a look.' He handed Bugsy a rather blurred photo from the file. 'It says here that in the summer months, Doomdochry Castle is open to the public and takes B&B guests. It's owned by the MacAlisters; their family has lived there since 1469.'

'Blimey, I shouldn't want their heating bills.' Bugsy was more impressed by creature comforts than admirable ancestors. 'There's a flipping great hole in the wall and half the tower's missing. The wind must whistle round the rooms like a fart in a colander. What must it be like living in a Scottish castle in this weather?'

'You'll find out tomorrow. DCS Cameron notified the MacAlisters that two Met officers were coming to investigate their suspicious death as their local plod's gone down with the flu. As there aren't any hotels or pubs close by, they've invited us to use their B&B facilities. Isn't that good news?'

'Blinding,' said Bugsy without enthusiasm and mooched off to order another round of decent ale while he still could.

CHAPTER SIX

DECEMBER 17TH

Constable Mellis was almost incontinent with excitement at the prospect of working with two Metropolitan Police officers on a potential murder investigation. An opportunity like this was as rare as grouse's teeth and she intended to make the most of it. She regarded the officers as her responsibility and she took that responsibility very seriously. She had been born and brought up in Baltasound, so she had local knowledge that might prove useful to them and she understood the Shetland dialect. Unattached and totally committed to her job, she hoped that if this turned out to be a murder and she made herself indispensable during the investigation, it could mean promotion or at the very least, a transfer to somewhere more exciting, like Scotland Yard. To that end, she would speak only her best English to prove to the Inspector that she could communicate clearly. At exactly eight-thirty, she bounced into the lobby of the Gordon Arms and marched purposefully into the dining room where Jack and Bugsy were finishing breakfast. DS Malone was buttering his fourth round of toast when Maggie fetched up at their table, eager to get started. Any keener, thought Bugsy wearily, and she'd be foaming at the mouth.

'Good morning, Inspector Dawes and Sergeant Malone.' She articulated each word in her 'posh' voice. 'I hope you had a comfortable night. The car is out front when you're ready.'

DC Mellis was working to a tight schedule. She needed to get them to the mortuary by nine o'clock, half an hour to view the corpse and speak to the pathologist, then an hour to reach the heliport in time for their flight. After some impressively subtle chivvying, she had both policemen and their bags securely installed in her car and they skidded off through the snow to the mortuary. She was longing to deploy the blues and twos, but since they'd only passed one other car since they started out, she feared it might appear ostentatious.

To Jack, one mortuary felt much like another and they all made him queasy. This one was small compared to the London ones, since it was not required to store as many cadavers, but small did not equate to cosy. It was icy cold with dazzling white tiles and a cloying, antiseptic smell that caught in his throat, leaving an acrid aftertaste of something nasty. The crusty mortuary attendant pulled open a drawer in the cabinet, uncovered the body and tottered out of the way to give the officers an unimpaired view.

This was the second dead woman Jack had seen in less than a week but this one was very different to Karen Baxter. In death, Astrid was small and thin with a look of childlike purity and innocence: not in the least like the brash, obvious sexuality of the prostitute with her tacky lingerie and long bleached hair. Astrid's auburn hair was neatly cropped and she looked as though she was sleeping peacefully despite her shattered bones. Karen Baxter's face reflected the manner of her death; a violent struggle ending in an ugly, gaping wound across her throat. Seeing Astrid in the flesh confirmed Jack's initial opinion that she didn't look like a typical junkie and goodness knows, he'd seen plenty. The door opened then, interrupting any further observations he might have made, and Dr MacLeod, the corroborating pathologist required by the Fiscal, hurried in. She was somewhat flushed and wearing a mask and gown to ward off the flu.

'Sorry I'm late, gentlemen. This epidemic's getting worse and there are even fewer of us left to cover the work.' She opened her copy of the report and glanced through the papers to refresh her memory. 'I don't know how much of this you've had time to absorb, Inspector Dawes, but time of death is a bit unreliable due to the body lying outdoors in freezing conditions. Doctor Snoddy and I have estimated it between midnight and one o'clock. Cause of death was a broken neck sustained by the fall from Doomdochry Castle tower.'

'Not from the heroin overdose, then?' Jack asked.

'No, she was alive when she hit the ground. But having said that, the dose was massive and it would have killed her, even if the fall hadn't. As you can see, she was thin and malnourished and as far as I can tell, this was her first experience of heroin or any other kind of drug abuse, come to that.'

'So I guess that rules out suicide,' said Bugsy. 'If you'd just given yourself a fatal fix, you'd hardly throw yourself off a tower just to make sure. That really would be overkill.'

Dr MacLeod glared at him. Bugsy was often accused of misplaced levity in these situations but gallows humour was his way of dealing with all the sickening crime scenes he'd witnessed without becoming an incurable depressive.

'It says in the report that Forensics found her fingerprints on the hypodermic syringe,' said Jack. 'Is it possible she could have injected herself, then overbalanced as the drug took effect? If she hadn't used heroin before, she might not have known how much to inject or what the effects would be.'

'It's possible.' Dr MacLeod's lips were pursed under her mask.

'But you're not convinced?'

'I'm not convinced it was suicide. There are a couple of factors that make me doubtful. In cases of a self-administered overdose, you'd expect to find the subject's thumbprint on the plunger. In this case, there wasn't one. Her prints were found only on the barrel.'

'And the second thing?' Jack was impressed with Dr MacLeod. Not as formidable and revered as Doctor "Big Ron" Hardacre, but smart nevertheless.

'She was three months pregnant.'

Jack wondered how he could have missed that fact when he studied the report. He blamed the seismic effects of the mince and tatties he'd been eating at the time.

'Now *that* could be a motive for suicide,' said Bugsy. 'Young girl gets herself pregnant; bloke doesn't want to know.'

Dr MacLeod sniffed scornfully. 'Really, Sergeant, this is the twenty-first century. Young women don't do away with themselves simply because they're expecting an unwanted baby. And it may surprise you to know that they can't get *themselves* pregnant; there's usually an eager male involved at that stage of the process. This girl must have known she was pregnant yet she allowed it to continue to thirteen weeks without doing anything about it. That suggests to me that she wanted the baby, so why kill herself?'

'Yeah, you're right, Doc,' conceded Bugsy. 'And why put the syringe neatly in her pocket rather than chuck it away? If I'd just given myself a lethal injection, dropping litter would be the last thing on my mind.'

'So what we're all thinking is that her death may have been caused or contributed to by the commission of a criminal act,' said Jack. 'Did she have any defence wounds?'

Dr MacLeod pulled a wry face. 'Impossible to tell with someone who has fallen eighty-odd feet and maybe bounced off a few battlements on the way down. There were bruises around the cephalic vein where the heroin was injected that might be consistent with someone gripping her forearm ante-mortem, but she was so badly cut and bruised by the fall, it's impossible to say for certain.'

Jack took one last look at the pathetic, broken body in the mortuary drawer. 'Thanks very much for your help, Dr MacLeod.'

Her eyes smiled above the mask. 'I'm sorry I couldn't give you more, Inspector.'

'You've given me enough to convince me that we need to investigate this death until we get a few more answers.'

On the way to the heliport, Jack sat in the back, silently mulling over the case and wondering how much resource he'd need when they got to Doomdochry. The Isle of Unst was just over 120 square kilometres with a total population of only around seven hundred. By comparison, the modern London Borough of Hackney totalled less than twenty square kilometres but with a population of around 212,000. Even if he had to interview everyone on the island, it wouldn't amount to more than a serious enquiry by the Met but they'd be more spread out, so harder to reach.

The heliport was a small one with just two helipads, one of which had been cleared of snow and had a powerful Robinson R44 sitting on it. The logo on its slim, dark blue flank read "Cameron Helicopter Services". Jack recognized a high-performance aircraft when he saw one; it was exactly the kind deployed by the Met's Air Support Unit, and he was impressed. At the same time, he was surprised that for a business enterprise, the fuel facilities and lighting were very limited and there were no hangars or a Customs presence. But he supposed it needed to be far enough away from towns and villages not to disturb the community with the considerable noise helicopters make taking off and landing. And, of course, the advantage of a helicopter is that, in total, travel is much faster and more immediate than most other means and in this case, speed was of the essence.

As they piled out of the car, a man wearing a "Biggles" flying jacket jumped down from the cockpit and trudged towards them through the snow, wiping his hands on an oily rag.

'Inspector Dawes and Sergeant Malone? I'm Donnie Cameron, your pilot. Good to meet you. Charlie phoned to let me know you were on your way; I'm all fuelled up and ready to go. The weather isn't too good but we should make Doomdochry by lunchtime if we don't hit any snags,' he finished cheerfully.

Bugsy gave him a watery smile and swallowed hard, trying not to imagine what the snags might be.

'Mr Cameron,' said Jack, shaking hands. 'No relation to the Chief Superintendent, I suppose?'

'Aye, she's the auld wifey,' he joked, 'but don't let on I called her that, for goodness sake. She'll lock me up in one of her cells.'

Nothing like keeping it in the family, thought Jack. When the DCS needs aviation cover, she just calls in her husband, and why not? It was good for husbands and wives to have symbiotic careers. He often helped Corrie prepare food when she was overwhelmed with orders, which happened quite often now that "Coriander's Cuisine" had become a successful catering business.

'Shall we climb aboard?' Cameron strode to his helicopter followed by DI Dawes, DC Mellis and a pale, reluctant DS Malone. 'Relax, Sergeant, it really isn't dangerous. If the weather gets worse or we have any kind of mechanical problem, I can land safely almost anywhere within a minute or two.' Donnie winked at Jack. 'Except over the water, of course. But I promise faithfully not to dump you in the Atlantic.'

They climbed in and belted up. Donnie opened the throttle all the way and soon the helicopter became light on the skids and eased into the air. Gaining speed to about fifteen knots, there was a slight shudder and they began to climb. Bugsy, now cold and sweating, suddenly saw his empty life flash before him; a misspent youth at football matches and dog tracks followed by thirty years of nicking villains and getting blood and puke down his clothes. He wished he'd been less humdrum, more in touch with his artistic side. Maybe he should have found time for the things that really mattered in life; the things other men took for granted. He thought of the wife he'd never had, his unborn children and the twenty-five quid he'd paid into the Metropolitan Police Social Club that he'd probably never see again.

'Why have you closed your eyes, Sarge?' asked DC Mellis. 'Are ye no' feeling well?'

He risked a peek through one squinty eye. Beneath them, a squall was whipping up ominous white caps on the ocean. Maggie put a reassuring hand on his sleeve. He shut his eyes again wondering if the last artistic thing he'd ever see would be the thistle tattooed on her brawny forearm.

CHAPTER SEVEN

DOOMDOCHRY CASTLE – SHETLAND

In the chilly Blue Sitting-Room that adjoined the even chillier Blue Bedroom, Alistair MacAlister, 20th Earl of Doomdochry, was taking tea and a 'piece' with his wife, as was his custom at this time of the morning.

'So the police are coming back.' With a deep sigh, Lady Alice dunked a shortbread finger in her mug and watched as half of it broke off and sank to the bottom. She wasn't surprised; it was turning into that kind of day. There was a longish silence.

'Aye,' replied Alistair, heavily. 'I'm no' surprised.' Now pushing seventy, the Earl had a look of bygone Jacobite affluence that had fallen on hard times. He was a tall, dome-headed man with long, thin whiskers, a faded kilt and a faded eye. He shook his head mournfully. 'It's a terrible thing that's happened. That poor wee lassie.'

Astrid's body had been discovered over a week ago but Alistair was still badly shocked that such a thing had happened on Doomdochry soil although clan history showed that it wasn't the first time a young woman had met a violent end there. The old Earl, steeped in Celtic superstition, feared Astrid might almost be the Lady Jean reincarnated, only to suffer another tragic death. But why, he asked himself, had the lassie chosen *his* tower to end her life? And how did she get up there without anyone seeing her? In the absence of any information to the contrary, MacAlister and most other Doomdochry folk had assumed her death was suicide and initially, the local bobby who attended the scene had been of the same opinion. But now the post mortem had been carried out, the Fiscal had instructed that further inquiries should be made.

'It's terrible right enough,' agreed his wife, emphatically. 'First it was young Constable Buchanan tramping snow all over our floors and sneezing his head off. Now he's away with the flu and the English police want to stick their noses in.' She sighed again. 'I wish you hadn't offered them rooms; it's asking for trouble.'

'If I hadn't, it would have looked like we had something to hide.'

She thought about it for a while. 'Aye, I suppose it would. And if they're determined to poke around anyway, it's better they bide here, where we can see what they're up to. How many are coming?'

'Three. Two detectives from London and a lassie from Inverness.'

Her expression was crafty. 'Tell Moragh to put one o' the men in the tower bedroom.'

He looked anxious. 'Are you sure, Alice? Won't we have to move everything?'

She tutted impatiently. 'Of course we will. We'd have had to do that anyway. Put it in the Guard Chamber. The police won't go down there; not with the rats and the leaking drains. Get Geordie to help and look sharp, before they get here.'

'What about the smell in the bedroom?'

'It'll no' linger for long. There's a wicked draught blows in through those tower windows.'

The Earl stroked his whiskers and frowned. 'They'll ask questions, the police always do. What if I let something slip? My memory's poor.'

Alice was a spry little body and in possession of all her marbles but she knew how to play the age card when it suited her. 'Alistair, you'll be just fine. Mack will deal with the police. We'll say we're upset and confused and if we have to speak, we'll use the Shetland. Now finish your tea and keep your voice down or Auntie will hear.'

They had talked in hushed tones. Whilst the walls of Doomdochry Castle were thick, they were not thick enough to prevent Aunt Flora MacAlister from eavesdropping in her room next door, which she invariably did. Flora was eighty-five and had not left her bedroom in the north wing for the last ten years. Despite this, she knew all the scandal that went on in Doomdochry; indeed, she was the instigator of much of it. Flora was Alistair's maiden aunt. His father, the 19th Earl, had died some years ago leaving his younger sister in Alistair's care, together with all the other crumbling chattels that constituted the ancient heritage of the Doomdochry MacAlisters.

Draining the dregs of his tea, Alistair shuffled off to find Geordie. He used the back staircase; a late 18th century addition that provided secondary access to the dining room and from there, into what was once the butler's pantry. Warily, he grasped the splintering handrail and placed his feet with practised care; the slightest tread on any of the stairs made a noise like an elderly oak-tree falling beneath the axe. Sometimes it did it at night without anyone treading on it. He dodged a piece of falling plaster. If he was honest, the castle was tumbling down around their ears. It was only a matter of time before one of their rare B&B guests had an accident and sued him. What if the death of the young lassie turned out to be negligence and he was liable? Maybe he should hand the whole place over to the National Trust, before the Scottish Tourist Board closed him down.

There was another alternative, of course; one that would enable them to live somewhere with modern luxuries like heating, sanitation and lights that didn't flicker on and off. He knew it was the option that Alice would choose and they were neither of them getting any younger. But the decision wasn't his to make because there was his son, Mack, to consider. The MacAlisters had held Doomdochry for over five centuries. When Alistair died, Mack would become the 21st Earl. It was his birthright and only his. Flora's mischievous hints about her deceased brother's *houghmagandie* and the existence of an heir born on the other side of the tartan were a wicked calumny and he refused to believe a word of it.

Cameron brought the helicopter in low, providing his passengers with their first glimpse of the spectacular Shetland landscape. He gave them the commentary he used for tourists, pointing out the nine hundred miles of coastline where deep-water waves were smashing against the mighty sea cliffs.

'No part of Shetland is more than five kilometres from the coast and it's the site of one of the largest bird colonies in the North Atlantic. Home to more than a million birds, they reckon, though how they count them beats me. The Isle of Unst, where you're going, is as far north as southern Alaska but the climate's milder than you'd expect. It's due to the warming influence of the surrounding seas although the winds can be pretty severe. Of course at this latitude, the winter nights are long and we're coming up to the shortest day so you'll only get around three and three quarter hours of daylight.'

'Oh bloody wonderful,' grumbled Bugsy. 'So we'll be stumbling around in the dark as well as in the snow.'

'Och, the snow seldom sticks for more than a day, Sarge,' said Maggie.

'I guess this is like a trip home for you, DC Mellis,' said Jack. 'I'm relying on you to help us find our way around Unst.'

Maggie glowed at the implied responsibility. 'I'll be glad to, but I don't know much about Doomdochry. As bairns, we were afraid to go there because folk said the castle was haunted but don't worry, sir,' she flexed her formidable biceps, 'it'll take more than a wee bogle to scare me!'

Jack glanced at her pugnacious profile and smiled to himself. It would take a very brave bogle indeed to try anything on with Maggie Mellis.

'I don't know about ghosts,' said Donnie, 'but a lot of the old Viking influence still exists. The name Unst comes from the old Norse *Ornyst*, which means "home of the eagle". Quite poetic for a race that prided themselves on raping and pillaging. Brace yourselves everyone, we're going in.'

Cameron set the chopper down as gently as a father lowering his new-born baby into its cot. Even Bugsy was impressed.

'This is as close as I can get to the castle so you'll have a bit of a hike, I'm afraid. Give my wife a ring when you're finished here and I'll come and fetch you. Good luck!'

Grabbing their bags, the three officers jumped out and ran clear, heads bent beneath the rotors' powerful down-draught. Donnie waved from the cockpit and lifted off, anxious to make it back to the heliport before the weather worsened and the Shetland fog grounded him. They waved back briefly then turned to take their first look at the focus of their investigation. For a while, nobody spoke.

Doomdochry Castle perched dizzily on a rocky promontory, almost detached from its estate and jutting out into the sea. It was roughly L-shaped to follow the odd contours of its cliff location but without any obvious architectural plan. The castle had been extended over time and as the Doomdochry Earls grew in power and dignity, so the stronghold became almost like a cliff-based village with a number of detached buildings and a large amount of land. The gatehouse entrance was at the head of a steep climbing track, fortified by three tiers of badly-disintegrated defensive walls with splayed gun loops.

Jack estimated that Donnie's "bit of a hike" was a good half mile, most of it uphill, and in this weather, the walk would be a challenging one. Sergeant Malone, who avoided any kind of exercise, particularly outdoors, opened his mouth to protest but the wind seized the words "Bloody hell, guv!" and hurled them back in his teeth. Jack pointed in the direction of the castle where a suspicious death waited to be investigated. This was not the time for issuing orders, it was the time to lead by example. He pulled up the hood of his jacket and began to stride out purposefully, with Bugsy and Maggie tagging along behind.

The virgin snow, whipped up by the wind, had formed drifts that were thigh deep in places, despite Maggie's assurance that it rarely settles on Unst. Jack cursed himself for not having the foresight to arrange for them to be met. The MacAlisters obviously had vehicles able to cope with such conditions; he could see some recent tyre tracks made by something big and sturdy.

DC Mellis forged ahead, yomping through the snow in her backpack like an SAS trooper on manoeuvres. Jack tightened the drawstring of his hood till it stopped the wind whistling round his ears. The driving snow showed no respect for his police-issue "waterproof" jacket and soaked into his trousers and through the lace-holes in his boots. The weather worsened with sleet showers racing across on a strong southerly. By the time they reached the castle, dragging their luggage behind them, the men were red-faced and gasping. Even DC Mellis had lost some of her relentless exuberance.

The arched gateway was thirty-five feet high and crowned with a parapet that used natural rock for added security and threat. The twin-tower gatehouse lay in ruins and unoccupied. Long ago, there had been a portcullis and a drawbridge too, but time and bloody battles had demolished both. High above the door, the device intended for pouring down unpleasant substances upon unwelcome visitors remained intact. DC Mellis reached out to tug at an iron bell-pull, but the heavy oak door began to creak open even before she touched it.

'Blimey, this place is like one of them old horror movies,' said Bugsy. 'Any minute now, a sinister old witch in black rags will stick her head out and cackle at us.' But the quip died on his lips as the door groaned back on rusty hinges to reveal an ugly, wall-eyed crone. She was very old, with brown leathery skin, wispy grey hair and a bloodstained sacking apron over a grimy black dress. She glared at them with her good eye and ran a thin, furred tongue over cracked lips.

'You're the police,' she told them, somewhat unnecessarily. She grimaced a smile, displaying a complete absence of teeth. 'Come in.'

Glad to be out of the biting wind, they trooped past her into a lofty, vaulted entrance hall where they stood about, making puddles of melting snow on the filthy flagstones. The old woman turned and left them without a backward glance, presumably to tell someone they had arrived. DC Mellis struggled out of a quilted parka the size of a sleeping bag, Bugsy lit a fag, and Jack took the opportunity to snoop around. His nose was assailed by a mixture of smells; stale fat, rotting food, paraffin and a lurking, earthy odour of something worse.

The hall was dominated by a life-size marble statue, standing between two Romanesque columns. It bore the inscription "To the Most Noble MacAlister, Earl of Doomdochry, as a mark of gratitude from King James III of Scotland 1469". Two carved stone panels set into the east wall displayed the arms of the early MacAlisters and gun loops and arrow-slit windows gave the castle a defensive command of all possible approaches, both by land and sea. It would have been from one of these early-warning windows, Jack decided, that their arrival had been spotted. Difficult, therefore, for anyone to sneak into the castle without being seen unless it was at night. And beneath their feet, he could envisage much scope for subterranean dungeons and passages, hewn out of the rocky foundations. It can never have been a comfortable place to live; he was surprised the MacAlisters remained there. And he still needed to find out what a young woman like Astrid was doing in such a dismal place and establish the circumstances that led to her death.

Bugsy's stomach growled loudly, echoing around the stone walls in the tomb-like silence. He hadn't eaten since his breakfast at the Gordon Arms. He wondered what the food would be like in a Scottish castle. Wasn't it Balmoral where royalty shot skinny little birds whose names he couldn't remember? The sooner they got this investigation over, the better. He strolled over to where DI Dawes was leaning out of a window, peering up at the tower.

'I'm feeling a bit uneasy about staying here, guv.'

Jack pulled his head in and grinned. 'Don't worry, Bugsy, DC Mellis won't let the bogle get you.'

'No, seriously, Jack, if this Astrid's death does turn out to be murder, it makes everyone living here a potential suspect. If we're their guests, won't it be a bit awkward if we end up having to nick one of 'em?'

'Possibly, but look at it this way. As guests, we're likely to see and hear a lot more than if we were just coppers calling to interview witnesses. It's very often the things people say to each other in unguarded moments that provide a lead to what really went on.'

DC Mellis was impatient to get started. 'Will I go and find someone, sir? I think that cross-eyed auld wifey has forgotten us.'

It was then that they heard a deep throaty growling coming from the rear of the castle. It became louder until a door flew open at the end of the flagstone corridor and a stern, cheerless old man in a tatty kilt cantered unsteadily towards them, towed by two enormous deerhounds. He was short and stocky with bushy red whiskers, sharp eyes and bow legs. The dogs came within inches of the police officers, straining on their leashes and baying. Bugsy could smell their fetid breath. He thought only Sheltie sheepdogs came from Shetland. Little hairy jobs, barely a foot tall. These animals were three times as big, more like Shetland ponies. Bugsy didn't like dogs and was lifting his size twelve boot to acquaint them of the fact when the old man shouted something unintelligible. Instantly, both dogs dropped onto their bellies, long grey muzzles on paws, silent but watchful.

DI Dawes pulled out his warrant card but the old man beat him to it.

'Good day, Inspector Dawes.' He said it without smiling. 'I'm Geordie, the Earl's ghillie. Please come this way.' He tied the dogs' leads around the surprisingly shapely ankle of King James III and lurched off on his wishbone legs. They followed him down the flagstone corridor, up some worn stone steps, around corners, down some more steps and through some sparsely furnished rooms that smelled of mildew. The old man had a remarkable turn of speed and Bugsy reckoned they must have covered a good hundred yards, some of it at a sprint, before Geordie finally stopped outside two shabby, panelled doors. He knocked, then put his shoulder to them, causing the badly peeling paint to scatter like confetti.

'The English police and the Scots lassie,' he announced and tottered off, giving the warped doors a good slam behind him.

As the police officers entered, the buzz of conversation ceased abruptly and seven pairs of eyes swivelled in their direction. If Corrie were here, thought Jack, she'd call this an 'Agatha' moment; that point in a Christie mystery when the detective assembles all the characters in the library and unmasks the murderer. What Jack could never understand was why the obliging murderer always turned up to be arrested when any normal person would have been half way to Brazil.

Ironically, they were indeed in the castle library, although the dusty books looked like they would fall apart if anyone so much as breathed on them. Jack tried for the second time to whip out his ID but a young man rose smartly from a chintz-covered armchair and strode towards him, offering a handshake.

'Welcome to Doomdochry Castle, Inspector. I'm Mack MacAlister. Maybe I should explain that all the first born male MacAlisters in Doomdochry are christened Alistair, including myself, but to avoid confusing me with my father, they call me Mack.' He shook Jack's hand, then Bugsy's and Maggie's. His handshake was warm and firm. 'Please consider yourselves our guests, although I appreciate the occasion is not a social one and you're here to carry out a serious investigation. My parents are no longer young and as you can imagine, they are very shocked by what has happened so they have asked me to deal with the formalities on their behalf. I hope that's all right with you.'

Mack MacAlister was thirty-six, just over six feet tall, muscular and handsome with a confident, relaxed manner. His reddish hair was streaked blond by the sun of some recent tropical holiday, and contrary to the tradition of the men in his family, he was clean shaven. He wore designer jeans, a cashmere sweater and expensive handmade loafers. Only a hint of Scottish was discernible in his cultured, English accent. Jack's and Bugsy's detective minds were working along much the same track: Jack asked himself whether this obviously well-educated, well-heeled son and heir still lived in the castle. Bugsy simply wondered what a bloke like that was doing in a dump like this. DC Mellis was thinking 'Phwoar! What a stud muffin!' and hoping he wasn't a murderer.

Mack smiled pleasantly. 'We assumed you'd want to start by speaking to everyone who was at Doomdochry at the time of the unfortunate incident, so here we all are, at your disposal. All, that is, except for my Great Auntie Flora who is eighty-five and too frail to leave her room. I believe you've already met Geordie, our ghillie and Moragh, our housekeeper. They've been with us since I was a child.' He waved an inclusive hand at the others. 'None of us knew the dead girl but we'll do all we can to help with your inquiries, Inspector. Should I introduce everyone now?'

Very open and direct, thought Jack. 'Yes, please, Mr MacAlister, that would be helpful.'

Mack strode to an elderly couple, sunk deep in a large, battered sofa, the springs long defunct. 'This is my father, Alistair MacAlister, 20th Earl of Doomdochry and next to him is my mother, Lady Alice.' The couple nodded, vaguely, but said nothing. 'And this stunning lady ...' Mack beamed adoringly, '... is Melissa MacAlister, my lovely wife.'

Damn, cursed DC Mellis.

Melissa MacAlister was gorgeous and dressed as though she had just stepped off a catwalk. Like her husband, Mack, she looked totally out of place in a medieval castle and not a little uncomfortable. She had the lithe figure of a supermodel, a great mane of black hair, trendily tousled, and tiny feet clad in killer heels. When she smiled, her expensively-capped teeth flashed white and even as a row of bathroom tiles. At Mack's soppy introduction, she lowered her huge brown eyes and peeped coyly at him from beneath impossibly long lashes.

The last time I saw eyes like that, thought DC Mellis, the owner was chewing the cud.

'I'm F-Fraser G-Grant.' The nervous stammer came from a restless young man, standing by the window. 'I f-found the body so you'll w-want to speak to me, w-won't ... y...?' He gulped several times but couldn't squeeze out the last word.

Mack took over in a seamless manner that suggested he'd done it many times before. 'Fraser is our factor, or property manager I suppose you'd call him, Inspector Dawes. He looks after the castle and the estate taking care of repairs, cleaning, landscaping, snow removal, you know the type of thing. He's lived here on Unst all his life. We used to play together as boys, didn't we, Fraser?'

Grant nodded, then went back to staring out of the window as if something would go badly wrong if he didn't keep watching.

'I'm Randall P. MacAlister from Seattle, USA.' The man rising heavily from his armchair beside the inglenook fireplace was around fifty, fat and balding with an aura that reeked of dollars. His lack of hair was offset by a magnificent red beard and moustache that seemed completely out of kilter with his clothes and his personality. He shook Jack's hand vigorously and indicated the woman sitting in the matching armchair. 'This here's my wife, Nicole. We don't live in the castle permanently. Not yet, anyway.' Randall guffawed loudly and winked at the Earl.

Nicole MacAlister was somewhat younger than her husband and much better preserved, thanks to frequent visits to the beauty parlour and a skilful cosmetic surgeon. She had the taut, wrinkle-free smile of a much-lifted face and breasts that owed more to the Silicone Health and Safety Council than to nature. On the downside, she had the sharp, beady eyes of a VAT Inspector and a mouth that would have caused panic in Amity Harbour.

'Randall and Nicole came here as paying guests to research Randall's family tree,' added Mack.

'That was six months ago, and we're still here. I can hardly believe my Scottish ancestors once lived in this great little castle, Inspector. We love it, don't we, honey?'

'We sure do.'

Jack thought Nicole sounded rather less in love with it than Randall.

'Now that you've met everyone, Inspector, shall I ask Moragh to show you to your rooms, so you can freshen up?' Mack asked.

'Thank you, Mr MacAlister. Then perhaps we might see the spot where the body was found. Would you show us, Mr Grant?' Jack thought he might relax more outside and they could question him about the girl and anything else he might have seen when he found her.

'Yes, of course,' said Mack, answering for Fraser yet again. Jack wondered if it was concern for his factor's speech impediment or whether he was uneasy about what Grant might tell them.

CHAPTER EIGHT

It was nearly half past two when Moragh reappeared. She was still wearing the grimy black dress but without the bloodstained apron, having finished disembowelling the elderly ewe whose demise would provide boiled mutton for dinner. Wordlessly, she set off at a loping trot around the castle, taking more or less the same route as Geordie. Eventually, DI Dawes and DC Mellis were allocated two of the cavernous, B&B bedrooms on the third floor where fires had been lit in vast, iron-clad grates and the four-poster beds made up. Bugsy, however, had further to climb. Moragh motioned to him to follow her, muttering malevolently under her mustard-gas breath. At this rate, he'd reckoned he'd need Sat Nav to find his way back again. It was a blooming great mausoleum of a place, even for a castle. The lively trot slowed to a wheezing climb until she finally stopped at the fifth floor. Bugsy waited for her to open one of the bedroom doors but instead, she led him to a heavy curtain at the end of the landing. She twitched it back, disturbing a cloud of dust and what might have been a small bat or a large moth, then she pointed to a narrow stone staircase, spiralling upwards. She showed no inclination to go up herself, so Bugsy assumed he was on his own from here.

'My room's up there, is it, love?' He shouted as he always did with members of the public who were old, dim or foreign. He reckoned she was all three. She stared at him. At least, he thought she was staring at him; her left eye had a strange sliding motion all of its own so it could have been looking at something up the stairs. She treated him to a gummy leer then hurried off on surprisingly nimble legs, cackling back at him as she went. He thought she said something like 'green beans' but he couldn't swear to it, and anyhow, it didn't make any sense unless they were on the dinner menu.

The corkscrew staircase seemed to go on for ever and became steeper with each twist and turn. At first, there was a rope guardrail to hang on to, but after a while, this petered out, leaving Bugsy with nothing to steady him but the stone walls. The steps were narrow with hardly room for his size twelve boots and the worn, sloping surface was lethal. He found the safest way to climb was to wedge himself and his bag firmly between the walls and take one step at a time. How the hell he'd get back down he had no idea but this was no time to turn round and look.

The tower bedroom was bleak and bitterly cold. A spiteful wind whistled in through gaps around the windows and gusted through a hole in the wall the size of a cannon ball. Surely the MacAlisters didn't put B&B guests up here? All he had was a bed, a rickety chair and a wardrobe. No heating apart from a small fire and no plumbing that he could see. Thin rugs covered the loose floorboards just as thin mildew covered the crumbling walls. Nobody sane would pay for this kind of accommodation. On the other hand, there was evidence that somebody had been up there quite recently. There were plenty of fresh footprints in the dust and scratches where something heavy had been dragged across the room. Probably just the housekeeper making up the bed. Good job he wasn't staying long. He unpacked his clothes then rolled up a sweater and stuffed it into the hole to keep out the worst of the draught. Despite the natural ventilation, the room had a strange smell. He sniffed the air like a bloodhound but although it was vaguely familiar, he couldn't quite identify it. He wondered what he'd do if he needed a wee during the night and looked under the bed but there was no receptacle, so it would either be a long trip down the spiral staircase or a short trip to the window.

By the time Bugsy had completed his epic stair descent, some of it in free fall, then wandered around the landings and corridors getting hopelessly lost, Jack was already in the drawing room with DC Mellis making a list of the people he needed to question and the places he wanted to see. Mack was there, being charming and hospitable. A little *too* charming and hospitable in Bugsy's view. He tended to categorize witnesses in a one-dimensional way and Mack came under the heading of 'smarmy bugger'. Experience had shown him that these were the ones to watch.

'I'm afraid you've missed lunch, Inspector, but Moragh has rustled you up a snack.' She was placing a tray on the table as Malone came in. 'I'll leave you to it. Just call if you need anything. Fraser is waiting outside to show you around when you're ready.'

They helped themselves to some thick, brackish tea and Bugsy took a large helping of the food. Jack waited until Mack was out of earshot.

'OK, Bugsy, first impressions.'

'They're a strange lot, guv. We've got three generations of MacAlisters, if you count the old girl in the attic; two elderly retainers straight out of the Addams family; a couple of wealthy Yanks digging up their roots and a property manager who's as jumpy as a cat in a Korean kitchen. None of 'em admits to knowing the dead girl except Fraser Grant and then only by sight.' He forked up a large mouthful of something oily and began chewing. 'You know what you always say, Jack. The murderer is usually the last person to see the victim alive or the first person to find 'em dead. Grant could be both.'

'He's certainly very twitchy about something. But we mustn't get too previous. We may find nothing suspicious here at all. Despite the pathologist's doubts, we've no proof yet that Astrid was murdered. We'll take a look at the spot where Grant found the body, ask him a few questions then spread ourselves about at dinner this evening and talk informally to everyone else. We'll meet up in the morning to discuss what we've learned and what more we need to find out. What do you say?'

'Can't say anything at the moment, guv,' mumbled Malone, 'me teeth are glued together.' He gulped hard. 'Flippin' heck, Maggie, what is this stuff?'

'It's haggamuggie, Sarge. It's a Shetland speciality, a bit like haggis. You take the stomach of a large fish, that's the "muggie", and stuff it with chopped fish livers and oatmeal. Then you tie up the ends and boil it.'

'Don't tell me anymore, I'll just have some bread. Roll on Christmas!'

Fraser Grant was pacing nervously up and down in the hall, waiting for them. Jack shook his hand to try to put him at his ease. It didn't work; his palms were cold and clammy.

'Thank you for sparing us some of your time, Mr Grant, I know you must be a busy man with this huge estate to look after. Do you live in the castle?'

'N-no, I live in one of the c-cottages on the estate. And I don't only w-work for the MacAlisters.' Nerves made his stammer worse. 'I d-divide my t-time between Doomdochry and s-several other p-proper-ties, n-necessitating frequent t-trips to the m-mainland.'

'Is that right, sir? Well, perhaps you'd be kind enough to let my constable have a list and details of when you were away.'

'Of c-course.'

'Could you show us where you found the young woman's body?'

The four of them traipsed around the castle walls in sub-zero temperatures. Finally Grant stopped at a patch of rocky ground where the snow had been cleared away. The local constable who had attended the scene had erected stakes and tied police tape around them but the savage elements had left it tattered and flapping in the wind.

'She w-was l-lying there, Inspector.' It was becoming increasingly hard for him to continue and there was little more they could learn from a week-old crime scene. It had gone cold in more ways than one. Jack took a few steps back and looked up at the blackened tower from which the girl had fallen. He knew he would have to go up there himself at some point but he wasn't looking forward to it. He decided to go back inside before they all froze to death.

'Shall we continue in the library? I don't believe there's much here.'

They had taken over the library as a makeshift incident room and now they sat round an old rosewood reading table with Grant, while DC Mellis made notes. Jack opened the file that DCS Cameron had given him.

'According to this report, you found the young woman lying dead at around three o'clock on the morning of December 11th. Is that correct, sir?'

'Y-yes. It w-would have b-been about three.'

'Two pathologists have estimated time of death between midnight and one o'clock so you must have found the deceased very soon after she fell.'

'Yes, I s-suppose I must. But she was already s-stiff and c-cold, almost covered with s-snow. I shouldn't have seen her at all if it hadn't been for that g-green shawl thing she always w-wore. It showed up in my flashlight.'

'In your statement you said you recognized her as Astrid, a young traveller from a nearby commune. How well did you know her, Mr Grant?'

'I d-didn't know her at all. I'd j-just seen her around once or t-twice. I didn't even know her n-name was Astrid until afterwards.'

'Did you see anyone else there? Maybe loitering about or coming out of the castle?'

'N-no. I wouldn't expect to s-see anyone at that time of n-night.'

'Which raises the question of what *you* were doing there, sir.' Bugsy rested his elbows on the table and leaned forward to eyeball Grant. 'Surely you're not required to patrol the estate at night as well as during the day?'

Grant gulped and opened and closed his mouth but no sound would come out. They sat in silence for over a minute, waiting for him to speak. He became more and more agonized with dark stains spreading from his armpits onto his shirt. Beads of sweat had formed on his top lip and the smell of second hand whisky oozed from him in nervous waves.

Bugsy tried again. 'Tell us what you were doing outside at three in the morning, Mr Grant. Had you arranged to meet Astrid?'

'N-no. I told you, I-I ...' he swallowed hard, 'I only knew her by s-sight. I s-saw her in the village once. She was a s-sad, skinny little thing. She l-lived at the commune with those Viking weirdoes. Why don't you s-speak to them?'

'Have you ever used heroin, Mr Grant?' Malone believed in shock-tactics.

'No, of course not! What are you accusing me of?' This came in a rush with no speech impediment at all now he was riled.

Jack spoke quietly. 'Take it easy, Mr Grant, we're not accusing you of anything. The Fiscal wants the death investigated and we need to find out as much about it as we can.'

'B-but why? She committed s-suicide, didn't she?'

Jack didn't answer that. 'Where had you been prior to finding Astrid?'

There was a long silence, then: 'F-for a w-walk.'

'It was chucking it down, sleet and snow, and cold enough to freeze the Niagaras off a brass monkey.' Bugsy returned to the fray. 'So you decided to go for a walk?'

'Yes, I suffer from insomnia. Is that OK with you, Sergeant?' He stood up. 'Look, I've had enough of this. I can't tell you anything more and I'm leaving now. I have work to do.'

Jack was intrigued at how the stammer disappeared when Grant became angry. 'Very well, sir, but we may need to speak to you again.'

Grant strode from the room and closed the shabby doors with rather more force than was necessary.

'There'll be no paint left on those doors by the time we've finished,' observed Bugsy, wryly.

Jack stroked his chin. 'I think he was a bit upset, don't you?'

'D'ye think he's no' telling us the whole truth?' asked DC Mellis

'I'm quite sure he isn't. For a start, if he'd only seen Astrid once or twice, how did he know she always wore a green shawl and lived on a commune? And I doubt you could tell that someone was sad enough to commit suicide if you only knew them by sight. No, he definitely knows more than he's letting on and he's scared. We'll question him again after we've found out a bit more. He was right about one thing, though. We need to speak to the people at that commune he mentioned. Do you know anything about it, Maggie?'

'Not much, sir. It wasn't set up till a year ago and I was away to Inverness by then. But I did a wee bit o' research after DCS Cameron mentioned it.' She opened her notebook. 'The commune's called Laxdale and the folk who live there have all taken Viking names. There're about a dozen of them, mostly older folk, and a few animals. According to their website …' she read from her notes '… it's a small, self-supporting eco-community with ideals and spirituality appropriate to the purpose and nature of the environment and some of the better aspects of the Viking culture. They welcome guests and some visitors end up staying there. It's ideal in its simplicity and practicality as long as you're mobile and can cope with outside toilets.'

'Laxdale …' Jack racked his brains, '… wasn't that an Icelandic Saga? If I remember rightly, it's a collection of stories about the early Celtic settlers.'

'Aye, I'm no' surprised, sir. There's a lot of Norse still thriving on Shetland.'

'Good work, Constable Mellis. We'll pay Laxdale a visit tomorrow.' He looked at his watch. 'Too late to interview anyone else, dinner's at six, so I suggest we go to our rooms, phone our families to let them know we've arrived safely, then meet up in the dining room. Let's use the opportunity to get a better picture of the set up here while everyone's relaxed. I doubt we'll get anything useful out of the Earl and Lady Alice, so I'll sit next to Mack MacAlister, Maggie you take his wife, Melissa, and Sergeant Malone can chat up Randall and Nicole from Seattle. We'll compare notes tomorrow morning in the incident room.'

Inside his room, Jack stoked the fire, loosened his tie and speed-dialled Corrie on his mobile. She answered straight away.

'Hello, darling. What's Doomdochry like? Is it a real fairy-tale castle?'

'Not unless Dracula was a fairy.'

'And the suspicious death? Was it a murder, do you think?'

'It's still early days, but something isn't right. I need to get answers to a few more questions before I make up my mind. It may be a while before I'm home. How are the Christmas orders going?'

'Great. Rushed off my feet. Have you got your dinner jacket with you?'

'We're never without one, me and James Bond.' He snorted. 'No, of course I haven't, you barmpot. Why would I need a DJ in a place like this?'

'Well, you never know. Cynthia Garwood says she and George go to a lot of posh events in Scotland, what with golf and the fishing and Burns' Night.'

'Burns' Night? That's the end of January, isn't it? I want to have this sorted out long before then. Incidentally, your chum Cynthia never told us Charlie Cameron was a woman, did she?'

'No, she didn't. Fancy that. No wonder she was so mysterious about it.' She paused. 'You will let me know how the case is going, won't you? I may be able to help with some ideas. I could even come up there after my Christmas rush is over and do a bit of sleuthing.'

Over my dead body, thought Jack. 'Thank you, but I think we can manage without your razor sharp powers of detection.'

'Must go, Jack, I have to box two hundred mince pies.'

'Well keep your guard up, darling.'

She giggled. 'They'll never whup me, they're too full of brandy.'

'I'll ring again tomorrow night. Love you.'

'Love you too.'

CHAPTER NINE

The Green Dining-Room was so-called because of the stained glass window bearing the Doomdochry coat-of-arms that dominated the west wall. When the meagre Shetland daylight hit the window, it clouded the room with a stagnant green murk. Alistair MacAlister Senior sat at one end of the heavy, mahogany 'D' end dining-table and facing him, some twenty feet away, was Lady Alice, making it impossible for them to chat to each other or anybody else, particularly the police. Around the table were sixteen dining chairs upholstered in cracked leather. Moragh trundled the food round on a trolley which, like its driver, had seen better days. In recognition of its historic effect on the English, Geordie strutted behind her playing the bagpipes so conversation was impossible until everyone had been served.

Jack pointed to the window. 'That's an impressive coat-of-arms.'

'It is, rather,' said Mack. 'The design depicts an escutcheon vert, that's a green shield, signifying the wild Shetland landscape. The figure is MacAlister, rampant, holding a dagger, argent, dripping blood or gules, after he'd negotiated a somewhat tricky settlement with the Vikings. The story goes that King Christian I of Denmark and Norway was in financial trouble, so when his daughter, Margarethe, became engaged to King James III of Scotland in 1468, he needed money to pay her dowry. MacAlister assisted by persuading Christian to pawn Shetland to the Scottish king as the dowry. Thus, in 1470, when James permanently annexed the islands to the crown, Scotland achieved its greatest ever territorial boundaries. It was in gratitude for this that the king awarded MacAlister a sum of money and a licence to build and fortify a private castle, hence Doomdochry. The window commemorates the event.'

'It must be very gratifying to be able to trace your ancestry back to such a noble Scottish figure.'

Mack MacAlister smiled wryly. 'If the Doomdochry ghost story is to be believed, there were aspects of his behaviour that were far from noble. In 1490, when he was in his fifties, he married Lady Jean, a beautiful young woman of eighteen from a very rich family.'

'Nothing wrong with that as long as you don't have a weak heart.'

Mack laughed. 'She was heiress to a vast amount of money and land. To begin with, all went well and after a year of marriage, a son was born. Then, Lady Jean mysteriously disappeared. The old Earl MacAlister was said to be a very possessive husband and there were suspicions that he'd murdered her in a jealous rage. He claimed she'd run off with a young lover but Lady Jean's family insisted she would never have left her little boy. From then on, strange manifestations began to plague Doomdochry. People reported seeing an apparition of the top half of a woman, just the head and upper torso, moving along the passageway towards the tower bedroom. Apparently, she's bathed in an eerie green glow and floats near the ceiling with an expression of dreadful sorrow on her face. It's said to be accompanied by a smell of rotting flesh. Disturbances became so common that the tower bedroom had to be abandoned for some time.'

'What a gruesome story.'

'It gets worse. Her lower half, from the waist down, dressed in blood-spattered green skirts, is reputed to walk near the family burial ground. There were several reported sightings in Victorian times and she became known as The Green Lady. Then, during some renovation work in the early part of the 20th century, the upper bones of a female skeleton were discovered under the floor boards of the tower bedroom. They never found the lower half so it could be buried in the MacAlister graveyard. The locals still won't go near it after dark and many of them, including Geordie and Moragh, claim to have seen Green Jean's bottom half walking there, although why she haunts in two halves remains a mystery. Her appearance is taken as an omen of imminent death, either an Earl of Doomdochry or a member of his family.'

'And what about you, Mr MacAlister. Have you seen her?'

Mack shrugged. 'No, I haven't. History and factual details are one thing but the ghost story has clearly been embellished down the years. There's no way to verify supernatural phenomena, you either believe in ghosts or you don't. Like all uncertainties in life, the believer will continue to believe and the doubter will continue to doubt. Personally, I can't understand why so many sane, rational and often previously sceptical people have uncanny and unexplainable experiences. But then, so much of a ghost story depends on the motives of the witness who's propounding it, don't you agree?'

Jack nodded. 'I take much the same view about suspects' evidence statements. So what happened to the old Earl in the end? Was he found guilty and brought to book?'

'Now that's the really chilling part. He fell from the tower parapet one dark, winter's night and smashed his brains out on the rocks below. Shortly before he fell, he was heard screaming in terror and begging to be left alone although there was no one up there with him. Locals believe he was driven mad by the perpetual torment of his wife's ghost and that he jumped to escape the terrible reproach in her demonic green eyes. Of course, it makes a cracking story for the tourists, who expect every Scottish castle to have an in-house bogle. Some of our B&B guests say they've heard banging and knocking in the night and heavy footsteps on the staircase. Difficult to know whether this was true or just their fitting the facts to the legend. All I can say for sure is that when Great Aunt Flora said she saw the phantom, I dismissed it as too much whisky and general senility. But when Melissa claimed to have seen The Green Lady, I had to believe her.'

'Your wife has seen the ghost?'

'So she says. She has trouble sleeping here in the castle, so rather than disturb me, she often goes for a walk, just as far as Doomdochry Burn and the estate cottages. On this particular night, it started snowing hard so she was hurrying back. As she passed beneath the tower, a piece of crumbling masonry fell at her feet, making her look up. She shone her torch upwards and saw the top half of a young woman in green, leaning over the parapet. As soon as the light hit her, the apparition disappeared according to Mel.'

First Fraser Grant, now Melissa MacAlister. Jack wondered how many more of the residents spent their nights wandering about outside in the freezing cold instead of staying tucked up in their beds. Or maybe they had been tucked up in bed; the same bed, in Grant's estate cottage. What if he and Melissa MacAlister were having an affair? That would set the wild cat among the gannets all right.

'Mel told everyone about seeing Green Jean the next day,' continued Mack. 'Randall was absolutely delighted but I think it may be why Fraser was so spooked when he found Astrid. All he saw in the darkness was the outline of a body and something green.'

'Yes, I can see how that would give you the creeps in the middle of the night.' Jack took a sip of the whisky that was served at every meal including breakfast, when the Earl poured it on his porridge. He gasped a bit and wondered which of the Highland Malt distilleries it came from. It was incredibly strong and smoky and tasted of peat. 'It'll be quite a responsibility taking all this on when you inherit the title.'

Mack frowned. 'Doomdochry has been in my family for more than five hundred years, Inspector. Naturally, my father expects me to carry on here after he's gone.'

Jack sensed a "but" coming.

'But Mel isn't at all happy with the idea, and that's putting it mildly. I can't blame her. You see, we've made our own life in Surrey.'

Jack raised his eyebrows. 'You don't live here in the castle, then?'

'Good Lord no. We came up here a couple of weeks ago to spend Christmas and Hogmanay with my mother and father. Just as well we did. It was a terrible shock for them when that poor girl was found dead.'

'So what do you do in Surrey, sir?'

'I'm a neurosurgeon and Melissa runs her own interior design company. We have a beautiful home, thanks to Mel's flair, and a busy social life. Living here would put an end to everything we've worked for but if I don't carry on the title, it'll break Father's heart. I've been trying to persuade my parents to sell up and live somewhere more comfortable but Dad won't hear of it.'

'I can see your dilemma, Mr MacAlister. What will you do?'

'God knows. I've been half hoping the damn place would just fall down of its own accord. Then the Historic Scotland people could preserve the ruins for posterity and we could all get on with our lives.'

'But it isn't it Mr Grant's job to ensure that it doesn't fall down?'

'That's right. Doomdochry would grind to a halt without Fraser.' Mack put down his glass. 'Don't lean on him too hard, Inspector. He's always been highly strung and at the moment, he has a few problems of his own.'

'Really, sir, and what would they be?'

'Well, I don't want to tell tales because Fraser and I go back a long way, but I think he has some bad debts. I've offered to help but he just clams up when I mention it. He's drinking rather a lot, too.'

'Difficult to see how anyone could get into debt here.'

'It's when he visits the other properties he services, on the mainland.

He has a gambling habit. He's also involved with a woman. I've no idea who.'

'Dear me. Gambling, drinking and women. Nearly all the vices a man can acquire in one hit. Does he use drugs, do you know?'

'No, I'm pretty sure Fraser wouldn't touch drugs and as a doctor, I think I'd spot the signs. But he's not coping at all well and finding that girl's body was the last straw.'

On the opposite side of the table, DC Mellis in her tartan frock, felt a complete muppet next to Melissa MacAlister, who was wearing very little yet looked amazing. Maggie had half hoped the inspector would let her question Mack but he obviously thought a female officer, speaking woman-to-woman, would get more information out of Mrs MacAlister.

Melissa poked languidly at her boiled mutton with a fork but as far as Maggie could tell, she hadn't put any in her mouth. Maybe that was how skinny women stayed slim, they never actually ate anything, just pushed it around the plate until someone came and took it away. Maggie's only diet dictum was "never eat more than you can lift". Bored, Melissa put down her fork and stared with amusement at her bizarrely-dressed dinner companion.

'You're from Unst, aren't you, Constable?'

'That's right, madam. I was born in Baltasound.'

Melissa snorted. 'Don't call me "madam" for Christ's sake; it makes me sound like a brothel keeper. What's your first name?'

'Maggie.'

'So tell me, Maggie, what on earth do civilized people find to do in a place like Doomdochry? It's simply gross! Everything's nine million years old. I mean, look at these knives and forks, they're like garden tools. And you should see the kitchen. It's full of enormous iron utensils, no sign of a microwave oven or a cappuccino machine anywhere. And God only knows how you'd get a Jacuzzi to work when there's thick green scum on the water and the electricity keeps coming and going.'

'So you're not happy living here with your husband, then?' Maggie would have willingly shared a bothy with Mack MacAlister, given the chance.

'You must be joking! I don't *live* here and I've no intention of moving into this ghastly castle when Father-in-law snuffs it, either. I'm a professional interior designer but frankly, I shouldn't know where to start with all this rotting timber and crumbling stone. And it's so frightfully cold, like living in the Dark Ages.'

Maggie noticed that when Melissa was determined about something, she stuck out her chin so far that her pert, unfettered little breasts lay in permanent shadow. She comforted herself with the knowledge that big trouble lay ahead when the old Earl died and Mack inherited the title and the castle. But that wasn't what she was here to find out.

'Did you know the lassie who was found dead here, Mrs MacAlister?'

'No. I didn't. She was some sort of vagrant, wasn't she?'

'What about your husband? Might he have met her?'

'Mack?' She did her Sloaney snort again. 'Hardly. Of course, he spends more time up here than I do, but as he told you in the library this afternoon, none of us had seen her before she turned up dead at the foot of the tower.' She paused and a tiny frown crinkled her carefully moisturized brow. 'Except perhaps Fraser.'

'So Mr Grant knew her?'

'Yes, I think he must have. Otherwise, why would he have made such a fuss when he found the body? I know it must be ghastly to find someone dead, but he completely lost it, weeping and wailing like a toddler having a tantrum. I'd have given him a good slap but Mack poured him a stiff whisky, gave him a sedative and calmed him down. He's been looking out for Fraser ever since they were kids. Something to do with his mother dying when he was born.' She grimaced. 'Oh God, here comes Moragh with the dessert. If it's stewed bog-berries, don't have any. I think she treads them in her bare feet.'

Sitting dutifully between Randall and Nicole MacAlister, Sergeant Malone was chatting to Nicole over a plate of stringy old ewe and the irony was not lost on him. Randall seemed deeply engrossed in replenishing his whisky and disinclined to join in the conversation. Bugsy paused to tweak a piece of gristle from between his front teeth and Nicole gave him her Botox, trout-pout smile.

'The food's crap, isn't it? I'll be glad to get back to Gainsborough.'

'I thought you lived in Seattle.'

'We do, Officer. Gainsborough's the name of our yacht. She's moored just off the Unst coast.'

'I thought I heard Mr MacAlister say you were paying guests here.'

'We are, but I go back to the yacht to chill out when I can't stand this god-awful nuthouse another minute. Randy's totally infatuated with it. He even grew that dumb beard so he'd look more like a Scottish MacAlister. In case you're wondering, Randy's just his name; it has fuck-all to do with his sex-drive.' She laughed and lurched towards him.

'When your husband said you didn't live here permanently *yet*, I took that to mean he intends to in the future.'

'That's right. Randy wants to buy Doomdochry and turn it into a theme park. Ever since he found out his clan ancestors lived here, he can't talk about anything else and now his mind's made up, he won't quit till he gets it. When it comes to private enterprise, he makes Donald Trump look like Forrest Gump.'

Malone whistled. 'It'll cost a bit, won't it? A castle and all the Doomdochry estate, never mind the development costs.'

'Randy can afford it. Can't you, honey?' She leaned across Bugsy, gripping his thigh in the process, and spoke loudly to her husband as if he were deaf or simple. 'I was telling Detective Malone that you're gonna buy this dump and turn it into Doomdochry World.'

Randall was trying to line up the whisky bottle with his glass. Distracted, he looked away and poured a generous treble over his hand. 'You bet. The old Earl's real stubborn, but I'll keep upping the ante till he gives in.'

'Randy retired last year and sold his IT company so big bucks aren't a problem. Boredom, that's his problem. He's looking for another empire to build.'

'And what are you looking for, madam?' Bugsy reckoned he already knew what this woman was after from the way she kept pressing her thigh against his and it was nothing to do with castles or computers. He wasn't flattered. She was the type who came on to every man in the room, regardless of race, sexual orientation or physical decrepitude. Most of the time, he liked women in a sad, baffled kind of way but this one had had rather more to drink than was seemly for a lady. She leaned very close and grasped his lapel as if to say something lewd.

'Art.'

'Actually, my name's Michael but people call me Bugsy because....'

She laughed. It was a raucous, bawdy laugh much louder and longer than the feeble humour of the misunderstanding warranted. 'No, honey. I mean art as in paintings. That's my thing. I travel round the world, collecting for my private gallery back home.'

That explained why their yacht was called the Gainsborough, thought Bugsy. He carried on eating, trying not to bend his fork in the mashed tatties. 'What do you reckon to the paintings here in the castle?' The dining room had oil paintings hanging on every available inch of wall, mostly of bellicose MacAlisters in kilts, brandishing primitive Highland weapons or young women with profiles like Red Rum surrounded by litters of snotty kids.

'They're all fakes. Pretty good ones, but fakes all the same.'

Bugsy couldn't argue on the basis that he wouldn't know a genuine Van Gogh from a quarter of jelly babies. 'Not worth much, then?'

'Zilcho, honey.'

'How do you get on with the MacAlisters?'

'Well, I guess they're Randall's folks in a lame kind of way. Christ knows how they stand it here. Mack's a hunk but that little wife of his is real flaky and so is Fraser, the guy who found that girl's body. I was asleep at the time, I'd taken one of my pills, but they say he howled the place down and he's been real edgy ever since. Weird wouldn't you say?'

'Did you know the dead girl?'

'Nope. The first time I saw her was when they loaded her into the meat wagon. And even if I'd seen her before, I doubt if I'd have remembered. I mean, she wasn't particularly memorable, was she?'

CHAPTER TEN

ELEPHANT & CASTLE – SOUTH LONDON
DECEMBER 17TH

While the MacAlisters were dining in Doomdochry, Lenny Lennox was lying low in South London. He'd heard a whisper that there was another warrant out for his arrest in connection with Angel's murder and decided it might be prudent to disappear until the heat died down. This time, it was Inspector Drake who was looking for him and he didn't play by the rules like the other bloke. DI Drake would fit you up soon as look at you, just so he could knock off work early. He'd even heard rumours that Drake took the odd bung.

The Old Bill had already turned over his flat. At least, he thought it was them. He'd come home from the pub to find the door kicked in and the place ransacked. Bloody cheek! They'd have to pay for the repairs. He knew his rights. When Harry Hoxton tipped him the wink that a couple of blokes had been in the bookie's asking for him, he did a runner. His lock-up, tucked away behind the junction of Elephant Road and New Kent Road was known only to a few trusted felons who occasionally slipped him a few quid to store their stolen goods. Currently, it contained a number of expensive electrical items rescued from posh houses with parlously inadequate security systems, and several cases of Bulgarian cognac that had apparently survived a fall off the back of a lorry. It also contained the wherewithal for a few days' camping out.

He'd got a small paraffin heater going and was plugging in his kettle to make himself a mug of tea when he heard a rattle, as though the steel roller door was being lifted. Either the wind was getting up or he hadn't shut it down properly. He got up from his patio chair and went to check. The door was closed again and he was about to return to his tea when he saw something that made his blood run cold. The two gorillas who appeared from behind the cases of cognac were not Old Bill and they didn't play by any rules. The taller of the two, muscle-bound and bull-necked, had a coil of rope over his shoulder. The other man, swarthy and of mixed race, had staring eyes like a snake watching its prey, ready to strike at the slightest movement. Snake-Eyes strolled to the door and leaned against it, casually peeling an orange with a small fruit knife and effectively blocking any means of escape. Both men wore latex gloves and heavy walking boots, selected for kicking rather than hiking.

'Hallo, Lenny.' The muscular man walked towards him, cracking his knuckles. 'We've come for a little chat. You see, the boss wants us to make sure you don't chat to anyone else … like the filth, for example.' He rubbed at a long scar on his cheek he'd got courtesy of an erstwhile cell mate with a cutthroat razor.

Terrified, Lenny backed away. 'But I wouldn't talk. He knows that. I'm not a grass. He can trust me.'

Snake-Eyes shook his head. 'But I'm afraid he doesn't trust you, Lenny. You're a stinking, cowardly little rat and he thinks that when the cops get hold of you again, you'll crack and tell them everything you know and he can't allow that. So he asked us to come and see you, to make sure it doesn't happen.' He swallowed the last segment of his orange then produced a pair of pliers from his pocket.

'No, please. Listen to me. I'm solid, I promise. I won't say anything; you've got to believe me.' Lenny edged sideways, his head jerking from one thug to the other, trying to gauge the speed of their reactions if he made a run for it. Desperate, he grabbed a sledge-hammer leaning against the wall and spinning around, he whirled it above his head in a two-handed grip, his eyes wild and frenzied. But even as he fought, he knew he was a dead man. Scar-Face leaped on him from behind, locking a bulging forearm across Lenny's throat in a strangling grip, making him drop the hammer. He held him there, weeping and begging, while the other man recovered the coil of rope and secured it to a joist in the lock-up roof. Then he made a noose. They fetched Lenny's patio chair, stood him on it and slipped the noose round his neck.

'Now you mustn't take this personally, Lenny. It's just a warning from the boss to any other miserable little bastard who feels like squealing to the police.' Scar-Face pinioned Lenny's arms with ease while Snake-Eyes forced his mouth open and grabbed his tongue with the pliers. Then he produced the sharp, serrated knife he had used to peel his orange.

It took longer than they expected for Lenny to die, given that he was a weak, pathetic little weasel. After he'd kicked the chair away, Snake-Eyes wiped the blood from his knife and peeled another orange, but still Lennox thrashed and gurgled at the end of the rope. In the end, they had to pull on his feet to finish him off. He was quiet now, though, swinging slowly from side to side, blood trickling from his mouth and down his greasy jacket, his trousers stinking where he had soiled himself in terror. Before they left, they carefully removed the cable tie from around his thumbs, extinguished the paraffin heater and unplugged the kettle. The boss wouldn't want the place to burn down before the police found the body and the underworld got the message. Outside, they pulled down the shutter door, peeled off their blood-stained gloves and lumbered away. The street was silent. Nobody had heard Lenny's last agonized shrieks. But sooner or later, some passing opportunist would notice the padlock was missing and venture inside.

CHAPTER ELEVEN

DOOMDOCHRY CASTLE – DECEMBER 18TH

Early morning, and a porridge-coloured dawn was beginning to touch the east battlements. The first gannet honked its gullet free of mackerel bones prior to shattering the silence with a harsh "Arrrh Arrrh". Up in the tower bedroom, DS Malone's toothpaste had frozen solid in its tube and his face flannel was a tile of ice. Before getting into bed, he had put all his clothes back on over his pyjamas and wrapped himself in the brown, utility blankets that were on the bed. Reluctant now to unwind them, he stumbled down the spiral stone steps to the bathroom like a giant twill sausage. By the time he reached the library incident room, his round face was shiny and his hair was tidy. The rest of him looked like it had been thrown together on a Friday afternoon when the factory was in a hurry to close down for the weekend. DI Dawes was his usual immaculate self and Maggie, in a thick sweater and sturdy trousers, was dishing out hot coffee and bannocks.

'Morning all.' Jack opened his file. 'Shall we start with a debrief of last night at dinner? Bugsy, you first.'

'Randall P. MacAlister made his millions from his IT empire in Seattle which he sold when he took early retirement, lucky bugger. He came to Shetland to trace his family tree and now he wants to buy Doomdochry and develop it, but the old Earl doesn't want to play. Nicole MacAlister's a bored American housewife who puts it about. In fact, I'd be surprised if any of "it" is still in the same place it started out; it's been lifted, pleated, re-sized or re-sited, probably with enough bits left over to make another one. I shouldn't want to see her first thing in the morning.' He shuddered. 'She travels a lot, collects fine art and owns a private gallery in the States. She reckons all the paintings in the castle are fakes. They own a whacking great yacht called the Gainsborough which is moored off the coast and she uses a speedboat to get to it when she's pissed off with living in what she calls "a medieval Big Brother House". Says she never knew Astrid but I'm not surprised; I reckon she's the type of woman who only notices men.'

'Nothing to suggest she gets her kicks chucking people off towers?'

Bugsy grinned. 'No, guv. One thing was odd, though. She behaved like she was as hammered as her old man but as far as I could see, she hardly touched the booze all night. Why would she do that?'

'If that's a multiple choice question, I'd say A – she was already drunk when she came down to dinner; B – she wanted you to think she was drunk so if she said anything indiscreet, she could deny it after-wards, or C – she was planning something extramarital and, if she appeared drunk, it would put Randall P. off the scent.'

'You have a very devious mind, guv.'

'So my wife keeps telling me. What about you, DC Mellis? What can you tell us about Melissa MacAlister?'

'She's bonnie but not smart. She hates Doomdochry and says she won't live here when her husband's the Earl. She didn't know the dead lassie but thinks Mr Grant did because of the fuss when he found her body. Greetin' like a bairn, she said.'

'That's interesting because Mack MacAlister told me Grant has a gambling and drinking habit and is involved with a woman. We have to consider that the woman could have been Astrid, even though he denies knowing her.'

Bugsy nodded. 'Nicole MacAlister confirmed Grant made a fuss when he found Astrid dead. A bit too emotional for someone who'd never met her, she reckoned.'

'But why lie?' asked Maggie. 'It wasn't as if he was married or anything.'

'Because she was up the duff, Constable, and it would make him an obvious contender. How about this for a scenario? Grant smuggles Astrid into the castle and up to the tower bedroom for a quickie but instead of getting the old Alan Whickers down, she tells him she's preg-nant. He doesn't want to know, says it's all over and legs it. She throws a wobbly, gives herself an overdose, staggers out onto the parapet and falls off. Case closed.' Bugsy bit into another bannock and put one in his pocket for later.

'It's a possibility, Bugsy. We could ask Grant to provide a DNA sample to see if he was the father, but I doubt if he'll agree. I certainly wouldn't in his position.'

'Why would she take a syringe of heroin with her if, like the pathologist said, she didn't do drugs?' asked Maggie.

'Good point, DC Mellis. Then, of course, there's Mack. As a surgeon, he'd have access to heroin and he'd know how and where to inject it. And he *is* married, never mind the threat to his professional integrity.'

Bugsy grinned. 'He's a surgeon, is he? I suppose that makes him Mack the Knife.' His mobile rang while he was still chuckling. He pulled it out and looked at it. 'It's Julie Molesworth, guv.' He sighed theatrically. 'The women won't leave you alone when you're sexy and lovable.' He strolled to the far end of the library, listening intently and grunting from time to time.

'Of course,' said Jack, 'the father of Astrid's baby could well be someone from the Laxdale commune. The sooner we find out what they know, the better. Rule One in the Dawes' Manual of Murder Investigation, Maggie. Find out how the victim lived and it'll give you a clue about why they died.'

'Right, sir. I've arranged a visit to Laxdale this morning. We could go as soon as Sergeant Malone has finished on the phone.'

'Good. After that, I think we'll have another talk to Fraser Grant.'

Bugsy returned looking grim. 'You're not going to like this, guv. Lenny Lennox is dead.'

'Dead? How?'

'Ducky Drake put out a warrant for his arrest for the Baxter killing; let all his underworld snouts know we were looking for him. They found the poor little bugger in the lock-up where he stashed his stolen goods. He was hanging from a metal joist in the roof and it looks like he'd bitten off his own tongue.'

Jack scowled. 'So what's Drake doing about it?'

'Nothing. DC Molesworth says Ducky's treating it as suicide. Reckons Lenny hanged himself in remorse for cutting Karen Baxter's throat. Two deaths, two results. Makes his clean-up rate look good and he doesn't need to lift a finger.'

'That's nonsense. Lenny Lennox would never hang himself, he didn't have the guts, poor little devil. What about the post-mortem?'

'Big Ron did it and she's not happy. Reckons he didn't bite through his tongue, it was cut out with a serrated blade to make it look like he had.'

DC Mellis went white. 'Och, dear Lord! Why would anyone do that?'

'It was a message, love. Someone thought Lenny was about to grass so they killed him before he got the chance. They cut out his tongue as a warning to anyone else who might be inclined to talk to the police. Now we'll never find out what it was he knew about Karen Baxter's murder. What will you do, Jack?'

'Not much I *can* do while it's still Drake's case. But I'm not going to let it go. I'll have a word with Dr Hardacre and then, maybe, DCS Garwood if he'll listen. Just because Lenny was at the bottom of the criminal food chain doesn't mean his murder's of no consequence. Ask Julie to keep us informed of anything new. Right now, though, we need to pay Laxdale a visit. Is it far, Maggie?'

'No, sir, but you won't want to walk. Not in this weather.'

Jack remembered the heavy tyre tracks. Probably a Land Rover or a big BMW model. 'Let's ask Mr MacAlister if there's a vehicle we could borrow.'

Bugsy had never seen a 1958 Volvo station wagon with the original AA badge still on it. It was mainly blue but the bonnet and one wing had been painted orange at some point in its life. The body filler used to disguise the rust was mostly what held it together. Mack handed him the keys.

'The old estate wagon's going well at the moment, Sergeant, so you shouldn't have any problems. Just make sure you don't overdo the throttle when you start her or the choke floods the carburettor. If it happens, just leave her for a bit, then have another go.' He shouted after them as they chugged away. 'Don't worry about the funny smell coming through the heater vents. It's probably a dead rat.'

The car lurched and juddered, sleet hammering on the roof, the windscreen wipers squealing as they tried to cope with the snowy onslaught. Driven horizontal by keen winds, it blasted in through the front passenger's window which was jammed permanently open. Jack, in the back seat, offered Maggie his raincoat which she put over her head in an attempt to stave off the worst of the blizzard.

The road to Laxdale was narrow, rutted and steep and tested the Volvo's springs to the limit. Finally, the old wagon jerked and spluttered up a single-track, barely wide enough for a wheelbarrow. The tall iron gates at the end of the approach road had rusted permanently open and swinging above them, a newly painted sign read, "Welcome to Laxdale". Beside it hung a logo, shaped like the head of a hammer and decorated with Viking symbols. Jack surveyed the bleak surroundings through the rear window and decided that "welcome" was the last word he would have used. If Doomdochry was remote, then Laxdale, set in this windswept, treeless wilderness, might almost have been on a different planet: a dank, desolate planet with a harsh and hostile atmosphere.

It had been a bumpy, uncomfortable ride so it was a relief when Malone finally coaxed the wagon to a halt in the untidy sprawl of the commune small-holding. Snow disguised piles of rubbish and battered corrugated sheeting, and rusty wire held in a few scrawny chickens who squawked in protest at the invasion of strangers. Nearby, a mangy goat nibbled at some scrubby weeds.

The main commune house was originally an old barn that had been hastily converted in a manner that suggested thrift rather than comfort. It looked neglected with some of the windows boarded up, peeling paint, and a section of guttering hanging limply down like a broken arm. Close by, a cluster of outbuildings in varying stages of repair, were optimistically labelled 'Workshop', 'Dairy' and 'Galley Shed'. The land immediately adjacent to the house was rocky and unproductive with thin, barren soil evidenced by an abandoned vegetable patch and a dearth of plants.

Reluctantly, the three officers climbed out of the comparative warmth of the car into a howling snowstorm, fighting their way to the door, heads down against the driving gale. Maggie, struggling to stay on her feet, reached the front door first but before she could knock, it flew open and a plump, middle-aged woman popped out. She was dressed as a Viking housewife with a woollen caftan over a hessian apron dress, held up by two large, ugly brooches. Around her neck, she wore several strings of beads and a Viking hammer pendant on a leather thong, like the one on the 'welcome' sign. As an authentic costume, it might have been more impressive without the pac-a-mac covering her shoulders and a pleated plastic rain bonnet of the kind sported by the Queen during a rainy day at Epsom. The woman beckoned to them.

'Quick! Come inside out of the cold.'

They followed her into a large, communal kitchen where a massive iron range dominated one end of the room, belching out acrid fumes and coating everything with dust. A large black cauldron festered balefully on the hotplate. The woman wriggled out of her plastic mac and shook the snow off it.

'*Heilsa!* I'm Thora Sharptongue.' She gave a snort of self-conscious laughter. 'Actually, I'm not really. That's just my Viking name.'

Jack was secretly amused. 'So who are you really?'

'Molly McGillicuddy. I'm from County Kerry originally but now I live here at Laxdale. When you come right down to it, Ireland, Scotland, Wales ... Celts and Vikings ... it's all a big melting pot, isn't it?' She spotted DC Mellis emerging from beneath Jack's raincoat. 'Oh dear, you haven't brought us another lost soul, have you? We seem to have become a centre of pilgrimage for the walking worried.'

'No, we're all police officers,' said Jack, showing her his ID. Malone and Mellis followed suit.

She smote her forehead so violently her rain hat flew off. 'Silly me, of course you are. The young lady constable made an appointment. It's about poor little Astrid, isn't it? What a terrible way to die, and so young.'

'Did you know her well?'

She chewed her lip. 'Not really. None of us did. She just turned up one day out of the blue. That would have been about six months ago. We took her in as a guest, initially, then she said she wanted to join the group permanently. It's not our policy to ask members about their past. They start a new life when they come to Laxdale.'

'Was Astrid her real name, Molly?' asked Malone.

She squirmed uncomfortably. Bugsy reckoned it was either embarrassment or hessian drawers.

'Please call me Thora. Group members are only supposed to use their adopted Viking names. You see, personal identity is bound up with personal possessions and here we practise strict egalitarianism. Everyone contributes what they can for the good of the community. In answer to your question, I've no idea what her real name was; she was always called Astrid, here.'

Jack sat down at the scrubbed pine table; Maggie joined him, notebook at the ready. 'Did she have a boyfriend at Laxdale? Someone she was particularly close to?'

'Definitely not. You'll see why when you meet the others. She was excessively shy and kept herself very much to herself. Her contribution to the community was dressmaking and she was very good at it. She could knit and sew almost anything we needed and in the Viking tradition. She made some very authentic jewellery, too. I asked if her mother had taught her but she said no and looked unhappy, so I didn't push it.'

'So what's your contribution here?' asked Bugsy.

'I'm in charge of housekeeping, guest admissions and candlemaking. Most of our income derives from visitors, paying-guests and selling our aromatherapy candles.'

'That's a very unusual pendant you're wearing,' said Jack. 'Did Astrid make that too?'

Thora fingered it, lovingly. 'Oh, no. This is Thor's Hammer, it's solid silver. We're all given one when we become members of the commune. It represents Thor, who, I expect you know, was the Scandinavian god of thunder. He was red-haired and bearded, like Ragnar, our founder, and he's the god of the common man. Thor was a major hero for mankind, fighting giants and defeating them with his weapon, a hammer called Mjolnir. It had special properties. When Thor hurled it at his enemies, it came back to him, a bit like a Norse boomerang, I suppose. The strike of the hammer caused thunderclaps. In Viking times, people wore Thor's Hammer as a symbol of protection. Nowadays, it represents our Norse heritage and we wear it for courage, strength and success. It's a kind of talisman. Laxdale members never take it off. Astrid was especially proud of hers. She wouldn't even take it off in the bath although I warned her it would weaken the thong.' She seized a large kettle and turned on the tap, fixed loosely to the wall above the large, yellowing butler's sink. Water gushed out in a cloudy stream. 'It's time for our mid-morning coffee break, Inspector Dawes. Will you join us? It will be a good opportunity for you to meet our group and guests and you can ask them about Astrid, although I doubt they'll be able to tell you much more than I have.'

At precisely eleven o'clock, the door opened and a dozen or so assorted Vikings trooped in and sat round the table. Jack reckoned most of the women were at least sixty and as all the men had full beards and whiskers, it was hard to estimate their ages. All the same, Thora was right; it was difficult to imagine an eighteen-year-old girl forming a relationship with any of them that might result in pregnancy. Thora introduced them to the police officers then busied herself with the coffee. The men had names like Knud the Great, Ragnar Redbeard, Ketill Flatnose and Erik the Red. The women were called Gudrun,

Helga, Valgerd, Kadlin, all names taken from the Laxdale Saga as far as Jack's limited knowledge could recall. They all wore Thor's Hammer pendants.

'Which of you is the leader of the commune?' asked Jack.

'We don't go in for anything as fascist as a leader at Laxdale, Inspector.' Ragnar spoke quietly, but when he did, everyone turned to listen. He was an unremarkable man, pale complexioned and dark eyed, with a bushy red beard, moustache and eyebrows. He wore a long-sleeved, hip-length caftan, belted at the waist and decorated with embroidery and appliqué, probably Astrid's work. His tight-fitting breeches reached to his knees with woollen winding-bands, wrapped around his lower legs for warmth.

Very Savile Row, thought Bugsy. Privately, he reckoned they were all barmy and he had no intention of joining in their charade. He was there to investigate a murder and he didn't care whom he offended in the process. 'Are you one of those fanatical religious sects that brain-washes young girls?'

Ragnar replied calmly and without rancour. 'No, Sergeant, we don't practise any kind of structured religion here. Some of us started out as Christians but found we could no longer sustain the delusion. The meek are supposed to inherit the earth, but look around you. Environmentalism must be the new religion or very soon, there'll be no earth left for the meek to inherit.'

'And was Astrid one of the meek?' asked Jack.

'Astrid was an innocent; a child without a family,' said Gudrun, an elderly woman with long grey plaits hanging down from beneath her linen cap. 'She didn't know how to survive in this wicked world. It was as if she'd been born without a set of instructions.'

'We tried our best to look after her, to be her family, but you simply couldn't get close to her,' said Thora, sadly. She handed Bugsy a mug. 'Here you are, Sergeant, homemade coffee. I roasted the acorns myself.'

'Why a *Viking* commune?' Jack was curious. 'They were hardly the epitome of caring and sharing.'

'You see, it's always the same!' protested Valgerd, an Oxford don who considered herself the intellectual of the group. 'From the moment they ransacked that priory at Lindisfarne in 793, the Vikings have had a bad press. They weren't all raping and pillaging, you know. Many of the Norse invaders were model immigrants. Within a relatively short space of time, the various cultures in Britain and Ireland started to intermingle. Emulating that process at Laxdale provides us with a paradigm of how diverse individuals can be absorbed into complex societies, contributing much to those societies in the process. There are still some important lessons for us to learn about cultural assimilation in the modern era.'

'But don't you find yourselves at odds with everyone else?' Jack was thinking maybe Astrid's irresponsible, traveller's way of life had made her some enemies.

Ragnar replied. 'We have our difficulties with bureaucracy of course, Inspector, and we share what are conventionally regarded as radical attitudes towards government and the police but on the whole our commune isn't persecuted by anyone. We aren't victims of oppression. We don't tolerate the use of drugs, alcohol or tobacco. Members here, and that included Astrid, are effectively screened from the world, disengaged. Many of us are cushioned by the belief that it's only a matter of time before everyone gets round to seeing things our way. We may be at odds with society, but we are not in conflict with it.' His smile smacked of superiority. 'We are aware that local people observe our antics with a high degree of scepticism, much of which comes from being brought up in an extreme environment where many idealists have come and gone with their new-fangled ideas in tatters. They will soon discover that Laxdale does not come into that category.'

Bugsy stood up. 'May I use your facilities, please? Must be all that delicious acorn coffee. Goes right through you.'

'Our lavatory is outside, Sergeant,' Thora said. 'Across the yard and to the right. Just follow your nose.'

Bugsy put on his overcoat, winked imperceptibly at Jack and hurled himself out into the snow like Captain Oates on a suicide mission.

'If you want to know my opinion, I object to people like Astrid abusing the commune by thinking they can simply stay here until they find something better,' complained Kadlin. She was a matron of some seventy summers, and if the down-turned mouth and the sour expression were anything to go by, seventy pretty miserable winters.

'Is that what Astrid said?' asked Jack.

Kadlin pulled a face. 'She said "I'm looking for a place to stay while I get myself sorted out". Well, naturally, I thought, oh oh, here's another little madam on drugs, or in debt, or trying to escape from some other consequence of her own silliness. Looks like I may have been right, doesn't it?'

Ragnar shot her a reproving glance and her mouth snapped shut like a rat-trap. 'What Kadlin means, Inspector, is that we prefer pair relationships here,' he explained. 'Singles cause practical, emotional and space problems.'

Jack wondered which one of the women was the other half of Ragnar's 'pair relationship', always assuming it *was* a woman.

'There's just one thing I didn't mention earlier, Mr Dawes,' said Thora. 'You see, I had more daily contact with Astrid than the others and recently, I noticed she'd started being sick in the mornings. I think … well, I'm almost certain she was pregnant. Since she'd been with us for over six months, it must have happened during her stay. Obviously the father was someone outside our community and she thought we'd disapprove, but she didn't have to kill herself. We would have looked after her and the baby, wouldn't we?'

'Of course we would,' chorused the women. Even cantankerous Kadlin.

So they knew about the pregnancy. But Jack decided not to confirm or deny their assumption of suicide, yet. And this was not the time to tell them Astrid's body contained a massive dose of heroin, despite their strict rules about drugs.

'Does anyone have any idea what Astrid was doing on the parapet of Doomdochry Castle at midnight on the tenth of December? Might she have gone there to meet someone?'

'You're wasting your time, Inspector Dawes.' This abrupt indictment came from the man introduced as Ketill Flatnose and it had the effect of terminating any further contributions from the others. 'Astrid was limp and pathetic. The slightest upset drove her into a state of panic and despair. She was just as likely to run up the tower and chuck herself off because …' he cast about for a reason, '… because one of the kittens had died or her knitting had gone wrong.'

'So you don't believe anyone else was involved in her death, then, Mr er, Flatnose.' Jack could see why he'd been given the name. The bloke's nose was spread across his face like a fried egg.

'No, I don't. And the best thing you can do is go back where you came from and stop wasting the taxpayers' money. We don't need law enforcers here, we police our own community.' He stood up and pulled on his coat. 'Come on, Helga, back to work.' He stomped back outside followed by his partner, pushing rudely past Bugsy who was on his way back in.

'I apologize for Ketill,' said Ragnar. 'He and Helga joined us only recently as guests and he hasn't yet relaxed into the easy rhythm of commune life. I think he may be battling some inner demons and we must respect that and support them both. Now, if there's nothing else, Inspector Dawes, we also need to get back to our labours.' They filed out like extras from a low budget costume drama.

Jack thanked Thora for her hospitality and they left, with DC Mellis still scribbling furiously in her burgeoning notebook. Back in the Volvo, Bugsy was too keen to get moving and overdid the throttle. As Mack predicted, the carburettor flooded and they had to sit and wait for it to recover.

'Any observations, Bugsy?'

'Yeah. That acorn coffee tasted like the goat had peed in it. Beats me where she gets the acorns, there isn't a tree for miles.'

Jack grinned. 'You're right, it was foul. But what I really meant was what did you observe when you were snooping around outside, even though we haven't got a search warrant?'

'Me, guv?' protested Bugsy innocently. 'I wasn't snooping, I lost me way looking for the bog. But since you mention it, there's a bloody great Viking ship in the outbuilding marked "Galley Shed".'

Jack stroked his chin thoughtfully. 'Is there really? That's very interesting. Is it seaworthy?'

'Why? What are you thinking?'

'Charlie Cameron said Shetland is one of the safest communities in the UK but they're always on the lookout for drug trafficking and the money laundering that inevitably goes with it. Shetland is at the crossroads of Scotland and Scandinavia, almost equidistant between Aberdeen and Bergen. The main transport links with the UK mainland are through Aberdeen. Think how easy it would be to get from Laxdale to Bergen in a Viking ship without arousing suspicion and with no Customs aggravation.'

'You haven't seen it, guv. That crappy ship would never make it to Norway, it's held together with superglue and Thora's knicker elastic.'

'All right, but what if it could sail part way? Just far enough to be out of sight of the Shetland coast? Then it's met by a powerful speedboat or maybe even a fishing vessel from Bergen. They transfer the loot, disappear up a fjord and Sigmund's your uncle.'

'In that case, what about Randall P. MacAlister's yacht?'

'Right. We've only got Nicole's word that he made his millions from

IT. Suppose he has a side-line in drugs and he's laundering the money using Norwegian casinos or dodgy investment banks?'

'So you reckon Laxdale's a cover for something else? Astrid found out and had to be silenced.'

Jack shrugged. 'I don't know, Bugsy, but we haven't found any other credible motives for someone wanting her out of the way.' He looked at Maggie in the passenger seat, still scribbling away. 'You're very quiet, DC Mellis. What did you think of Laxdale?'

'Och, they're just a wee bunch o' muesli-munchers, sir. Not proper, vicious criminals like the ones you have in London. Will we try the engine now, Sarge? My lug's awful cold.'

Jack pondered on this while Bugsy threaded the old Volvo down the narrow lane. Maggie could be right. Working with the Met made you see master criminals lurking under every stone and incidents like the brutal murders of Karen Baxter and Lenny Lennox did nothing to dispel that view. The Laxdale Commune was probably just what it seemed, a harmless collection of eco-nutters seeking an alternative society by recreating some of the better aspects of Viking culture. Astrid had obviously been one of the 'lost souls' that Thora mentioned, drawn to the commune's pseudo-family as a substitute for the one she'd either lost or never had. She'd been young and naïve and her hunger for affection had resulted in pregnancy. He was aware it was a rather glib analysis and that he was no nearer to unravelling the mystery surrounding her death, but he felt sure about one thing; the answer lay not in Laxdale, but somewhere in Doomdochry Castle.

CHAPTER TWELVE

'You know what I want and I've got what you need. Seems like a straight deal to me.' While the police were drinking acorn coffee at Laxdale, Nicole was in the castle library, sipping the real stuff that she could only get if she brewed it herself. She always carried her own Brazilian beans with her. In her experience, coffee in the UK tasted even worse than the tea.

'Nicole, I'll g-get it, I promise, but I n-need more t-time. You have to help me.'

Nicole put down her cup and strolled casually to the rosewood reading table. She flicked idly through the papers on it. 'There's no "have to" about it, honey. You're in the shit and you want me to get you out of it. I've told you my terms, take it or leave it.'

'B-but we've been so c-close.'

Nicole laughed, a coarse contemptuous laugh. 'Close? I let you shag me and you call it "close"? You Scots, you're so tight-assed.' She opened a file and glanced briefly at the contents. 'Tell me, were you screwing little Miss Muffet at the same time?'

He bridled then, stammer gone. 'No, of course I wasn't! Astrid and I were just friends. She was struggling with some tough decisions and didn't know what to do. She was still a child in lots of ways. She needed to confide in someone she could trust. I'd never have taken advantage of her while she was in that state. What do you take me for?'

'Exactly what you are, baby. A sad little man who drinks too much and owes some bad guys a lotta big bucks.' She glanced slyly at him. 'These tough decisions, they must have been pretty heavy to make her jump off the tower.'

His eyes narrowed. 'They were ... but I d-don't believe she j-jumped. I think s-someone wanted her out of the w-way.'

'Why?'

'I'd rather not s-say but I'm sure she was m-murdered and I'm p-pretty sure I know who did it.'

Nicole scoffed. 'You're just bragging, pretending you're smart. You don't know diddly-squat.'

'Oh yes I do!' Fraser's anger was stutter-free. 'Astrid told me things about certain people that even you would find shocking. She knew stuff so dangerous it got her killed.'

'OK so why haven't you told Dawes? Why did you lie about even knowing her?'

'That's my business.'

'Suit yourself.' She tried the drawer in the table but it was locked.

'Sh-should you be d-doing that?' Fraser asked nervously. 'Those p-papers are p-police p-property, aren't they? I th-think they're using this room as their office.'

She sneered. 'For Chrissake, Fraser. Those old dames who brought you up didn't just mollycoddle you; they cut off your balls. You're so fucking repressed, you can't even talk straight. Anyway, the door wasn't locked and nobody said we couldn't use the library. If they didn't want anyone to see, they shouldn't have left them on view.'

'S-so w-what about it, Nicky? W-will you h-help me?' He went across and tried to put his arms around her. She shrugged him off.

'Sure, I will. Just get me what I want and keep your goddam mouth shut. Then all your problems will be over.'

At four o'clock, the Procurator Fiscal turned up. He was a fastidious little man with a thin moustache and a thick accent. He bustled about the crime scene, demanded an update on the investigation, complained when told there wasn't an update and implied it was all Dawes's fault. Then he climbed back into his mighty beast of a four-by-four which explained the big tyre tracks leading up to the castle and pushed off, threatening to return very soon.

Jack wanted to speak to Big Ron urgently, before the Lennox case was filed away and forgotten. If she'd performed the post mortem, she'd have very definite views about how he died. He punched in her number and waited, hoping she wasn't up to her elbows in some poor devil's entrails. 'Doctor Hardacre? Sorry to ring so late.'

'Is that you, Inspector Dawes?' She sounded surprised. 'I thought you and Malone had pissed off to Scotland to avoid doing any work over Christmas.'

'Something like that, Doctor. But I still have an interest in the Karen Baxter investigation that I had to abandon half way through.'

'I thought it was DI Drake's case now.' She sniffed. 'He's a lazy bugger.'

'Yes, I know. I heard Lennox committed suicide. I was hoping you could give me your opinion.'

'Glad to, although your colleague chose to ignore it. Even before I performed the autopsy, DI Drake decided that Lennox killed the prostitute then hung himself in a fit of depressive remorse. I believe Lennox was murdered. I'll tell you why. He was found hanging from a joist in his lock-up where he'd clearly made provision to lie low for a while. There was a bed, food, heating and a crate of beer. When "uniform" found his body, he'd made himself a sandwich and had started to brew tea, the kettle was full and the tea-bag was already in the mug. If you're planning to hang yourself, you don't make yourself a snack first. SOCO went over the place with a fine tooth comb and found fingerprints, DNA, boot prints from just about every burglar, fence and petty thief in London, just as you'd expect. The place was a Fagin's Kitchen, full of stolen goods. But more specifically, they also found recent marks from a heavy walking boot on the chair that was kicked out from under him. Lennox was wearing trainers. And his neck wasn't broken, he hung there until he choked to death. DI Drake says if he'd been murdered, they'd have tied his hands. It's true there were no marks on his wrists, but if his hands weren't pinioned in some way, why didn't he grab at the rope and try to pull himself free? It's an automatic reaction in people who try to hang themselves, a basic instinct to survive that kicks in if the neck doesn't snap immediately.'

DI Dawes, always squeamish about violent death, swallowed hard.

'I can hear you gulping, Jack. Brace yourself, there's worse to come. Someone tied his thumbs together. I found marks consistent with some simple device, strong enough to restrain the hands but not sharp enough to bruise the skin.'

A cable tie, thought Jack. The mandatory accessory without which no self-respecting gangland thug would leave home.

'And lastly, he didn't bite through his tongue in his final death throes. It was cut out using a small knife with a serrated blade, the kind used for peeling and slicing fruit or vegetables. The SOCO team found a fragment of orange peel with minute traces of the victim's blood on it. No DNA from the user of the knife, unfortunately. I think your killer peeled and ate an orange after he did the deed. What kind of callous bastard could do that?'

'I don't know, Doctor, but I'm going to find out. Thanks for your help.'

Jack made several abortive attempts to contact DCS Garwood at the station only to be told by Miss Braithwaite that he was entertaining the DAC and couldn't be disturbed. He finally reached him at home that evening, just as he was sitting down to dinner. The Chief Superintendent wasn't pleased. His appraisal hadn't gone as well as he'd hoped. At the very outset, the DAC had asked how the investigations into the two murders were progressing. When Garwood told him DI Donald Drake had solved one murder with the subsequent suicide of the killer, he looked sceptical and asked why DI Dawes wasn't on the case. He hadn't been at all impressed with Garwood's explanation of his reassignment to the Northern Constabulary and told him in no uncertain terms that it wasn't good practice to reassign your best officer when there were serious crimes on the patch. He expressed his surprise that Garwood had sanctioned such a move. He then devoured three mince pies with a couple of drams of Garwood's thirty-year-old malt whisky and pushed off in his shiny, chauffeur-driven Lexus without so much as a Merry Christmas. Garwood slunk home, tail between his legs, wondering where it had all gone wrong and blaming Jack Dawes. He was still in this slough of despond when the phone rang.

'Mr Garwood? It's Jack Dawes here, sir. Sorry to ring you at home but I couldn't reach you at the station. I need to speak to you about the Lennox killing. I've discussed it with Doctor Hardacre who did the post mortem and we both agree it needs further investigation. The forensic evidence indicates there might have been foul play and I'd like to direct my MIT team in London to continue working on it. There's very little development up here at present, sir, so I could easily steer the enquiry from Shetland.'

This was the last straw. Garwood felt a vein throbbing in his temple, indicating that his blood pressure was threatening to blow. His pulse pounded on the back of his eyeballs. 'Oh, could you?' he said, nastily. 'Could you really? Well, let me remind you that this is policing, Inspector Dawes, not pick and mix. You don't get to choose a case because you like the look of it; you work on what you are given. DI

Drake has cleared up both the Baxter and Lennox cases to his satisfaction and mine, just as I knew he would. There is absolutely no
reason for you or your team to interfere, either here or from a distance.
I suggest you concentrate on DCS Cameron's suspicious death and stay
out of matters that don't concern you. Do I make myself clear? Good!'
He slammed down the phone.

Jack's mobile rang as he was getting ready for bed. It was Corrie. She'd
had Cynthia Garwood bending her ear for the last hour; time she could
have put to better use sticking robins on chocolate Yule Logs.

'What on earth did you say to George?' she demanded, without
polite preamble. 'Cynthia says he's absolutely livid. Something about
you undermining his authority and threatening to re-open the Lennox
case.'

'Hello, my little food processor. I'm very well, thanks. How are
you?'

'Sorry, Jack. How are you, darling? Is everything going well up
there?'

'Absolutely marvellous. Like paddling through porridge. I've got a
suspicious death that somebody must know something about, but
everyone's dancing around it like a handbag at an Essex wedding.
Meanwhile, back at the ranch, Ducky Drake has succeeded in sodding
up two murder investigations, *my* murder investigations, which the
team might well have cracked by now without his masterly inactivity.'
He sighed. 'Sometimes, I feel like I'm standing on the touchline of life,
watching the human scrum kick itself to destruction.'

'Dear me, that's very profound. Are they feeding you properly?'

'Depends how you feel about mutton, neeps and tatties. Remind me
to give you the recipe for haggamuggie; you might want to put it on the
menu at Garwood's next dinner party.'

'Which is tomorrow night, incidentally; he's invited the DAC. Only
six days to Christmas, now, darling. Any chance you'll be home?'

'I've been thinking about that. I interviewed a Viking today who
accused me of squandering taxpayers' money. He said I should go back
where I came from and stop wasting my time. He was quite convinced the
suspicious death was a suicide. I'm beginning to think he may be right.'

'Is this a bad line or did you just say you interviewed a Viking?'

'Yep. A bloke called Ketill Flatnose. He was quite aggressive; obviously resented my presence.'

Corrie giggled. 'If he's like that with all Anglo-Saxons, it probably explains his flat nose.'

'He lives on an eco-commune called Laxdale with a dozen or so other Vikings. I read the leaflet setting out their mission statement; it's all about anthropogenic global warming and the downward spiral in societal degeneration. They aim to be entirely self-sufficient in heat, power, water and food, while leaving an almost non-existent carbon footprint on the planet.'

'Blimey! I'm still struggling to remember which wheelie bin to use.'

'Little Astrid seems to have left an almost non-existent *human* footprint on the planet.'

'Is that the young woman who fell from the castle tower?'

'Mmm. She lived on the Viking commune. It seems nobody knew where she came from, what her real name was or why she was up on that parapet at midnight. She was three months pregnant and her system was full of heroin. The general view is that she was fanciful and flaky and she committed suicide.'

'Maybe she did. Do you have hard evidence that suggests otherwise?'

'No, only circumstantial; I've nothing concrete that would convince the Fiscal her death was the result of a criminal act. I can't make a case based purely on the intuition that you keep telling me I haven't got, and no good detective lays himself open to speculative imagination. I'll give it a couple of days, see if anything turns up. Then I think I may take Ketill Flatnose's advice and stop wasting the taxpayers' money. I'll make my report and come home.'

'Only if you're sure, darling. Don't worry about me, I'll be busy.'

'I know, sweetheart, but there's DC Mellis and DS Malone to consider, too. No point in keeping them here over Christmas if there's no case to investigate. It's just that when I saw Astrid's body lying in the morgue, she looked so small and irrelevant. What a terrible waste of a young life. She came and went without making any lasting impression on anybody, but that doesn't mean we shouldn't bother to find out why and how she died. I guess I feel exactly the same about Lenny. '

After she'd put down the phone, Corrie poured herself a glass of Chardonnay and stood at the kitchen window, watching the snow fall and mulling things over. Jack sounded uncharacteristically despondent. If there was one thing he hated, it was not completing a job efficiently and there had been three deaths now, none of which had been resolved to his satisfaction. She ought to be able to help, but how? Then she had one of her inspired ideas. There was something she could do, by way of gathering background information. Something Jack couldn't do himself, even if he were here. Of course, he wouldn't approve so she wouldn't tell him. Not until afterwards and not unless she turned up something useful.

CHAPTER THIRTEEN

For the next couple of days, DI Dawes, DS Malone and DC Mellis examined and re-examined the facts, always ending up with the same inconclusive assessments. Jack had an uneasy feeling that a wall of silence had been erected at Doomdochry long before they arrived. Apparently undaunted by the police presence, the MacAlisters simply worked around them. It was business as usual but with an indefinable air of equivocation that hung over them like the angels' share of the whisky in a Highland distillery.

Mack and Melissa were secretly counting the days before they could return to the comfort of their Surrey home. To pass the time, they had decorated a huge Christmas tree, put up garlands of greenery and generally prepared the castle for the imminent festivities. In unguarded moments, they could be seen whispering earnestly in corners with Melissa doing most of the whispering. Now, she looked down at her stomach, still flat and hard, and frowned. This was no place to bring up a child and she must have it out with Mack or it would ruin the rest of their lives. She found him on the main staircase sitting astride the hand rail, nailing holly to the minstrel's gallery and hoping to God the newel post wouldn't snap.

'Darling ...' Melissa sat on the stair beneath him, '... we won't *really* have to live here after your father dies, will we? I mean, think of your career. How many successful neurosurgeons do you know who have their consulting rooms in a mouldy, medieval castle miles from civilization?'

Mack looked down at her, the love of his life. She was the product of a happy, privileged childhood and hadn't really grown up since. Thanks to the support of her wealthy parents, she had spent her winters skiing in the Swiss Alps and her summers in the Greek Islands, pretending to crew on a yacht, which was where she met and married Mack. As his wife, with no obligation to earn a living, she had drifted into interior design and was surprisingly successful. By using hi-tech computer graphics, she was able to show her clients how their homes would look after redecoration but before they actually took the plunge and painted the walls puce.

Mack climbed down and put his arms around her. 'Sweetheart, there have been MacAlisters at Doomdochry for over five centuries. It would break Father's heart if I didn't inherit the earldom from him.'

'But what about *my* heart?' whimpered Melissa.

'I'm sorry, Mel, but unless Dad accepts Randall's offer, I can't see a way out and at the moment, he's pretty determined he won't sell.'

'Why not? Goodness knows, he and Alice could use the money. They'll die of pneumonia if they stay here many more years. Couldn't Randall carry on the earldom? He's a MacAlister after all.'

'I've suggested that but Dad seems to think he'd be selling my birthright despite my efforts to persuade him I don't want to be the 21st Earl. Then of course, there's Great Auntie Flora. According to Grandfather's will, she has to give her consent, too, and she says she'll only leave Doomdochry in a coffin.'

'Will your father change his mind, do you think?'

Mack thought about it. 'There's a small chance he might if Randall made him an offer too big to refuse and we could persuade Aunt Flora.'

In that case, thought Melissa, somebody needs to do something to help the deal along a bit. She clapped a hand to her mouth. 'Sorry, darling, must dash. Think I'm going to be sick. Must be something I ate.'

The Earl and Lady Alice spent as much time as possible in their private Blue Suite, waiting for the police to leave and staying well out of their way in the meantime. They reappeared only to dine, when they said very little and always in unintelligible Shetland. Nicole had taken the fast speedboat across to the Gainsborough, where she intended to pamper her abused body. She claimed her digestion had been ravaged by Moragh's disgusting food and her complexion ruined by the god-awful climate and the filthy living conditions in the castle. Randall stayed behind, apparently contenting himself with planning what he'd do with Doomdochry when he'd finally persuaded the Earl to sell. He could be seen strolling about the castle in search of spots where reception was good, making long calls on his mobile to the States. At the same time, glass in hand, he was systematically working his way through a considerable quantity of MacAlister's whisky. Moragh and Geordie maintained a hostile but watchful distance and Fraser Grant continued to drink, stammer and look shifty.

Jack was running out of inspiration. He'd never conducted a murder enquiry in a castle before. He reckoned it would make a good training exercise for would-be inspectors. It was impossible to be sure he'd investigated thoroughly. They'd searched as far as was feasible with such a small team and found absolutely nothing of relevance, although there could be evidence buried under all the accumulated clutter that nobody would ever find. As Bugsy observed: 'You should see the state of that gunroom, guv. Never mind a murder, you could wipe out a cavalry regiment in there and no one would notice. I haven't even attempted to search the underground chambers. One sniff was enough; they're full of rats and raw sewage. Forensics like a challenge but that would really be taking the piss.'

Similarly, they'd interviewed everyone who might know something, yet learned absolutely nothing. Everyone, that is, except Aunt Flora. Whenever he'd suggested speaking to her, Dawes had been met with a salvo of reasons why it wasn't possible: she was too frail; she was confused; she was confined to her room so knew nothing about the dead girl or anything else beyond her immediate surroundings. She was a sick, bewildered old lady and to tell her about the incident would distress her. It could even prove fatal, he was told. Flora simply wouldn't be able to help him.

Jack couldn't insist on questioning her, but he had a feeling she might be able to provide some useful facts about the family's past; facts that the others were reluctant to divulge. Maybe the real reason they wouldn't let him near her was their fear that she might say something indiscreet. He wondered whether he might just tap on her door and ask if he could have a quiet word, strictly in confidence and without tiring the old dear too much. It was a murder investigation, after all. In the event, he didn't need to. DS Malone and DC Mellis had been passing Aunt Flora's room on their way down to dinner when the door suddenly flew open and she popped her head out. Looking swiftly up and down the corridor to ensure she was not observed, she grasped their sleeves and dragged them inside.

Unlike the rest of the castle, the room was very warm and stank of lavender, whisky and rancid fish. It was crammed so full of heavy Victorian furniture and ugly bric-a-brac that there was barely room to move. Likewise, the walls were covered entirely with paintings, ranging from a life-size Scottish warrior to tiny animal miniatures. All fakes if Nicole MacAlister were to be believed, thought Bugsy. Great Aunt Flora MacAlister was dressed in a purple satin evening gown with a fluffy, pink bed-jacket and matching bed-socks. She jangled with jewellery; a hotchpotch of heavy necklaces, rings, bracelets and brooches. Her copious grey hair was stuffed into a snood with a thistle stuck in it, by way of traditional adornment. But most bizarrely, she had a dozen or so yellow post-it notes with messages scrawled on them, stuck to the front of her dress. She hopped back in bed and motioned the officers to two armchairs.

'So …' she folded her arms, '… ye've come to speak to the head of the MacAlister family, and no' afore time!'

'We understood you were too frail to be interviewed, ma'am.' Bugsy didn't think she looked at all frail. Batty but not frail.

She made a hawking noise as if she were about to spit. 'Heuch! I'm fit as a flea.' She turned her piercing gaze on Maggie. 'Pour us a wee dram, lassie, over there on the table. Then I'll tell ye what ye want tae know.'

Maggie went to the dressing-table and poured the whiskies. Bugsy sipped his cautiously. It was like fire water, scorching his throat as it went down. He panted a few times to dispel the worst of the heat. Christ only knew what proof it was, but the old girl downed hers in one. She smacked her lips. 'Och, that's good. Doomdochry Malt's the best.'

'Is there a distillery near here, then?' croaked Bugsy, still gasping for breath.

She chuckled. 'Aye, boy, nearer than you think. But ye haven't come to ask about whisky, have ye?'

'No, Miss MacAlister.' DC Mellis thought she'd better start carefully. The old lady might be alarmed when she heard about a dead body being found in the castle grounds. 'What bonnie paintings. Which one's your favourite?'

'My wee doggie.' She pointed to a small frame tucked away among the portraits. It was the head of a deerhound, painted in oils and obviously old. Malone stood up to admire it. He was no expert but he thought it looked rather better than the others. The signature was faded, but he could read the date – 1834. Maybe that one wasn't a fake, who could tell?

DC Mellis decided it was safe to ask some serious questions and ventured, cautiously: 'There was an unfortunate incident here about ten days ago. It involved a young woman and we wondered if you saw or heard anything ...'

'Don't beat about the bush, lassie, I ken fine what happened.' Flora plucked off one of the post-it notes. 'See here. It was the tenth of December. The lassie's name was Astrid and she was murdered in cold blood, pumped full of filth and pushed off the tower. Isn't that why you're here? To catch the devil who did it.'

Malone and Mellis exchanged glances. So much for the frail old lady who lives in a vacuum and mustn't receive any shocks. Aunt Flora caught them staring at the yellow notes adorning her bosom.

'Great age is no blessing when the body outlives the strength o' the mind. My memory's not what it was. I can recall when Doomdochry had paraffin heaters and candles but I can't recall what I had for breakfast. I write these notes to help me remember the important things.'

Bugsy wondered what else she had written on her chest but decided not to look too closely as she wasn't beyond giving him a clip round the ear. 'Why do you think Astrid was murdered, ma'am?' he asked.

She glanced sideways at him and answered his question with another. 'Have you spoken to Fraser, yet?'

'Yes, but he couldn't help us. He didn't know the young lady.'

'Is that what he told you?' She shook her head sadly and wisps of grey hair escaped from the snood. 'The boy's troubled. He's been part of the MacAlister family since he was a wee bairn, but then he went abroad to England and lost all sense of what's proper. Now his coat's hanging on a very shoogly peg.' She lowered her voice and murmured to Maggie. 'I blame that foreign trollop. She's no better than she should be and she's after....'

They were never to find out what the "foreign trollop" was after because the door flew open and Mack MacAlister strode in. 'There you are, officers. Your dinner's getting cold.'

'Sorry about that, sir, but your great aunt was just giving us her thoughts on the suspicious death.'

Mack sat on the bed and put his arm around her. 'Now then, Auntie Flora, what have you been saying?' He turned to Malone, with a condescending smile. 'You mustn't take her too seriously, Sergeant. She gets muddled and tends to imagine things, don't you, dear?'

Furious, she slapped his arm away. 'Don't speak like I'm senile, boy! I know what I saw.' She snatched off another post-it and waved it at them. 'The Green Lady ... floating up the stairs to the tower. I heard her wailing and I could smell the stink of her poor rotting body. It was the night the lassie was murdered.' She grabbed Bugsy's arm in a pincer-like grip. 'When ye see Green Jean, somebody in Doomdochry is going to die.'

'Now you know very well that's just fanciful rubbish, Auntie.' Mack picked up her empty glass. 'When you've had too much whisky, you can't tell fact from fiction. This ghost story of yours is just for the tourists.' He turned to Malone and winked. 'And hopefully, it might increase the price if Father finally decides to sell to Randall. You know what the Americans are like about haunted castles.'

Aunt Flora went scarlet. 'You forget, boy!' she roared, jabbing Mack painfully in the ribs with a bony elbow. 'Alistair can't sell Doomdochry without my permission and I'll never give it. Never, d'ye ken?'

Mack patted her arm. 'Now, Auntie, you know very well you'd be much better off in a nice nursing home with proper care and modern facilities. And I'd far rather that you, Mother and Father were comfortable for the rest of your days than inherit Doomdochry.' It was the worst thing he could have said.

'Over my dead body! When I leave Doomdochry, it'll be in a box!' she shrieked, then her voice dropped to an evil cackle. 'Besides, we're not sure who'll be the rightful Earl of Doomdochry once your father's gone, are we?'

Mack's face darkened and he was about to retort but Flora's angry outburst had exhausted her and she sank back on her pillows. 'Go away, I'm tired.' Her head drooped onto her chest and she began to snore gently.

During the Fifties, the old hunting-room had been converted into a lounge where MacAlister gentlemen sat and enjoyed cigars, whisky and a blether after dinner. DI Dawes, being there on official police business, had not taken advantage of this amenity, but that particular night, he and DS Malone were cornered by Mack MacAlister who was anxious to speak to them.

'I feel I should correct one or two little inaccuracies that your sergeant may have picked up from my Great Aunt Flora, Inspector.' He crossed to the old oak drinks' cupboard and picked up a decanter. 'Would you like water with your dram, gentlemen? The well was relatively scum-free today.'

Words like *typhoid* and *cholera* came into Bugsy's mind to join other words like *Moragh* and *salmonella*. 'No thank you, sir. I prefer it neat.' With any luck, spirit of that intensity would kill off any fatal organisms. Mack shepherded them to armchairs well away from the Earl and Randall, who were discussing business.

'As you may have gathered, Aunt Flora is very fond of Fraser. He has always been her favourite.'

'Where is Mr Grant this evening? asked Jack. 'I notice he didn't dine with us.'

'No, Fraser is busy with estate work.' Mack picked his words carefully. 'He has a rather tragic background, as I believe my wife may have intimated to Constable Mellis. His mother was Elspeth Grant, a young woman who was employed here in the castle as housemaid, to assist Moragh. She became pregnant and this was in the seventies when to be an unmarried mother on Shetland still carried something of a stigma so she kept her pregnancy secret for as long as she could. That meant she didn't have proper ante-natal care which could have identified the potential complications before she went into labour. Unfortunately, there were insurmountable difficulties and she died in childbirth, but her baby, Fraser, survived. He was born just a month before me, so being the same age, we grew up together. And because he had no mother or father, he was doted on by four surrogate mothers; my grandmother Lady Eleanor; my mother Lady Alice; my Great Aunt Flora and of course, Moragh, our housekeeper, who looked after him like the son she and Geordie had never had. Fraser was never strong, emotionally, and when I left Doomdochry to study medicine at university, Fraser remained here and was given the job of factor and a cottage to go with it.'

Mack took a gulp of whisky, clearly ill at ease. 'This next part is rather embarrassing so I'd be grateful if you could keep it confidential; it has nothing at all to do with the death that you're investigating. My grandfather, the 19th Earl, had a reputation as a womanizer. Whether it was justified or not, I have never asked and I have no wish to know. Unfortunately, Auntie Flora takes great delight in fabricating salacious and wildly exaggerated stories about her older brother's *houghma-*

gandie as she calls it, one of which involved Elspeth Grant. The way Flora tells it, my grandmother, Lady Eleanor, caught Grandfather naked in the pantry with Elspeth. Well, clearly, that's nonsense because Elspeth was only twenty when Fraser was born and my grandfather was in his fifties.' He laughed, awkwardly. 'Gentlemen that age don't form sexual liaisons with young girls, do they?'

They bloody well do if they get half a chance, thought Bugsy. What planet is this geezer on?

'And if the story were true,' continued Mack, 'that would make Fraser my uncle.'

'Which would presumably muddy the waters somewhat when it came to things like inheritance? I don't understand how earldoms work, especially Scottish ones, but I imagine it's like royalty, it would depend on who had male issue and when. Have you gone into the legal aspects at all?'

'No, of course not, Inspector.' Mack brushed it off. 'The whole thing's preposterous. But unfortunately, Flora has put all sorts of ideas into Fraser's head and he's weak and impressionable enough to believe them.'

'You mean, if the Earl sells Doomdochry to the Yanks, Grant will demand his share?' said Malone, cutting straight to the chase.

Mack nodded. 'I really wish Auntie wouldn't encourage him with her crazy notions; it unsettles him and causes ill feeling.'

'Are you saying your Great Aunt Flora's barmy?' asked Malone.

'Yes, but not certifiably so. She simply won't accept that none of us knows who Fraser's father was; Elspeth took her secret with her to the grave.'

'Was she buried in the family cemetery?'

'Yes, she was, as a matter of fact. She was part of the household and had no relatives; it was only common decency for the family to take responsibility.'

The conversation ended abruptly when Randall shouted across: 'Mack, will ya get over here and talk some sense into this old guy?'

The Earl was shaking his head, morosely. 'I can't sell Doomdochry, Randall, not at any price. There's the clan birthright to consider.' He smiled blearily, squinting at Mack through a haze of cigar smoke. 'My boy has a wife and the bairns will come along soon. One day ...' he raised his glass, sloshing most of its contents down his Prince Charlie jacket, '... Doomdochry will belong to them.'

'But it's a damn good deal, Alistair. The folks back home would pay big bucks to stay in a real Scottish Castle and drink your Highland Malt.'

'Maybe, but a Shetland Theme Park, Randall? Are you sure?'

'Sure I'm sure! We'll call it Doomdochry World. I'm just kicking a few ideas around here but how about bungee-jumping from the battlements? And an eighty foot roller coaster over the tower; that big sonofabitch that the girl fell from. We could bill it as the Death Ride. I'll fix up sound systems blasting out, "When You Wish Upon a Star" on the bagpipes and get little guys dressed up like cute dwarf Vikings to go round shaking hands with the kiddies.' Randall was in his element, doing what he did best. 'And don't forget the spin-off merchandise. Gift shops selling plastic Viking helmets with horns, fake red beards for the guys and long blonde braids for the gals. We'll host stag nights with real stags!'

'Then half the Green Lady appears with blood all down her frock and scares the shit out of everyone,' said Bugsy, who was fast losing his grip on reality.

'Way to go, Detective Malone!' cheered Randall. 'A gen-u-ine ghost! It's a licence to print bucks. Think about it, MacAlister. You won't get a better deal.' But the Earl, muttering anxiously to himself, had fallen into a merciful slumber.

CHAPTER FOURTEEN

Sergeant Malone had little truck with life's unexplained mysteries so it was with some surprise that he turned a corner on the fifth floor landing of Doomdochry Castle and came face to face with the Green Lady. To begin with, he just stood there, trying to work out exactly what it was. He could see the hazy contours of a girl, shimmering and luminous, standing with her back against the stone wall. She wore old-fashioned clothes; a tightly-fitting green bodice with billowing sleeves and a long, emerald cloak with a hood that partially obscured her head. He stared hard and could just make out a small, pale face wearing a desperate, doleful expression. He glanced down to see if her feet were on the ground or floating above it. That was when he realized she had no bottom half. She ceased abruptly at the waist. He shut his eyes for a few seconds then opened them again. She was still there, drifting in and out of focus, glowing bright green one minute and murky grey the next. He didn't believe in ghosts, it had to be some kind of hoax, a clever illusion with smoke and mirrors. He walked briskly towards the figure and put out a hand to touch her but as soon as he came close, she vanished into the solid wall, leaving him standing there with his hand out, like a twit. As he told Inspector Dawes later, he wasn't drunk and he hadn't imagined it.

'Are you sure, Bugsy? You know what you're like when you don't eat properly. It makes you light-headed.'

Bugsy was never entirely sure about anything. Thirty years in the police service had taught him unshakable scepticism. As a result, he believed nothing he was told and only half of what he actually saw.

'I'm sure it wasn't a ghost, guv, but I certainly saw something weird and now I know what Moragh said when she left me on the fifth floor. It wasn't "green bean" as I thought. It was Green Jean. The old girl might believe in the supernatural, but I reckon somebody in this dump is taking the proverbial.'

Jack frowned. 'Yes, but who? And why? And is it connected to the suspicious death that we're here to investigate or something else entirely?'

'Bugger only knows. I reckon we should talk to Grant again. The old aunt was about to tell us something about him and a "foreign trollop" before Mack stopped her. And she was convinced that Astrid was murdered. She must have got the idea from someone and I'm betting it was Grant. She dotes on him and she kept dropping hints that he's really an illegitimate MacAlister and should have some rights to the estate.'

'A concept that Mack went to great lengths to dispel. But matters of inheritance and a potential deal with the Americans are nothing at all to do with the police unless they constitute a motive for crime. Great Aunt Flora might well be starting rumours of murder and mayhem to spice up a dreary old age. And she's totally against selling Doomdochry because Mack's planning to put her in an old folks' home.' He scratched his head. 'As I see it, we've been here four days and discovered nothing to suggest a crime has been committed.'

'What Randall's planning to do with Doomdochry's a crime,' observed Bugsy.

'I agree, but similar projects have proved otherwise. Doomdochry World could create enough work to empty the Jobcentre and generate a load of revenue for Shetland.'

Bugsy frowned. 'I've still got serious doubts about Fraser Grant. If he didn't know Astrid, like he claims, why make such a fuss about her death? And the old girl hinted that he knew more than he's told us. Let me give him another tug, Jack.'

'OK, one last try, if only to stop you seeing spooks round every corner.'

'What will you do, guv?'

Dawes was going to do something he'd been dreading since they arrived; something he knew he had to do before he could consider the investigation complete. 'I'm going up to take a look around the tower.'

'Well, go careful, Jack. It's a bloody long way down.'

Sergeant Malone and Constable Mellis took the station wagon and crawled through the snow to Fraser Grant's cottage on the estate. He wasn't pleased to see them and he was nursing a black eye and a badly swollen jaw.

'I thought you'd f-finished with me,' he said, petulantly. 'You're w-wasting your time ... and m-mine. I c-can't tell you anything more and I'm b-busy.'

'That's a nasty black eye you have there, sir,' said Bugsy, making himself comfortable in an easy chair. 'How did it happen?'

'I w-walked into a t-tree, not that it's any of your damn b-business.'

Malone eyeballed him. 'Bit of advice, mate. Don't bugger about with the police. We can play dirtier than you and there're more of us.'

They went over his statement asking the same questions and getting the same stonewalling. Then Bugsy decided it was time for some straight talk.

'Astrid was three months pregnant when she died, Mr Grant. Was the baby yours?'

'No, of course it wasn't!' blurted Grant, stammer gone.

'You don't seem surprised at the news. Were you already aware she was pregnant?'

Grant began to sweat. This fat, scruffy sergeant was playing with him. Oh God, what if they were really here about the other business? But they couldn't have found out, could they? The room was closing in, he felt cornered; he wanted to run, get away. Now he knew why that brawny woman detective had remained standing. She was blocking the door; preventing him from escaping. They had him trapped. He was finding it difficult to breathe. The sergeant was staring at him, waiting for an answer. He lost control.

'How many times must I tell you? I didn't know the girl!' he shouted. 'She was just someone I'd seen around and I was unlucky enough to be the one who found her body. How could I have known she was pregnant? It didn't show when she was lying dead on the ground.'

'Maybe she told you,' Bugsy kept chipping away. 'Maybe you arranged to meet her that night, took her up the tower. You had an argument. She wanted you to take responsibility for her and the baby. There was a bit of a scuffle and she fell. Was that how it happened?'

Grant calmed down a little. So they didn't know, after all. 'If I were the father of a girl's baby, Sergeant Malone, I assume I'd recall having sex with her,' he said, sarcastically.

DC Mellis sniffed audibly. 'You'd be amazed at the number of men who don't, sir.'

'Maybe, Constable, but I assure you I'm not one of them! Now, if that's all, I have work to do.'

The police officers were almost out of the door when Malone turned back. 'Just one more thing, sir. When Doomdochry's sold, are you planning to mount a claim to some of the proceeds as the present Earl's illegitimate half-brother?'

Fraser Grant stared at him, his mouth opening and closing like a goldfish. That stopped the little shit in his tracks, thought Malone.

'I d-don't believe that's any of your b-business.' The stutter was back. 'You've b-been harassing Aunt Flora, haven't you? She's a d-dear old l-lady, k-kind and c-caring, which is m-more than you can say f-for the rest of this rotten f-family. Just leave her alone. '

Bugsy continued, undaunted. 'All the same, I daresay you could use the money, sir. I understand from Mack MacAlister that you're in considerable debt. He told us you had financial problems due to gambling and were experiencing some kind of trouble with a woman. May we ask the identity of that woman, sir?'

Grant's face was like thunder. 'No, you bloody well may not! MacAlister had no business telling you anything.' He sneered. 'Mack, the golden boy with the expensive education, thinks he can treat people how he likes. We aren't all lucky enough to be overpaid surgeons, sitting back waiting to inherit a fortune that may rightfully belong to someone else. If you want to know the truth, I *am* in debt, *huge* debt, to some characters who don't mess about. And I have no idea how I'm going to raise the money. If I'm really lucky, they'll only break my legs. Now, if you don't mind, I'm going to work.'

Detective Inspector Dawes knew he was regarded by his colleagues as a murder-solving automaton. No detail escaped his keen eye and no stone was left unturned. So why, he asked himself, had he drawn a complete blank this time? Standing on the wall-walk of Doomdochry's massive tower, he leaned over the parapet between the battlements. Bugsy was right, it was a bloody long way down and Dawes wasn't good at heights. He stood back and closed his eyes until the nausea subsided. It was early afternoon on the shortest day of the year and already dusk was falling after barely four hours' of daylight. The wind howled like a soul in torment and hurled freezing sleet at him that stung like gravel. Jack tried to imagine what it must have been like up there at midnight. Had the girl really injected herself with heroin and jumped off? Or had someone else manhandled her over the edge? In either case, she must have been terrified. He wasn't really sure why he was up there or what he was expecting to find. The incident had happened over ten days ago and the forensic team, although drastically depleted by the flu, would already have searched and bagged anything relevant. The violent weather would have destroyed everything else. DCS Cameron had warned him that the storms on Shetland were severe and December was one of the wildest months. Gales had been recorded with gusts exceeding 90 knots and here, in the north of Shetland, the wind speeds were even greater with a gust of 150 mph recorded from the Muckle Flugga lighthouse, which he could see in the distance. Could Astrid have been caught up in one of these gusts and blown off the tower? He could feel the squall tearing at him now, threatening to lift him off his feet and hurl him over the parapet. He was six foot three and fourteen stone and even so, he had to cling to the balustrade for safety. Astrid was small and very thin, barely six stones at a guess, hardly sufficient to anchor her to the wall-walk. And if she'd been foolish enough to sit on the low stone between the crenellations, a gust might simply have plucked her off. He recalled Donnie Cameron telling him that as recently as 2007, Unst was rocked by an earthquake measuring 4.9 on the Richter scale. It was reckoned to have been one of the most powerful earthquakes in the Norwegian Sea area in the past ten years. Clearly, this was an island prone to violent meteorological incidents. Maybe Astrid's death wasn't murder or suicide; just a terrible, unfortunate accident. But that still begged the question, why was she up there at all?

It was nine o'clock on the evening of the twenty-first of December. Dinner was over and DI Dawes had joined DS Malone and DC Mellis in the library to compare notes.

'Not surprisingly, I found nothing on the tower wall-walk to help us.' Jack looked hopefully at the other two. 'Anything on your side, Sergeant?'

Bugsy pulled out his notebook. 'We didn't get much more out of Grant, guv. He still denies knowing Astrid and says he had nothing to do with her pregnancy. He's got a chip on his shoulder the size of a King Edward and he's jealous of Mack MacAlister's privileged position in the family because he reckons he has a prior claim to the Earl's estate. He also admitted he was badly in debt to some heavies who are likely to damage him if he doesn't come up with the readies. He was sporting a real shiner of a black eye. He didn't deny there was a woman involved, but he wouldn't tell us who, only that it wasn't Astrid. Have I missed anything, Maggie?'

'No, Sarge. Except, he's awful fond of Miss Flora MacAlister.'

Jack thought while the fire crackled in the grate. 'DC Mellis, remind me where everybody said they were at the time of Astrid's death.'

Maggie opened her file and took out the statements she'd laboriously written out in long hand. The creeping Doomdochry damp had somehow infiltrated her laptop which resolutely refused to function. She'd asked, more in hope than expectation, whether anyone had a computer and printer in the castle that she might borrow. Mack and Melissa said they never took their laptops on holiday and Randall said he had enough of technology back home and didn't carry it around with him. Nobody else in the castle even knew how to use a computer let alone owned one. DC Mellis began to read out loud.

'According to the pathologist's report, time of death was around midnight on the tenth of December. The Earl, Lady Alice, and Mack and Melissa MacAlister were all in bed and asleep by eleven. Mr Randall MacAlister said he was tired and went to his room early. His wife says he was drunk and passed out as usual, so she took a sleeping pill and was asleep by ten. Miss Flora never leaves her room. Nobody saw or heard anything which is no surprise as the walls are so thick. Mr Fraser Grant says he woke in his cottage about two-thirty, couldn't get back to sleep and went for a walk in the snowstorm. He found the body at three o'clock. The ghillie and the housekeeper have rooms on the ground floor at the back of the castle and wouldn't hear anything going on up in the tower. Geordie locks up at midnight after feeding and walking the dogs and checking the stock. He says if the lassie sneaked in during the day, there are plenty of places in the castle where she could hide till night time, but he couldn't think of a reason why she'd want to.'

'So each of the couples used their partners as an alibi. Except for Fraser Grant who has a key to the main castle door.'

Bugsy nodded. 'He smuggles Astrid in after dark when everyone's gone to bed and takes her up the tower. Then he gives her a shot of heroin, shoves her off, goes back down, locks the door behind him and pretends to find her body.'

Jack looked doubtful. 'But why go to all that trouble? If he wanted to get rid of her for whatever reason, why not lure her to his cottage and bump her off there? Then, given the wild nature of the terrain, bury her body where it wouldn't be found for some time, if ever. The girl was a traveller with no relatives; it's unlikely anyone would have reported her missing. The Laxdale lot would simply have assumed she'd moved on. Why would Grant take the risk of someone in the castle seeing them together? And why be the one to find her and make a big fuss, casting suspicion on himself? No, I don't think so, Bugsy. Not unless he's even dafter than he seems.'

'Then why is he acting so shifty?'

'Maybe ...' began DC Mellis cautiously, 'maybe he didn't do it himself but he knows who did and he's shielding them?'

'Or he's scared of 'em,' added Bugsy.

They carried on kicking ideas around, building hypotheses then knocking them down again until, two hours later, Jack called a halt. They were going over the same ground and coming up with the same conclusion. It looked increasingly like an open verdict; the death was suspicious but there was insufficient evidence to prove the cause.

'I think we've reached the end of the line, folks.' Jack tried his coffee, but it had gone cold hours ago. 'Unless anyone has any better ideas, I'll ring DCS Cameron tomorrow morning, tell her the position and ask her to arrange for Donnie to pick us up and fly us back to Inverness. Thanks for all your help, DC Mellis. I'll mention it in my report to the Fiscal. I don't think there's anything to be gained by carrying on here. Time to go home.' He jabbed a thumb at Bugsy. 'Apart from anything else, Sergeant Malone here is suffering from hallucinations. He reckons he saw the ghost of the infamous Green Lady.'

'Och, I've seen her twice,' announced Maggie, nonchalantly. 'Only the top half, but plain as day. Floating down the corridor towards the staircase, close to the ceiling. Green bodice, big sleeves and a long dark cloak with a hood over her head.'

'Why didn't you say something, Constable?'

'I didn't think you'd believe me, sir. But now that the sergeant has seen her too....'

'There you are, guv, what did I tell you?' said Bugsy, exonerated.

Jack grunted. 'That settles it. We're going home, before *I* start having hallucinations!'

*

Back in his room, Jack sat on the edge of his bed, thinking. He knew he'd done everything conceivably possible. There was no justification for staying any longer. It wasn't simply that he wanted to get back home to Corrie in time for Christmas, although the prospect was appealing. He consulted his watch; eleven thirty. Late but not too late. Corrie had been known to work well past midnight at this time of year. He fished out his mobile. There was a slight delay before she answered. Maybe she'd gone to bed after all. But when she spoke, she sounded more excited than sleepy.

'Hello, Jack, how are you?'

'I'm fine, sweetheart. Sorry to ring so late. I didn't wake you, did I?'

'No, course not. I've only just got in.' She was slightly breathless as though she'd sprinted to reach the phone. 'You'll never guess where I've been this evening.'

'Surprise me, my little plum pudding.'

'I've been having a drink with Ray Hadleigh at the Blue Ray Club.'

'WHAT?' Jack shouted loud enough for the whole of Shetland to hear.

'Now, don't go into one of your rants, darling. He's a really nice bloke.'

'That's what they said about Harold Shipman!'

'Now you're just being silly.'

Jack tried to stay calm. 'All right, tell me what you were doing at the Blue Ray Club.'

'Well, the last time we spoke, you sounded so despondent. As if you felt the murders were slipping through your fingers without proper investigation, especially after George Garwood whisked you off to Scotland right in the middle of the Baxter enquiry.'

'Corrie, I know you mean well but how many times have I asked you not to interfere?'

She carried on, undaunted. 'Then, Cynthia Garwood told me in strict confidence and under the influence of a whole bottle of Cabernet Sauvignon, that George got rid of you because the DAC was coming to do his appraisal and he didn't want you around to upstage him. Well, I didn't think that was fair, so I decided to help out; put in a bit of leg work on your behalf. I couldn't help much with your suspicious death in Scotland but I could do a bit of digging down here, so I—'

Jack was still processing this. 'Hang on a minute. Are you telling me that Garwood did a secondment deal with DCS Cameron just to get me out of the way?'

'Yes, darling, but never mind that; listen to what I have to tell you. Tonight, I went to the Blue Ray Club, just to have a general nose around. After all, Karen Baxter used to drink there and Lenny Lennox worked there so it was the obvious place to start. I know your team turned it over and came up with zilch, but people are less guarded chatting to a customer than when they're being questioned by a copper. Anyway, I sat at the bar and bought myself a glass of Pinot Grigio. It was surprisingly good, actually; crisp and dry with fresh lemon and lime flavours but with a slight hint of orange blossom on the ...'

'Never mind the bloody wine! What happened?'

'Ray Hadleigh came and sat beside me. I recognized him by his blue dinner jacket. Armani, not cheap.'

'You didn't tell him who you were?' groaned Dawes. 'Please promise me you didn't say you were snooping on behalf of an Inspector in the Met.'

'No, of course I didn't. I'm not daft. I said my husband was away on business and I felt like some company.'

Jack clapped a hand to his brow. 'Oh my God, it gets better! He thought you were a bored housewife on the pull.'

'No, he didn't. I told him I ran a catering company and wondered if he might put some business my way. He said he was sorry but his clubs only provided the customers with bowls of crisps and nuts. He didn't have a licence for food, but I could leave some of my cards on the bar in case any of his customers needed catering services. We chatted for a bit then I happened to mention, casually, that I'd read about the murder of Karen Baxter in the local paper and wasn't it awful? He agreed and said he was shocked when he learned that Lennox, his pot-man, was the killer. He thought hanging himself was probably the only honourable thing Lennox had ever done. Saved the taxpayer the expense of a long investigation and a trial. Then he bought me another drink and I agreed to drop him off a Christmas cake next time I was passing. I thought he was perfectly charming and I had a very pleasant evening.'

'I'm thrilled for you,' said Jack, caustically.

Corrie ignored this. 'But here's the interesting bit. Before I left, I had a chat with some of the waitresses and bar staff. Very discreetly, you understand. They all said there was absolutely no way that Lenny would have harmed Karen, let alone cut her throat. He was very fond of her because she was the only person who was ever kind to him. Neither did they believe he'd hung himself. It was completely out of character because the general view was that he was a spineless, scruffy little thief with halitosis and no bottle.'

'Popular with his work mates, then.'

'Shut up. They all felt that because the victim was a sex worker, the police had just gone for the easy option rather than look for the real killer. A "bunch of idle wankers" was how one girl described you.'

'Thanks a lot. Mind you, in the case of Ducky Drake, that's probably close to the truth.'

'Then I bumped into Ray Hadleigh's chauffeur on my way out. He'd come to drive him home. He wasn't particularly forthcoming, actually, tried to fob me off, but I suppose discretion is an important part of a chauffeur's job. Eventually, he told me Hadleigh lives alone in an expensive apartment in Knightsbridge. No wife, but lots of girlfriends. I'm not surprised. He's a real hunk with a very seductive manner and a lovely sexy voice – just a hint of a lilting Irish accent. And simply divine aftershave. Very distinctive and probably costs a bomb, like his dinner-jacket. Anyway, his cleaning lady who also cleans at the club, told me there's one girlfriend in particular who spends occasional weekends with him. Nobody knows much about her; he keeps her under wraps, but she's glamorous, wears expensive designer clothes and probably lives and works abroad because when she leaves, Hadleigh always drives her to the airport himself.'

'I don't suppose you managed to interrogate the bloke who empties Hadleigh's bins, as well?'

'There's no need to be sarcastic. I think I did pretty well. Hadleigh's a fit, well-mannered, astute businessman with a taste for the good life. Did I mention he's incredibly handsome?'

'Sounds like you were smitten.'

'Mm.' She hesitated. 'Rather too much fake tan for my taste.'

'Maybe Mr Wonderful has something to hide after all.'

'Jack, *all* men with fake tans have something to hide. Usually their inadequacies. He's probably got a small dick.'

'That's very Freudian for a caterer.'

'The point of all this is that I believe your initial instinct was right. Lenny Lennox knew or guessed who murdered Karen Baxter and why, so they killed him to shut him up. What would you like me to do next?'

'Nothing, thank you. That's what I was ringing to tell you. I've done pretty much all I can up here so I'm coming home. If I can get a flight from Inverness tomorrow, I should be home by the evening.'

'Good. I've missed you. What would you like for dinner?'

'Anything but mutton.'

CHAPTER FIFTEEN

DECEMBER 22ND

Nine o'clock next morning, Chief Superintendent Cameron put down the phone in her Inverness office and sighed deeply. The tip-off had been from a senior officer in the Scottish Crime and Drug Enforcement Agency so she knew it was serious.

The activities of a major international crime organization dealing in drug trafficking and illegal immigrants had been tracked to an area under her geographical command. The main operation was centred in London Docklands, but SCDEA had evidence that the money laundering side of the business was using the Northern Isles as a remote springboard to Norway. From there, the 'dirty' money was cleaned by running it through a complex business network of shell companies and trusts based in tax havens around the world. It was known as 'smurfing' in banking industry jargon: the practice of using financial transactions which were structured to avoid record-keeping and reporting requirements. This process effectively concealed the identity, source, and destination of illegally gained money. Charlie Cameron knew about the practice, she'd been to police seminars on the subject, but she'd never envisaged coming face to face with it on her patch.

So far, she'd been given very little of the detail because a sophisticated, intelligence-led initiative was underway to trap the main protagonists and the intervention tactics SCDEA were to employ obviously had to remain top secret. For some time, they had suspected a leak as the criminals had managed to stay one step ahead, so from now on, information would be provided on a need-to-know basis only. All she had been told was that this multi-million pound crime organization had the capacity and resources to severely damage local economies, the community and anybody else foolish enough to get in their way.

Dismantling the infrastructure of this criminal empire was proving dangerous and challenging and required close collaboration with all law enforcement agencies both here and abroad. To this end, the SCDEA had told DCS Cameron that they would stay in regular contact with her and might require her to provide immediate support when the action kicked off. Exactly from where she was expected to draw the manpower for this support they hadn't indicated. The flu epidemic had claimed more victims over the last two weeks and she'd already cancelled all leave despite Christmas looming. Meanwhile, the snow, a white blanket of obstruction, continued unabated.

She switched on the kettle and dropped a tea-bag in her mug. This type of crime was shaping the future of the police service: the increasing ease and speed of trade and travel meant that organized criminal groups would continually expand to collaborate with their foreign counterparts and operate on an international level. She was lamenting this rapid escalation of serious crime when the phone rang again. It was DI Dawes. He explained, apologetically, that his suspicious death investigation had failed to produce anything substantial that could be placed before the Fiscal.

'That's fine, Jack. As long as you're satisfied, then so am I. I know you'll have done your best and I'm grateful. You'll let me have your report for the PF?'

'As soon as I can link up with modern technology.'

She laughed. 'I guess Doomdochry isn't exactly bristling with cyber cafés. Thanks for all your help especially in such awful conditions. I'll arrange for Donnie to come and pick you up as soon as possible. It may not be until this afternoon as he has a commercial job on this morning, but if I get him to take you straight to Inverness Airport, you should be back in London by this evening.' After she'd put down the phone, DCS Cameron wondered briefly about Astrid. But sadly, the death of one wee lassie from a heroin overdose paled into insignificance compared to the numbers who would be irreparably damaged if this international crime organization were allowed to prosper.

Mack MacAlister drove the police officers from the castle to the helicopter landing site in the old Volvo, saving them the arduous trek through the snow that they'd undertaken when they arrived.

'Thank you for your efforts, Inspector Dawes.' Mack shook Jack's hand warmly. 'My parents are very relieved that you found no evidence of criminal activity at Doomdochry, although naturally, we're all sad that a young girl's life should end so tragically, myself especially. You see, in my profession, we regard drugs as a vital element in healing and prolonging life. It's a poor indictment on our society that the irresponsible use of those same drugs for so-called recreational purposes should result in so many unnecessary deaths, whilst lining the pockets of unscrupulous dealers.'

'I agree, Mr MacAlister,' said Jack, 'and please thank the Earl and Lady Alice for their hospitality. I hope you and your family can now enjoy a peaceful Christmas without any further intrusions.'

'I'm sure we shall, Inspector.' He hesitated, feeling awkward. 'I hope you didn't place any credence on Great Auntie Flora's little outburst as we were leaving? I fear she's beginning to exhibit all the classic symptoms of Alzheimer's disease; disorientation, irrational behaviour, impaired judgement, and of course, problems with abstract thinking.'

As they'd been loading their bags into the Volvo, Flora had flung open her window and leaned out, dangerously. She waved a post-it note and shrieked at them. 'I saw her! Last night, outside my room. Lady Jean, howling and stinking of rotten flesh. There's going to be another death in Doomdochry! She's warning ye but ye'll no' listen!'

Jack smiled. Privately, he doubted very much if the old girl had Alzheimer's; she was sharp as a tack. And this probably wasn't a good time to mention that both his sergeant and constable claimed to have seen the ghost.

'Please don't worry about it on our account, sir.'

'Thank you, Inspector. I knew you'd understand. You must witness a lot of bizarre behaviour in your line of work.' He pointed to the sky where rotor blades were swirling the snow into a white tornado. 'Here comes your transport.'

As arranged, Donnie Cameron put his helicopter down where he'd dropped them some five days earlier. The three police officers grabbed their bags and sprinted, leaving Mack giving them a regal wave from the Volvo.

'Hello again!' Donnie shouted over the noise of the engine. 'Did you find what you came for?'

'In a manner of speaking.' Jack belted himself in, far from sure that he had, but there was no point in dwelling on it. He'd made a decision and now it was time to get back to London and pick up where he'd left off.

'Home in time for Christmas, eh?' Cameron turned and laughed cheerily. 'Just the job. You don't want to hang around here any longer than you need. Too bloody cold. I bet you didn't realize it but Shetland's closer to the Arctic Circle than to London. Everybody belted in? I promised Charlie I'd have you back to Inverness Airport well in time for your flight to Gatwick. Hang on to your hats!' He twiddled a few knobs, pulled a few levers and they lifted off into the swirling snowstorm at an alarming rate of knots.

'Have they gone?' Alistair MacAlister popped his lugubrious face around the library door where Mack was checking to see if the police had left anything useful behind.

'Yes, Father.'

The Earl trotted in, followed by Lady Alice. 'You see, Alistair,' she said briskly, 'I told you it'd be fine.'

'Aye, but what if they'd found out? I'm too old for prison, it'd be the end of me.'

Mack made his parents sit on the large, battered sofa with the busted springs while he poured them tea. Then he pulled up a chair opposite and eyeballed them, sternly.

'Now listen to me, both of you. You have to stop this right away. If those police officers had done their job properly and searched the Guard Chamber, you'd have been in big trouble and so should I. I thought any minute that Fraser was going to give the game away, he was in such a state. He's a loose cannon at the best of times and so is Great Aunt Flora. It was sheer luck that I managed to burst in when that scruffy Sergeant and his fat Constable were trying to wheedle information out of her. You know what she's like, she'd have told them everything, just for devilment. Fortunately, she told them she'd seen the Green Lady so they've gone away, believing she's batty.'

Lady Alice looked defiant. 'It's all very well for you, son, you're not here most of the time. How are we supposed to manage? We've done deals with some powerful folk through Randall and his American companies, we can't go back now.'

'Well you can't carry on.' Mack was adamant. 'The death of that girl on Doomdochry land has attracted the unwelcome attention of the authorities and the whole enterprise has become too risky. Promise me that's an end of it.'

The Earl and Lady Alice looked at each other doubtfully and nodded.

They were over the Atlantic when the call came through. Donnie's radio crackled into life and they could just make out his side of the conversation above the noise of the chopper.

'Hello, Charlie.' Donnie had DCS Cameron on the line. 'Yes, we're well on our way to Inverness – about another hour in this weather, I reckon. What?' His expression was suddenly grave. 'I understand. Yes, I'll tell the Inspector. See you later. Over and out.' Without a word, Donnie twisted the throttle lever and decreased the pitch of the tail rotor. The helicopter gave a slight lurch then began to turn smoothly to the right in a wide circle until they were facing back the way they had come. Once safely on course, he turned to Jack, his mood transformed from cheerful to grim. 'Charlie wants me to fly you back to Doomdochry. There's been another death. Obviously she couldn't give me the details, but she said to tell you that the body they've found has been identified as that of Fraser Grant.'

By the time they reached Doomdochry, the news had spread as quickly and as devastatingly as the swine flu epidemic. Only DC Mellis was happy. She tried hard not to show it but she was elated at the prospect of working with DI Dawes and DS Malone for a while longer. It had to be the real thing this time. A proper murder and in the nick of time before she ended up back in uniform for Christmas, chucking drunks out of Inverness pubs.

Mack MacAlister waited edgily for the helicopter to return. Two hours earlier, he'd been sighing with relief as the police left. Now he was cursing vociferously while he waited for them to come back. Bloody Fraser! He'd been a feckless, weak, attention-seeker for most of his life. Always the spoilt brat, demanding special treatment and affection from the women. And now, even in death, he was creating an almighty fuss. And it was fuss that Mack decidedly didn't need.

At Jack's request, Mack drove them straight to Fraser Grant's cottage on the estate. The doctor was already at the scene, but had touched very little, waiting for the police. The Deputy Fiscal had been and gone. Grant was lying on the bed, naked. He was stretched out on his back, his arms and legs in a normal, relaxed position. To the casual observer, he might easily have been asleep until the eye travelled upwards to the blue freezer bag over his head, concealing the gaping mouth and bulging, bloodshot eyes. The doctor was leaning over him, examining the tape that secured the bag around his neck. She straightened up when the police officers entered the room.

'We must stop meeting like this, Inspector Dawes.' It was Jenny MacLeod, the pathologist from Inverness.

'Dr MacLeod. This is a surprise. What are you doing here?'

'Right this minute, I'm trying to calculate the time of this unfortunate man's death because I know that's the first thing you'll ask me. But if you mean how come I'm on Shetland, it's to help out with the swine flu epidemic. Quite a few of the doctors have gone down with it and there are children and elderly patients with severe symptoms who need attention, so I'm trying to relieve some of the pressure. I hadn't expected to find myself dealing with another suspicious death, though.'

'Well, it's good to see you again, whatever the reason.'

'First thoughts on the time of death, Doc?' asked Bugsy, keen to get down to the nitty gritty.

'An informed guess? Late last evening but before midnight. I'll have a better idea after the PM.'

'Cause of death?' asked DC Mellis, who had whipped out her ever-present notebook.

'Asphyxiation by plastic bag. That's the easy bit. Whether he did it himself or it was placed over his head by someone else is going to take a little longer, Constable. What I can tell you is that there are no obvious defence wounds. And if it's suicide, I would expect to find some kind of depressant to make him pass out before oxygen deprivation triggers instinctive panic and the urge to escape. It's called the hypercapnic alarm response. He smells very strongly of alcohol and there are fresh semen stains on the sheets so it's probable that he had sex and a good deal of whisky shortly before he died. Right now, I can only tell you that he died by asphyxiation. It's your unenviable task to establish the circumstances.' She snapped her bag shut. 'The Fiscal wants me to perform the autopsy as soon as possible here on Shetland, Inspector Dawes. I'll try to do it later today and I'll let you have my report.'

'Thanks, Doctor.' Dawes dropped his voice to a murmur. 'Do you think you might also compare his DNA with that of Astrid's foetus? It might give us some kind of a lead. At the very least, it would help to tie up a few loose ends.'

*

Muttering malevolently, Moragh was remaking the beds that she'd stripped only a couple of hours earlier, whilst bringing down the wrath of God on whoever was responsible for Fraser's death. She still regarded him as her little boy and was devastated. Meanwhile, the library at Doomdochry Castle had re-acquired its status as an incident room with existing files resurrected from DI Dawes' briefcase and some fresh ones opened in respect of the new case.

Moragh's husband, Geordie, sat on one side of the rosewood reading-table opposite Sergeant Malone, who was asking the questions. DI Dawes had withdrawn to a nearby armchair so as not to appear intimidating.

'I believe it was you who found Mr Grant, sir. You went to look for him when he didn't turn up for work,' said Malone.

'Aye.' Geordie met Malone's stare. 'Will ye be staying long?'

'We'll be staying as long as it takes to establish how and why Mr Grant died.'

'I can tell ye that,' declared Geordie. 'It was gangsters from England. The lad owed 'em money from his gambling.'

'Really, sir? And how do you know that?'

'I've seen 'em afore. Couple o' nights ago when I was out late, checking the sheep. Two big 'uns kicking in the lad's front door. Must've come back and done him in.'

'Why didn't you tell us this before, Geordie?' asked Maggie.

'Fraser wasn't dead then, was he?'

There was no questioning his terse logic and although they tried for some fifteen minutes, he either didn't know any more or he wasn't telling. After he'd gone, they sat deep in thought.

'Barmy Aunt Flora was right about one thing,' said Bugsy. 'Fraser's coat was hanging on a very shoogly peg if mobsters came all the way from England to do him in.'

But Jack's crooked nose told him there was more to it than that. They needed the results of that autopsy. Strange that the ghillie displayed so little emotion at the unexpected death of a young man who had been brought up almost as a son. Jack turned to Bugsy who was checking Maggie's notes.

'Sergeant, promise me if I die suddenly, you'll show a little more grief than that.'

Bugsy face creased with sincerity. 'Course I will, Jack. I'll be gutted. I mean … if *you* kick the bucket, I'll be left on me own with Ducky Drake and DCS Garwood. Bloody tragic!'

Later that afternoon, Jack rang Corrie. This new development meant he definitely wouldn't be home for Christmas as he'd hoped.

'There's been another murder.'

'Dear me, Jack, you're starting to sound like something from a very old *Taggart* movie. Who is it this time?'

'It's the young man that I originally had in the frame for killing Astrid.'

'He still might have, mightn't he? Maybe someone found out and got to him before you did. It sounds very spooky. I wish I could come and help you.'

'No, you don't. It's perishing cold, everybody hates us and the food preparation would give you apoplexy. You're much better off where you are. And there's nothing spooky about this last death. One theory is that he got into debt with some evil bastards and a couple of them came up here from England and bumped him off. A witness saw two strangers kicking his door down a couple of nights ago. That could have been the first warning. Then, when he didn't come up with the loot, they could have come back last night and finished him off. In any event, they're probably back in England by now.'

'If the man died last night, the thugs must still be there on Unst because all flights from the Highlands and Islands have been suspended due to the heavy snow. I've been watching the weather forecasts and travel news, wondering how you were going to get home.'

'Maybe they have a fast car and drove up from England.'

'Even so, they'd still have to get from Shetland to the mainland and I assume divine intervention didn't enable them to walk on water.'

Jack thought about it for a long time after he'd said goodbye. Corrie had a point as usual. Geordie had told them that the men he saw were strangers; men he'd never seen on the island before. So if they're still on Doomdochry, where were they hiding?

CHAPTER SIXTEEN

A man and a woman stood on the lip of the Unst cliffs from where they had a perfect view of Out Stack, the most northerly point in the British Isles. Beneath them, massive waves crashed against the jagged sea stacks and seals lolled on the rocky shore, but they were not there to admire the dramatic scenery. The woman had chosen this place because they could not be overheard above the fierce, howling wind and they were unlikely to be observed by anyone who mattered. She was dressed in designer jeans, a Stella McCartney silk parka and a headscarf that flapped frantically in the wind. The man shouted above the furore of the wind and sea.

'Nice outfit. Must have cost a packet. Business is obviously booming.'

She yelled back. 'You must be sitting on a decent little nest egg yourself, by now.'

The man, restless and uneasy, scowled and flicked his cigarette butt over the cliff edge into the wild Shetland landscape. 'It wasn't the money that dragged me into this.'

'But you took it, didn't you?'

'Yes and I was a fool. I always knew there'd be another time, another favour, but *two* bodies. For Christ's sake! Where will it end?'

She was calm, dispassionate. 'You knew what the business was about; what he does.'

'Yes, he kills people.'

'That's right, he kills people. You haven't seen them, but I have. I've watched them die. Now, I've stopped looking. They're just statistics to me.' She took a mirror from her handbag and checked her lipstick. 'Look around you. Everyone's on a rake-off from something. It doesn't matter whether it's tax evasion or drug trafficking and prostitution. I don't care who's selling what or who's buying whom; every bastard's

124

on the take. Even here, in Doomdochry. So wake up and smell the coffee.' She opened her bag and took out a bulging envelope, but held on to it as the man went to take it. 'Just keep your mouth shut and do your job. You saw what happens to people who talk too much.' She released the envelope and the man snatched it and stashed it inside his jacket. Then he turned on his heel and strode away.

Following Fraser's death, an even greater sense of foreboding hung over Doomdochry. The opinions of the local gossips were split. Some believed, like Geordie, that he had been killed by 'foreign' mobsters from the city gambling dens and he probably had it coming to him. Others held the view that he had in some way been responsible for the death of the wee lassie who fell from the tower and could no longer live with the guilt so had done away with himself. The seriously unhinged declared that Grant was an illegitimate descendant of the first Earl and that the Green Lady had come back from the grave to wreak terrible revenge upon him. The general consensus was that so few suspicious deaths had ever happened in Doomdochry that two in less than a fortnight had to be linked in some way.

Jack requested just sandwiches and tea in the library that evening, instead of joining the MacAlisters for dinner in the dining-room. With this second death so close on the first, he felt it was time for some straight talking and for that, he needed to distance the police from the family, apart from formal questioning. The room was unnaturally silent while the three detectives tried to make sense of the new situation.

Despite the improbability, Jack couldn't help seeing parallels with the two cases he'd left behind in Southwark. He started to jot some notes on a sheet of scrap paper, hoping it would help to arrange his thoughts into some kind of logical order. (1) Victims (a) Karen Baxter and (b) Astrid murdered. (2) Close friends of victims (a) Lenny Lennox and (b) Fraser Grant found dead. Jack linked the names with arrows for he knew Karen and Lenny had had a kind of friendship, unlikely though it was, and he believed that despite Grant's denials, he and Astrid had been friends, if not lovers. He scribbled another line underneath. (3) Death of friends. Remorseful suicide or murder (?) The vicious execution of Lenny Lennox had been only thinly disguised as suicide for the benefit of 'idle wankers' like DI Drake. The manner of Fraser Grant's death had still to be determined by autopsy. But if it was murder, why? Another line. (4) To stop friends from revealing something they found out from victims. Such as what? Karen Baxter, the prostitute, had been worldly enough to be mixed up in something dangerous, but what could an eighteen-year old waif and stray like Astrid have done to warrant this kind of violence? He screwed up the sheet of paper and threw it at the wall. It missed. He was probably barking up the wrong tree entirely. After all, it was just guesswork. He didn't even know if Astrid *had* been murdered although now, he was becoming more receptive to the idea. Neither did he know that Fraser *hadn't* committed suicide. Everyone seemed to agree that he was a pretty pathetic, ineffectual kind of bloke. He might just have been emotionally unstable enough to get drunk and top himself, having been scared to death after being beaten up. Maybe each case was just as simple and straightforward as it appeared on the surface and these apparent similarities with the London killings were macabre flights of fancy brought on by spending five days in a haunted castle full of congenital eccentrics and over-exposure to a diet of mutton stew. Bugsy's familiar growl burst his morose bubble.

'I bet you all the neeps in Moragh's tattie-pit that Grant turns out to be the father of Astrid's baby.'

Jack shrugged. 'You could be right, Sergeant, although it wasn't Astrid he had sex with the night he died, was it? Which seductive lady provided the stimulus for all that semen on his sheets?'

DC Mellis sniffed. 'My money's on Melissa MacAlister, sir.'

'And what's the reasoning behind that hypothesis, Constable?'

Maggie sniffed even more disdainfully. 'Because she looks like she's never worn a decent pair o' knickers in her life!'

Jack smiled. 'Do you think we might attach a little more relevance to the facts rather than emotionally-loaded sartorial observations, Constable?'

Maggie flipped open her notebook. 'The shameless besom claims she can't sleep here in the castle, so she goes for walks late at night instead of stopping in bed with her lovely husband who'd be much better off with a good Shetland girl. Fraser Grant said he had insomnia and wanders about the estate at night. What if they cooked that up between them in case someone spotted them on their way to commit a mortal sin in his cottage?'

'That's better, Constable.' Jack had considered more or less that same possibility himself. 'What are your thoughts, Sergeant?'

Bugsy leant back on two legs of his antique chair. It creaked, ominously. 'Yeah, I'm with Mags. Gotta be Melissa, hasn't it? I mean, who else? Given the wilderness and the weather, we have to assume it's a female in the Doomdochry vicinity unless he's bussing them in from outside. It isn't Lady Alice, Aunt Flora or Moragh which only leaves Melissa and Nicole the Mercenary Ball Breaker, and Grant wasn't her type. No money and no balls.'

'Aye, and not much of a dick either,' said DC Mellis, casting her mind back to his naked body on the bed. 'Nicole MacAlister's not short of a few bob right enough, what with her yacht, her art collection and her silicone tits. Why would she waste time on a loser like Grant when she's married to a billionaire?'

Malone frowned. 'What d'you make of Randall MacAlister, guv? I mean, all that crap about creating a Highland Theme Park called Doomdochry World. Is he serious, or what? Surely nobody, not even a Yank with more money than taste, would seriously consider a venture as tacky as that?'

'Maybe he has another motive for wanting a base in the Shetlands. Remember when we were kicking ideas around at Laxdale? We said how easy it would be for Randall to use the Gainsborough to smuggle drugs or dirty money or even illegals across to Norway without attracting unwelcome attention. Doomdochry World would be the perfect cover for it. Did we ever check out his IT Company?'

'Yes, guv. I got Julie Molesworth to do it. He's kosher all right. Made a shed-load of dollars out of microchips and then sold his empire to enjoy himself before his liver packs up.'

'Maybe, but that genial old drunk routine could just be an act. It wouldn't take a massive leap of faith to see him as the head of a different kind of empire: one that makes money out of serious crime and kills people who get in the way.'

Bugsy was still doubtful. 'Yeah, but it's hard to imagine a vast criminal organization having the head of its control centre here. Shetland's like Garwood, all wind and water.'

'It would have been hard to imagine anyone being murdered here until it happened. Maybe Randall's original headquarters got too hot so he needed to move his set-up somewhere safer. All he had to do was pretend to be researching his family tree and the Shetland MacAlisters did the rest.'

At nine o'clock, Jack's mobile rang. It was Doctor MacLeod. He switched her to speaker-phone so they could all hear.

'Inspector Dawes? I've got the results of Grant's autopsy.'

'Thanks for giving it priority, Doctor.'

'Time of death is confirmed at between ten o'clock and midnight and the evidence points to murder, not suicide. He'd snorted a considerable amount of cocaine and he'd drunk the equivalent of a bottle of whisky.'

'He was known to be a heavy drinker, Doc,' Malone called out.

'He may have liked a drink, Sergeant, but I can assure you he didn't want this last one. I found blood and a sliver of glass inside his mouth from the neck of a whisky bottle. It had been forced down his throat so viciously that it splintered against his teeth on the way. Also, at some point prior to his death, his thumbs were tied together behind his back with something small and narrow, possibly a cable tie. None was found in the cottage so the killer must have brought it with him and taken it away again.'

The mobster's favourite appliance of restraint, thought Jack. The same MO that was used on Lenny Lennox while he was hanged. Another parallel, nagged the small voice in his head. He ignored it.

Doctor MacLeod continued with more of the detail until she came to the freezer bag, then she hesitated. 'This may be relevant or it may not but I think it's worth mentioning. The freezer bag that was used to suffocate the victim wasn't a new one, it had been used before according to the young lady in the laboratory, who, incidentally is struggling on alone, her male colleagues having all fallen victim to swine flu. Without her, you'd have had to wait much longer for any forensic results. She found traces of the freezer bag's previous contents.'

'Don't tell me,' yelled Malone. 'It was mutton.'

'Good guess, Sergeant,' Dr MacLeod shouted back, 'the bag had originally contained frozen mutton, but there were traces of something else. At some point recently, the bag had held money, paper money. I'll send over the full report, Inspector. One last thing, the DNA didn't match. Grant wasn't the father of Astrid's baby.'

They drank tea and risked choking on the bones in Moragh's fish paste sandwiches while they mulled over the post-mortem findings.

'Now we know this one's definitely a murder, don't we, sir?' DC Mellis, trying hard to contain her excitement, was anxious for confirmation.

'Yes, Constable, Fraser Grant was murdered all right. What we have to ask ourselves now, is whether the woman in his bed was an accessory to that murder, or ...'

'... whether the bloke enjoyed one final shag before the bad guys caught up with him,' finished Bugsy.

There was a sharp tap at the double doors and they flew open almost immediately before anyone had time to shout 'come in' or 'stay out'. Mack MacAlister strode in, flakes of paint down the front of his immaculate, charcoal suit, evidence that he'd been leaning against the door, most probably to eavesdrop. Jack wondered how much he'd heard. They'd been shouting to Dr MacLeod on speaker-phone about the violent manner of Fraser Grant's death.

'It's getting late,' Mack observed, tetchily. 'May I ask what's been going on?'

'You may ask, sir, and if you get an answer from anyone, perhaps you'd explain it to me,' said Jack, evenly. He selected a sandwich, peeled it apart to inspect the scaly, viscous filling and then put it back on the plate. 'You see, Mr MacAlister, I have a disturbing suspicion that not everyone here has told us the whole truth, and that includes you.'

Mack began to bluster. 'I'm sure I don't know what you mean, Inspector. We've all tried to assist you as much as possible. You've admitted yourself that you couldn't find any evidence of foul play regarding the young woman who threw herself from the tower and, as I understand it, Fraser was killed by thugs from England to whom he foolishly owed considerable gambling debts. It's sad, of course, but he brought it on himself and I don't see that it has anything to do with my family.'

'Fraser Grant was employed by the MacAlisters, sir. He was brought up as one of your family and he was murdered in a cottage on the castle estate. I find it hard to believe that nobody, apart from Geordie, has admitted to knowing anything about the man's activities or his death. For that reason, I intend to question everyone again and I mean everyone, so that will include Miss Flora MacAlister and the Earl and Lady Alice.'

Mack's face was crimson with rage. 'That is completely out of the question. My mother and my great aunt are in mourning. They were very fond of Fraser and his death has come as a terrible shock; I really can't permit you to harass them at this time. Nor do I wish you to pester my wife. She knows nothing that is relevant to Grant's death. She didn't want to spend Christmas at Doomdochry and only came here to please me. I forbid you to ...'

During this tirade, Dawes stood up and braced himself to his full six foot three, which gave him a slight but nevertheless significant psychological advantage. His voice was quiet but firm. 'This is a murder enquiry, Mr MacAlister, and that means you are not in a position to forbid anything that may lead to the identification and arrest of the killer. To do so may result in a charge of obstruction. Constable Mellis, please explain "obstruction".'

Maggie stood up and chanted in text-book English. 'The offence of obstructing a police officer in the course of his duty includes any intentional interference by physical means, threats, telling lies, giving misleading information, refusing to co-operate or warning a person who has committed a crime so that he can escape detection.' She sat down again.

'Thank you, Constable.' Jack turned to Mack and gave him the full force of his laser-beam glare. 'I shall require an accurate, detailed account of everybody's movements on the night Mr Grant died and anything else about him that anyone may hitherto have failed to disclose for whatever reason. I shall be the one who decides what is relevant, not you.'

The gloves were off. Without another word, Mack MacAlister turned on his heel and marched out, slamming the doors behind him.

It was quiet after he'd gone. Then Bugsy broke the taut silence. 'Like I said, there'll be no paint left on those doors by the time we've finished.'

It was midnight and the church clock hurled a salvo of sonorous chimes over the sleeping London suburb. Corrie Dawes poured herself a well-earned glass of Cabernet Sauvignon and stood at the kitchen window, watching the snow fetch the tiles off next door's roof. She wondered what she'd do over Christmas without Jack. It wouldn't be the first Christmas she'd spent without him; there wasn't a moratorium on murder simply because it was supposed to be the season of goodwill. Just the opposite, very often. Something to do with people being cooped up together in a confined space with nothing to do but eat, drink and pick a fight with each other. Sooner or later someone snaps and lashes out. She was about to take a sip of her wine when the phone rang. It was Cynthia Garwood.

'Hello, darling, only me. George and I were wondering what you were doing over Christmas now Jack has to stay in the frozen north. I heard about the second murder. Charlie Cameron phoned George to ask if Jack could help out a while longer. Awful isn't it? You imagine Shetland to be full of fat little ponies and salty old fishermen in cable-knit sweaters not serial killers armed with freezer bags. Anyway, we wondered, well, I wondered actually, whether you'd like to come over and enjoy the festivities with us.'

I bet you did, thought Corrie. She knew Cynthia had several parties planned because she'd ordered all the food from Coriander's Cuisine. She'd like nothing more than to have her old school chum on the spot to serve it and do all the skivvying.

'I'd love to, Cynthia, but I'm afraid I'll be working all over Christmas. I have to prepare all my New Year orders. Thanks all the same.'

'Oh.' Cynthia sounded disappointed. 'Well, if you change your mind, you'll be very welcome. Bye, darling.'

Corrie smiled. Cynthia never ceased to amaze her. She was so transparent and the only person she knew who could telephone at midnight without thinking it was anti-social. She put down the phone and it rang again immediately. Obviously Cynthia wasn't the only person with insomnia. This would be Jack ringing to say goodnight. She snatched it up. 'Jack?'

There was silence for a few moments then a gruff, female voice said, 'I wanna speak to Inspector Dawes.'

Corrie tried to place the voice and couldn't. 'I'm sorry, I'm afraid he's away on a case. Who's that speaking?'

'Never mind who I am. When will 'e be back? I've got some information for 'im. It's urgent.'

'I really don't know when he'll be back, he's in Scotland. It could be several days or even weeks. Can you tell me what it's about?'

'Karen. It's about Karen. She called 'erself Angel.'

'Oh. In that case, you should speak to Detective Inspector Drake. He handled the murder investigation and—'

'Yeah and 'e let the killer get away. I don't wanna talk to 'im, he's a sleazy wanker. I'll only tell DI Dawes.'

Corrie sympathized. She wondered if she should give the caller Jack's mobile phone number if it was urgent, but she knew he'd go into one of his rants about security if she did. 'Can you give *me* the information? I'm Corrie Dawes, Inspector Dawes' wife.'

'Yeah, I know who you are. I took one of the cards you left in the Blue Ray Club.'

So that's how she got this number.

The girl hesitated, curious. 'Is your name really Corridors?'

'Something like that, it's a long story. Listen, if you give me the information, I promise I'll pass it to DI Dawes immediately.'

The girl hesitated. 'OK but not on the phone. I wanna meet.'

'All right. Shall we say around eleven tomorrow? We could go for a coffee.'

The girl gave a scornful laugh. 'I'm a working girl, love; we don't do nine to five wiv a break for coffee and cream buns. I'll meet you in half an hour on the corner of Portsmouth Street and come dressed like you're looking for business. I don't wanna to be seen talkin' to a copper's wife.'

Corrie recognized the address; it was right in the heart of the red light district. 'But it's half past twelve! I really don't think I could ...' But the girl had put the phone down.

At precisely one a.m. Corrie was walking down Portsmouth Street towards the corner where several working girls stood chatting and smoking, waiting for a punter. She was amazed at how little they were wearing on a freezing cold, December night with snowflakes the size of dinner plates coming down. She felt overdressed in a red satin mini skirt and fishnet tights she'd bought years ago for a "vicars and tarts" party. Her frilly blouse had a couple of buttons left undone to show some of her ample cleavage and since all her shoes were chosen for comfort, she'd put on her high-heeled boots. The sheepskin coat, bobble hat and scarf added at the last minute could be whipped off if necessary. She was wondering whether she should walk along swinging her handbag when a skinny young woman in a low-cut top with a bare midriff and a skirt that barely covered her knickers, left the pack and fell into step beside her. She linked her arm through Corrie's and muttered out of the corner of her mouth.

'Keep walking, Corridors.'

'How did you know it was me?' Corrie muttered back.

'Do me a favour, love. If you were a real tart, you'd have starved to death years ago.' The girl stopped under a street lamp and Corrie could see her face. Underneath the slap, she looked about sixteen and Corrie's soft heart gave a lurch of anxiety. 'Why are you doing this job? It's so dangerous.'

'You're tellin' me,' the girl answered, grimly. 'Now listen up, coz I daren't stop long. Karen was my friend. She was older than me and she looked out for me when I first went on the game. It was 'orrible what 'appened to 'er and I know who did it. If I tell you, will Inspector Dawes get the bastard and put 'im inside for good?'

'He'll have a bloody good try. What's your name, so Inspector Dawes can get in touch with you?'

'It don't matter what my name is, all you need to know is the name of the slime-ball what killed Karen. He …' Her eyes suddenly saucered. She was staring over Corrie's shoulder at a black Mercedes with tinted windows that was speeding towards them down the deserted road. Only yards away, it mounted the pavement and showed no sign of stopping. Suddenly, the girl shoved Corrie hard into a pawn shop doorway and ran. Taken by surprise, Corrie hit the steel security shutters head on. Dazed, she struggled to her feet with grazed knees and what felt like a sprained elbow. She heard the squeal of tyres as the driver executed a fierce handbrake turn and prowled the road, hunting for her. Instinctively, Corrie ducked back into the shadows and flattened herself against the wall until the driver finally gave up and roared away; then she stumbled out into the road. The girl was lying, motionless, on the pavement, her head in a spreading pool of blood. Corrie ran to her, mobile phone already in her hand, desperately dialling 999.

It was dawn when the traffic police finished with her. She gave them all the information she had which was pathetically sparse. No, she didn't know who the girl was and no, she hadn't managed to get the licence number of the Mercedes that killed her. Although the uniformed officer didn't say as much, he was clearly thinking how unobservant she was for a policeman's wife and what a lousy eyewitness she'd make if they ever caught the driver, whom he automatically assumed to be someone over the limit who lost control and was scared to stop. He said they might need to speak to her again, but didn't hold out much hope of an arrest. All sorts of men cruised that part of town from High Court judges in Rollers to pensioners in mobility buggies. The paramedics looked her over, proclaimed her only slightly damaged, patched her up and let her go home. Mercifully, they didn't comment about the way she was dressed.

Back in the familiar warmth of her kitchen, Corrie poured herself a large brandy. She was ashamed to see that her hands were trembling violently as she unscrewed the cap. Jack had been right all along. Drake should never have closed down the Baxter case. Lenny Lennox hadn't slit her throat, it was much more complicated than that. Why hadn't this young girl come forward when Jack's team were asking the women on the street for information about Angel? If she had, she might still be alive. The answer was obvious, she was too scared to risk even a suspicion of co-operating with the police while the case was still being investigated. Now she'd been killed because she'd been seen speaking to a policeman's wife.

It was no use ringing Garwood or Drake. As far as they were concerned, the case was closed. Corrie had to tell Jack what had happened and fast. She reached for the phone then stopped. Baxter, Lennox and now this young prostitute had all been murdered because of something they knew, something they could tell the police. Whoever did it had no idea how much the girl had told Corrie before they ran her down. If they knew she was Inspector Dawes' wife, they'd try to find her. She shivered and it wasn't from cold. This might be a good time to disappear for a while. She wouldn't ring Jack; he'd only lecture her and start to worry. She'd get herself up to Scotland despite the weather and tell him in person. He'd know what to do. She hurried upstairs to pack a bag.

CHAPTER SEVENTEEN

DECEMBER 23RD

Two days to Christmas and any festive spirit that might have existed at Doomdochry Castle had now evaporated entirely, following the discovery of Fraser Grant's body. Outside, the snow continued to fall and the spiteful Shetland wind flung it in through the arrow-slit windows where it piled up on the stone floor and melted into dismal grey puddles.

True to his word, Jack tasked DS Malone and DC Mellis with taking fresh and comprehensive statements from each of the MacAlisters with instructions to take no nonsense from any of them. Proof would be required for any alibi put forward for the times of the deaths and corroboration from a partner was not sufficient. For his part, Dawes decided to speak first to Great Aunt Flora. So far, they hadn't met and Bugsy's view was that 'the old duck might be a bit diddlo, but she's nobody's fool and knows more than the family give her credit for'. Also, Flora had been closer to Grant than the others and he might have told her things in confidence that she wouldn't have revealed while he was alive. Now he was dead and couldn't be harmed by anything she said, she might feel more inclined to help the police get to the truth. Conscious that the old lady was frail and might be taking an afternoon nap, Jack tapped gently on her door. If she didn't answer immediately, he'd try again later. But her reply when it came was swift and firm.

'Come in, Inspector. I've been expecting you.'

She wore a dress of black bombazine, the favoured fabric for the mourning clothes of her youth. It was brightened by a sash in the MacAlister tartan and several yellow post-it notes adorning her bosom. A black snood contained her dishevelled hair and she'd tied a black ribbon around her throat. She seemed to Dawes to be stuck in a time

135

warp – a Victorian caricature from a Stevenson novel. She motioned him to the armchair beside her bed and he sat, while she perched on the edge like a small black crow; her arthritic, bird-like hands folded in her lap. Jack began gently.

'I'm sorry for your loss, Miss MacAlister. I believe you and Mr Grant were close.'

She sighed heavily. 'Aye, I loved him fine. I'm no' but a gizzened old maid and Fraser was the bairn I never had. This'll be the death o' me.'

'I wonder if you feel up to answering some questions? I need to know if he told you anything that might help me to catch his killer.' He saw the brief flicker of shock. 'You did know that Fraser was murdered?'

'Not for sure, but now you've told me, I'm no' surprised.' She sighed again and muttered to herself. 'So the bastard got him. I was afraid he would.'

Dawes pushed, gently. 'Who got him, Miss MacAlister?'

She continued as though she hadn't heard him. 'I warned the boy. Didn't I tell him he was playing with fire? But he'd no' listen. When I saw the Green Lady, I knew.' She pulled a lace hankie from her sleeve and dabbed at her eyes. 'The Doomdochry MacAlisters live in a veil of tears, Inspector Dawes. Violent death is in our history and in our destiny. The bogles know it and we ignore them at our peril. Will ye tell me how Fraser died? Nobody here tells me the truth and they won't tell you, either.'

Jack explained how they'd found Grant with a freezer bag over his head but left out some of the more sordid details such as the cocaine, the whisky bottle forced down his throat and the semen on his sheets. Even so, the thought of her boy suffocating to death upset her terribly and she wept bitterly.

Jack spoke quietly, trying to offer some comfort but desperate to get to the truth. 'What do you know, Flora? What did Fraser tell you? Help me catch his murderer.'

'We brought him up, Eleanor, Alice and I. What else could we do? His mother was no more than a bairn herself and she died bringing him into the world, leaving the poor wee boy all alone. He was never strong, like Mack, and he inherited his father's weaknesses; the drinking, the gambling and the loose women, especially that foreign bitch who deserves a good thrashing!'

Jack wondered what was Flora's idea of foreign. It could be

anything; Scandinavian, Norwegian perhaps. Then again, given the insular nature of Doomdochry, foreign could mean American or even English. Grant's father was another mystery. 'Who was Fraser's father, Flora? Was it your brother?'

She seemed not to hear Jack's questions and carried on with what amounted to a monologue about Grant's childhood. He decided to let her ramble, hoping that she'd come to the part of the story that interested him.

'Then, a wee while ago, he met that lassie, Astrid. I know he told ye he never knew her, but he did. Found her sitting in the castle grounds, weeping. He took her home to his cottage, she told him her troubles and they became friends. They were kindred souls, you see, Inspector. Both victims, both vulnerable, both weak. But it wasn't my Fraser who got her pregnant.' Her face darkened with anger. 'It was *him*, the other one.'

Jack became anxious. He could see Flora was tiring and he needed to find out what she knew before she became too exhausted to carry on. 'What other one, Flora?'

She hissed him silent. 'Whisht! I'm telling ye, aren't I? Astrid wasn't a Shetland lassie. Her home was a long way from here.'

'Where, Flora? Where did Astrid come from? Was it somewhere in the UK or farther than that, like America perhaps?'

'*He* brought her here, the wicked one. Sent her to live in that farm place with those strange folk, so he could use her when he felt like it. Told her he loved her and promised her the world. He was rich and powerful, a lot older than her, and she was infatuated so she believed him, like silly young lassies do. Then she got pregnant and when she told him, he said she had to get rid of it and go back where she came from. He was tired of her.' Flora's hooded eyes narrowed. 'But the lassie knew things about him, things that could ruin him, put him in prison for a long time.'

At last, thought Jack. A motive for Astrid's murder was emerging. 'But when she found out he was a criminal, why didn't Astrid tell the police straight away?'

Flora smiled at him, pityingly. 'You don't know much about women, do you, Inspector?'

He smiled ruefully. 'That's what my wife keeps telling me.'

'Astrid loved him so she turned a blind eye to his crimes, pretended they didn't happen. It wasn't his law-breaking that finally turned her against him, it was finding out he was planning to go away with his other woman. Astrid was a lassie scorned, Inspector, and you know what fury that can spawn.'

'Who *was* the man's other woman? Was she his wife?'

'I don't know. Nor did Fraser. Astrid wouldn't tell him, but it was then that she threatened to go to the police so she had to be got rid of, didn't she?' She paused and took a deep, shuddering breath.

'How do you know all this, Flora? Did Fraser tell you?'

'Aye. The evening Astrid died, she'd been to see him in his cottage. She was very happy, he said, full of hope and excitement. She told him she was away to meet her man at their special place. He'd changed his mind and wanted to take care of her and the bairn, after all. Then, later that night, when my boy found the lassie's poor broken body at the foot of the tower, he knew what must have happened. The wicked devil had lured her up there then pushed her off. Threw her away like a piece of old rubbish.'

'If Mr Grant suspected Astrid was murdered, why didn't he tell us when we questioned him? Why did he lie?'

'You don't understand, Inspector. Fraser was in debt to some very bad people. They'd beaten him up more than once. He saw a way to get enough money to pay them off.'

'Do you mean blackmail? Did Mr Grant try to extort money from the man he suspected was Astrid's killer?'

'Aye. I warned him. I told him it was dangerous, but he was desperate. He said it would be revenge for Astrid, but I knew his days were numbered. The last time I saw him, his aura was green. Clinging all around him like a rotting shroud. The colour of lust, decay and evil. Green is the colour of death, Inspector, and now he's dead. My Fraser, my wee boy.' Exhausted by her outburst, Flora's head slumped onto her chest, her eyelids drooping.

Jack leaned closer and spoke quietly. 'Who is this man, Miss MacAlister? Do you know his name?'

Her voice was weak, querulous. 'The Green Lady knew. Lady Jean warned us.' She closed her eyes and began to snore, gently.

Grinding his teeth in helpless frustration, Jack realized he'd get nothing more until after the old lady had slept. He looked at his watch. Half past three. He'd come back around Flora's tea-time and speak to her again. If he found out who Astrid's lover was, he believed he'd have the man responsible for two murders which would more than justify the cost to the taxpayer of his continued presence. He had no way of knowing that he had stumbled upon a criminal empire of such magnitude and power that its resources were infinite, and to its henchmen the killing of two young people was as routine and inconsequential as swatting a couple of troublesome flies.

Further interviews to establish alibis for the time of Fraser's death had been meticulous and in DS Malone's case, rigorous. In DC Mellis's view, his approach was dangerously close to harassment, particularly with regard to Mack MacAlister, and afterwards she hinted as much. Bugsy was unrepentant.

'The smarmy git reckons he was in the Red Drawing-Room wrapping Christmas presents till midnight. He says nobody can confirm it because he didn't want anyone to see what he'd bought them until Christmas morning. I ask you! Talk about bollocks.'

'But Mack doesn't have a motive, Sarge?'

'Oh doesn't he? How about this? Grant was a thorn in Mack's side all the time they were growing up. Poor little Fraser without a mummy was fussed over by the women and treated like one of the family; he even threatens to demand his cut of the loot if the Earl sells. Then, to top it all, Mack finds out Grant's been shagging his wife. No, Mags, the bloke's up a tree on this one and it's our job to kick the ladder away. He'll have to come up with something better than wrapping presents if he wants us to eliminate him as a suspect.'

Melissa MacAlister claimed she'd spent the hours between nine and midnight in the ghastly little "garderobe" next to the kitchen with the door locked. And no, she said shirtily, of course there weren't any witnesses. She wasn't in the habit of inviting an audience when she took a bath. When asked why it had taken so long, she replied that heating enough water to fill a bath using Moragh's ghastly witches' cauldrons took absolute yonks, never mind fishing out all the wildlife first. She'd been sick twice just from the stink.

According to the Earl and Lady Alice, they were in bed by nine o'clock as was their custom. Moragh had woken them with tea at eight-thirty next morning. They never left their room. It was tempting, Dawes observed, to dismiss them as suspects until you recalled what Great Aunt Flora had said about Grant mounting a challenge to the Doomdochry title as an illegitimate heir. The Earl was fiercely protective of his son's inheritance and determined to ensure the honourable continuity of the MacAlister line. The scandal of such a claim, and by a putative half-brother, might be considered a strong motive. Even if the Earl eventually succumbed to pressure from Randall and Mack to sell Doomdochry, Grant might, as Bugsy said, have been standing on the side-lines with his hand out for a cut. People had been bumped off for considerably less.

The only person with a cast iron alibi was Nicole MacAlister. She'd been taking a break on the Gainsborough, enjoying the luxury of edible food, proper sanitation and a fit, all-male crew who would swear that she was on board at the time of the murder. Her husband, Randall, had spent the evening on the phone to his realtors, whilst working his way through a bottle of MacAlister Malt. He passed out around ten-thirty and was helped up to bed by Geordie. It was hard, Jack thought, to see what motive Randall might have had for disposing of Fraser Grant, unless of course, he turned out to be the 'wicked devil' described by Flora MacAlister and Grant was putting the screws on him. It was Jack's interview with Aunt Flora that had produced the best lead they'd had since they arrived. In fact, as DS Malone was quick to point out, it was the *only* lead they'd had.

'Don't get too excited,' cautioned Dawes. 'The old lady seems to swing between relatively lucid and completely crackers. One minute she was describing Grant's dissolute life-style and his attempt to black-mail a vicious killer, then she went on about his aura being green and how it was the colour of death. She said the ghost of Lady Jean had warned her.'

'Green Jean never said anything to me,' grumbled Malone. 'You'd have thought she could at least have come up with a winner at Hackney or a few lottery numbers.'

'Speaking metaphysically,' began DC Mellis, 'green *is* considered to be the colour of death. In medieval Celtic tradition, it signified evil and green was avoided because of superstitions associating it with decay, misfortune and death. Folk like Miss MacAlister, who can see with their third eye, say that someone with a green aura is typically a person who works with nature and the outdoors, and we know Fraser Grant did exactly that as a factor.'

Bugsy stared at her with a pained expression. 'Bloody hell, Maggie, what a load of bollocks. You really should get out more.'

'Third eye or not,' said Jack, 'I'm far from sure Flora hasn't made the whole thing up or at best, imagined some of it. Nevertheless, it's all we have and we need to take it seriously as a viable explanation until facts prove otherwise. According to her, the man we're looking for is rich, powerful and much older than Astrid. He's involved in some kind of unlawful activity and he has a wife, or at the very least a partner, whom we must assume knows nothing about his affair with Astrid or his criminality. She might tolerate the latter, but not the former.'

'It has to be Randall, doesn't it, sir?' asked Maggie. 'He's the obvious suspect: an American multi-millionaire with contacts all over the world probably in the Mafia, too. I bet if we got a warrant and searched his yacht we'd find drugs and firearms and....'

'... horses' heads?' teased Bugsy. 'My money's still on Mack.'

'He's not rich and powerful!' protested DC Mellis.

'Maybe not to you, but he might seem that way to an impressionable young girl like Astrid,' said Bugsy. 'He's just the sort of smarmy git who'd feed her a load of oily chat, just to get her into bed. And I wouldn't be at all surprised if he isn't up to something dodgy, too. Drug dealing, just for starters. He must have plenty of opportunities to lay his hands on 'em as a surgeon.'

Jack stroked his chin thoughtfully. 'We're assuming it's someone here in Doomdochry. It could just as easily be a bloke we know nothing about who has now legged it across to Norway or back to England until the heat's off.'

Bugsy shook his head. 'Doubt it, guv. Not in this weather. Like your missus said, unless he can fly or walk on water, he has to be still here on Shetland. Look at it this way; where would you go around here if you wanted to lie low for a bit? Assume a different name, disguise yourself in funny clothes and keep out of sight till the heat dies down.'

They looked at each other. 'Laxdale.'

'What say we have another word with Ragnar, king of the tree buggers?'

Jack smiled. 'I think you'll find the term is tree huggers, Sergeant.'

'If you say, so, guv. Either way, he could be providing refuge to a murderer on that commune; either knowingly or by accident. Why don't we storm in and ask 'em all for ID? Real names, not that load of Viking bollocks.'

'Tomorrow, Bugsy, depending on what more Flora MacAlister has to tell us.' DI Dawes looked at his watch. 'We'll give her another hour, then we'll speak to her together. You can give me your opinion on how much weight we should attach to her evidence. It's all hearsay, so far.

Just a lot of paranoid stuff that Fraser Grant told her. I'm not even sure she can tell us who the killer is with the kind of accuracy that would cut it with the Fiscal.'

'The question is,' said Bugsy, 'does the killer believe she can?'

Flora MacAlister was a light sleeper and rarely slept for long, existing on short naps between which she would wake, take a wee dram or a cup of tea and a 'piece' and drop off again. That afternoon, exhausted by grief and talking to DI Dawes, she was having one of these catnaps when her bedroom door opened quietly – or as quietly as a five-centuries-old oak door on rusty iron hinges will allow. She awoke immediately and sat up as a familiar figure entered and stood at the foot of her bed. Flora tutted irritably.

'Och, not you again! What do you want now? Can't you see I'm grieving for my poor Fraser? If you had a morsel of decency, you would be, too. I've told you once; I don't want to talk to you. Go away and leave me be!' She lay down again and closed her eyes, indicating that any attempt at conversation would not be reciprocated.

The intruder stepped swiftly forward and pulled one of the pillows from beneath Flora's head. 'You aren't going to speak to anyone ever again, you interfering old hag. You've made mischief for the last time.'

It was a simple matter to push the pillow down over Flora MacAlister's face and hold it there. The old lady fought back, tearing blindly at her assailant's clothes, but soon her feeble screams, muffled by the dense, duck-down pillow, ceased altogether and she stopped thrashing and kicking and lay very still. The pillow was neatly replaced beneath her head, where her long grey hair lay tangled and wild. The black mourning snood, having come loose during her helpless struggles, fell unnoticed to the floor. The execution lasted less than three minutes and that included the time taken for Flora's killer to remove some items from the room on the way out.

CHAPTER EIGHTEEN

The kitchen in Doomdochry Castle occupied half the west wing. At one end, a cheerless fire smouldered, its acrid smoke escaping up the blackened wall and drifting over the pine table darkened by age and grime. A cauldron of thick porridge burped flatulently on the hob. Ravenous, DS Malone sneaked in looking for a snack that wasn't fish or mutton. He'd found a bowl and helped himself to some of the porridge when he caught a familiar whiff of damp tartan and Old Sporran Ready Rubbed. Turning, he stared straight at a shabby tam o' shanter. Beneath it stood Geordie, pipe clamped firmly between tobacco-stained teeth. Malone used the opportunity to do a bit of digging.

'You've lived on Doomdochry most of your life, Geordie. You must know everything about the people here. Why do you think Fraser Grant was murdered? Was it because of debts, or was it really because he was an illegitimate MacAlister?'

Geordie's expression was inscrutable. He took his pipe out of his mouth and rooted idly in his matted beard with a grimy fingernail. 'Fraser was a very bitter laddie. He'd always been jealous of Mack and like I told you, he was in a heap o' trouble. As for the heir to Doomdochry ...' he struck a match on his knee and sucked at his pipe stem, '... some say he was and others say he wasn't. It's not important, now he's dead.'

Malone strolled outside to eat his snack on the bit of covered court-yard immediately below Great Aunt Flora's tower bedroom. He'd scarcely taken a spoonful when he heard screams; blood-curdling, female screams that raised the hair on the back of his neck. He dropped the bowl and ran.

*

Bugger and double bugger! Malone rammed a cigarette into his mouth with such force that it broke in half. Even before the results of the post mortem, there was little doubt that Great Aunt Flora had been smothered. The pillow under her head had been replaced by the killer but the underside was still damp with her saliva and there were bloodstains where she'd bitten through her lip as she fought for her last breath. How could it have happened under their very noses? In any normal circumstances, Malone would have sealed off the crime scene and prevented anyone from leaving or entering, but here, it was pointless. Anyone could get into this bloody great castle and out again without being seen; there were so many entrances, exits and blooming great holes. He took one last, saddened look at her. Poor old cow, her third eye hadn't been a lot of good to her this time. He stubbed out his fag and went to find Jack.

'How is Lady Alice?' DI Dawes intercepted Mack MacAlister as he emerged from the Blue Bedroom where his mother was lying on her bed, sedated.

'She's suffering from severe shock, Inspector, as you would expect. The whole family is deeply traumatized. My mother had gone up to the tower, as usual, to wake Flora with a cup of tea. It was quite bad enough that she should find my Great Aunt dead, but the contorted expression on her terrified face was too much. Mother screamed, as we all heard, and then collapsed.'

'Who was the last person to see Miss MacAlister alive, sir?'

Mack's smile was more of a sneer. 'I imagine you're asking that, Inspector Dawes, because of the ridiculously obvious theory that the last person to see the victim alive is usually the murderer. As you know, my aunt didn't have many visitors; indeed, there were very few people she would allow into her room apart from my mother and Fraser. Fraser is dead and I assume even you don't suspect my mother, so ...' he paused for maximum effect, '... since no one has been up there since breakfast, it appears, in this instance, that the last person to see her alive was ... you.' He snapped shut his medical bag and turned on his heel.

The Fiscal arrived in his hefty four-by-four, cursing the snow and the time it had taken him to get there. He was even more critical of the performance of the Met team than on his last visit and showed the unmistakable signs of beginning flu. He blew his red, inflamed nose, constantly: it didn't improve his temper.

'Until you came up from your magnificent metropolis to "help" us, Inspector Dawes, murder was virtually unheard of on Shetland. Now we've had three in less than a fortnight, this last victim being a senior member of an ancient and highly-regarded Shetland family dating back to the fifteenth century. As I understand it, the intention was that you should investigate the initial death then leave. It was not that you should hang about, drumming up more business, until the Doomdochry community has been wiped out entirely!' He left, still trumpeting into his handkerchief, having instructed that Flora's body be removed immediately for autopsy which he proposed to attend in person. More work for the beleaguered Doctor MacLeod, thought Jack. She'll be starting to think suspicious death followed him around, which, in his profession, it invariably did.

The Earl and Lady Alice were distraught when Flora was taken away. 'They will permit us to lay her to rest in the MacAlister family graveyard, won't they?' asked the Earl, his thin whiskers drooping even more.

Dawes assured him that once the investigation was complete, the body would be returned to Doomdochry for burial. Rashly, he also assured him that the killer or killers of Astrid, Fraser Grant and Flora MacAlister would be caught and very soon. They had several leads, he declared, which they were following up and the police were relying on the total co-operation and honesty of the household.

'I wish I shared your optimism, guv,' said Bugsy, afterwards. The team was in Flora's bedroom, searching for anything that might give them a clue as to what had taken place there. They were all shaken by the turn of events.

'Who'd want to do away with a nice old lady like Miss MacAlister?' asked DC Mellis. 'I thought she was a dear old soul. It's wicked and brutal.'

'At present, Maggie, I'm inclined to believe it's the same people who "did away" with Astrid and Grant and for the same motive: to shut them up. It's a chain of events and so far, the killer has stayed one link ahead of us.'

DC Mellis chewed this over. 'Astrid was having an affair with a "rich, powerful man" but only threatened to go to the police about his criminal activities when she found out he was leaving her for another woman. He pretended he loved her then lured her up the tower and killed her before she could talk. Only by then, she'd already told Fraser Grant everything and when he tried to blackmail the murderer, he had to be silenced, too.'

'That's pretty much how I see it. Unfortunately, when we took an interest in Flora MacAlister and continued to interview her, the killer became uneasy about how much Grant had told her. He must have known that Fraser was Flora's favourite and that he spent a lot of time talking to her in her room. Even though she was generally regarded as batty, he couldn't risk what she might say to us, so he nipped in when he had the chance and put a pillow over her face. It couldn't have taken long; there was hardly anything of her.'

'So, in a way, we're responsible for her death.' Maggie was sombre.

'You mustn't think of it like that, DC Mellis. We have a job to do and that means interviewing everyone who might know something. Right now, the killer will be wondering how much we've found out about him. He'll have guessed that Flora didn't give us his name, otherwise we'd have already grabbed him. But now we have to work fast. As soon as the weather permits, he'll want to get as far away from here as he can. We have to stop him.'

'And how will we do that, sir, when we don't know who he is?'

Bugsy pulled on latex gloves and browsed the room, examining the paintings and picking up bits of the bric-a-brac that adorned every square inch. Having gone full circle, he fetched up next to Jack and Maggie. He was frowning. 'Is there something missing from this room?'

Maggie nodded. 'I can't put my finger on it, but something isn't the same as when we were in here before.'

'Did either of you notice anything different about Flora MacAlister before they took her body away?' asked Dawes.

'Not really, sir, apart from the awful look on her face. I shall mind that for the rest of my days,' shuddered Maggie.

'No, I mean something different about her clothes.'

'Yeah,' said Malone. 'The post-it notes had gone off her frock.'

'Right, Bugsy. And since none of us removed them, we have to work on the assumption that the killer took them, in case she'd written something incriminating. He wouldn't have had time to read them so he took the lot.'

'Flamin' heck, I wish I'd read them when I was in there before, only it didn't seem polite to stare at an old lady's bosom.'

'Never mind, Bugsy, they might not have meant much to us, anyway. Probably just a few jottings to remind her of things that were important to *her*.'

Bugsy muttered. 'Yeah, like maybe the name of the bloke we're after.'

It was as they were leaving, having decided there was nothing more in Flora's room to help them, that sharp-eyed Maggie Mellis spotted it. She'd been having one last look under the bed. Something shiny gleamed from behind the chamber pot. It was partly covered by the old lady's snood, ripped off in the struggle and kicked under the bed. Maggie retrieved the object and held it up.

'I wonder how this got here, sir.'

Dawes and Malone stared at it. It was a Thor's Hammer pendant on a broken leather thong. Jack examined it. The thong had snapped which must have taken some force. The death throes of an old woman, fighting for her life, perhaps.

'Fetch the car, Maggie; we're going back to Laxdale.'

It was 5.30 and pitch black. Sitting at her desk in Inverness, Chief Superintendent Cameron received two phone calls within ten minutes of each other. Their proximity prompted her to make what might otherwise have been a very illogical connection. The first call was from her contact in the Scottish Crime and Drug Enforcement Agency.

'Charlie? Good, glad I caught you. This is it, the big one we've been waiting for and we need you to be ready. We've had a tip off from our contact in the Netherlands that a large consignment of Class A drugs is to be smuggled into the UK over Christmas.'

'Dear God, not at Christmas. Is nothing scared? How will they do it?'

'It's a typical scam; illegal immigrants from Eastern Europe are brought in to London docks via Holland, hidden in large shipping containers. They're given condoms of cocaine to swallow in Amsterdam which they then have to hand over when they, and the condoms, reach "the other end". This is in addition to paying large sums to be smuggled in on forged papers. It's a simple choice; no condom, no new life in the UK.'

'What happens to them after they've handed over the drugs?' Charlie wasn't sure she wanted to know.

'When they get here, they're placed in filthy accommodation and have to work in sweat shops for fourteen hours a day, at a pound an hour. These factories are run by members of their own ethnic community, but we know they're financed and controlled by the head of the UK branch of the organization and his associates. The younger women come here expecting to work as waitresses or cleaners, but they're forced onto the streets as sex workers. And they can't complain to the authorities because they're illegals. And it gets worse. Sometimes they die. After the last big operation, the Met's Marine Policing Unit found the body of an Albanian boy, no more than sixteen, dumped on a Thames garbage scow. He'd been poisoned by a condom of cocaine that burst in his stomach. We have to smash this organization, Charlie. Put them out of business for good.'

'I agree, but if it's all kicking off in London, where do I come in?'

'You're going to have to trust me on this one because I can't give you all the details. Last time we spoke, I told you we'd discovered that Shetland was being used as a springboard to Scandinavia where the dirty money's laundered. Well, for the last six months, we've had a couple of operatives working undercover on your patch and they're pretty sure this new consignment of drugs is to be smuggled out of the UK by the same route; Shetland to Norway and from there to the drug barons in Russia and the USA. It's a very dangerous assignment because if their cover's blown, they're as good as dead, so I can't give you their names or their whereabouts. Not yet. What I can tell you is that the point of export has been tracked to Unst.'

DCS Cameron chewed her lip. 'Smart of them to choose such a remote location and at Christmas, when police and Customs are bound to be at a minimum, never mind the swine flu that's decimated my manpower up here.'

'Oh, they're clever all right, and completely ruthless. We've been after the head of the UK end of the business for some time but he's always stayed one step ahead of us. The Met boys are sure that police intelligence is being leaked to him by an informer on the inside, which is why we're keeping dissemination of details to a minimum.'

'I understand, but you surely don't suspect the leak's at my end?'

'Dunno, Charlie. Can't take the risk. Not with our officers working undercover. Trust me, this bloke would have them taken out in a nanosecond, if he got so much as a smell of coppers.'

'So what do you need me to do?'

'The Met and the SCDEA are planning synchronized raids in London and on Unst. I can't tell you when, yet, but what we'll need from you is backup but without getting in the firing line. And it *will be* a firing line. We know the villains we're after are armed, so my team will be, too. How many officers do you have available in the Doomdochry area of Unst over Christmas?'

Charlie was about to say "none" when she remembered Jack Dawes and his team. 'Call it a strange co-incidence, but I've got two men on secondment from the Met; a DI and a DS. They also have one of my constables working with them.'

'Only three?'

''Fraid so. The flu has hit us hard. I can be available, too, of course.'

'Thanks. Don't tell your men anything yet. I want as few people in the loop as possible until the last minute. Sorry about the short notice, but that's how these strikes have to work. I'll be in touch.'

'Before you go, do you know the identity of this man we're after?'

'Oh yes. We know who he is, all right. We've known for some time, but we've never had proof; never been able to make anything stick. We've picked up some of his henchmen in the past, small fry doing the dirty work, but they've either been too scared to talk or he's had them topped before they got the chance. But this time we'll get him. This time, we're going to nail the bastard before he has a chance to flee the country. I can't say any more now but get yourself to Doomdochry as soon as possible and expect fireworks some time on Christmas Eve.'

Charlie put down the phone, took out a bottle of whisky and a glass and poured herself a dram. She didn't normally drink on duty or this early in the evening but she felt in need of a stiffener. What was the world coming to? She'd been a copper all her working life; most of it in the Highlands. All right, she knew cities like Aberdeen and Inverness had their share of crime, but finding out that a multi-million pound crime empire was using a beautiful, unspoiled place like Unst to export drugs and dirty money stuck in her throat. She knocked back the whisky in one. Maybe she was getting too old for this job. She looked at her watch. Donnie would be back from his trip to Leeds tonight and they'd be able to cook supper together. He'd been flying some businessmen home for Christmas, after their scheduled flight had been cancelled due to the snow. Sometimes, she envied him his job. It must be very relaxing up there in the sky; no criminals, no violence, no stress, nothing to worry about except the odd bit of turbulence and the occasional wayward seagull. Poor Donnie, he probably thought he'd finished work until after Christmas, but now she needed him to fly her out to Doomdochry as soon as possible next day. She should let Inspector Dawes know she was coming and was about to pick up the phone when it rang. It was Jack, right on cue, almost as if he were telepathic. He told her they'd found Flora MacAlister murdered in her bed earlier that afternoon. The old lady had been about to give him the name of the man she believed had killed Astrid and Fraser Grant.

'I expect you'll hear from the Fiscal very soon; he seems to think I'm encouraging murder and mayhem to create work for myself and prolong my secondment. Mind you, three suspicious deaths in two weeks would be pushing it a bit on *my* manor, let alone on Unst. They're obviously connected and I think I know how. I propose to stay until I find the killer if that's all right.'

Charlie's expression was grim. 'I'd be very grateful if you could all stay, at least until after Christmas.' Mentally, she crossed her fingers, hoping that she wasn't putting the three officers in danger. Common sense told her the sudden spate of murders was linked to the criminal organization and the imminent drugs transaction. On a tiny island like Unst, it was too much of a coincidence to think otherwise, but she couldn't warn Jack yet. 'I'll be coming to join you on Christmas Eve, in case there's anything I can do to help.' She still felt uneasy about what she might be letting him walk into. 'What's your plan of action, Jack?'

'I've got a lead, of sorts. We found something in Flora MacAlister's room that suggests another visit to Laxdale might be useful. That's the commune I told you about.'

Charlie breathed a little easier. They could hardly come to any harm on a funny farm with a bunch of eco-nutters pretending to be Vikings. 'Right. Keep me up to date with any progress, and Jack ...'

'Yes, Superintendent?'

'You will be careful, won't you?'

CHAPTER NINETEEN

Working in the dark, DI Dawes decided, was both literally and metaphorically a permanent feature of this Shetland job. At five o'clock it had been snowing for most of the day which made the drive to Laxdale even more challenging than on their first visit. Similarly, while he had been speaking to Chief Superintendent Cameron, something told him there was more to this investigation than she had revealed. Possibly, more than she was able to reveal. Why, for example, did she feel the need to come all the way to Doomdochry at Christmas "in case there was anything she could do to help". And even more out of character, why had she warned him to be careful?

Maggie was in the driving seat and the car heater was playing its usual tricks, blasting them with cold air. They were frozen by the time she hurled the old station wagon between Laxdale's iron gates then slewed it to a hair-raising halt just inches short of the main house. This time, they were not expected. They piled out and DC Mellis went to hammer on the door. Jack stopped her.

'Hang on, Maggie, no need to let them know we're here just yet. We'll have a snoop around first. I want to take a look at that Viking long ship.'

They trudged through the bitter wind to the building marked 'Galley Shed'. Inside, the big Viking ship was shored up on resting-blocks. Jack had to admit, it was pretty impressive. It was around ten metres long with a hull made of overlapping planks held together with iron rivets. The beam was a good two metres across and in Jack's estimation, the vessel would be capable of holding a crew of at least ten if required. A three metre high dragon's head with baleful eyes adorned the bow and the brass plate on the side predictably named it 'Laxdale'. They admired it in silence for several moments.

'It's a big bugger, isn't it?' observed Malone.

'It is indeed a big bugger,' agreed a female voice from inside the hull. A head popped up. It was Valgerd, the Oxford don and self-appointed Viking expert. 'To what do we owe the pleasure, officers? I understood you were finished with us now that Astrid's death has been investigated to destruction.'

'Not quite, madam,' said Jack. Obviously, news of the two new murders at Doomdochry hadn't yet reached Laxdale. He wasn't surprised. This community functioned in a protective bubble and they preferred it that way. 'There are just one or two points that still need clarification.'

'You won't mind if I carry on painting, only we need to have the Knarr ready for the Up Helly Aa. It's Europe's largest fire festival, held in Lerwick on the last Tuesday in January every year, so it'll be Laxdale's second since we set up. It's a big occasion on Shetland. Of course, our little celebration is much less grand, but we like to maintain the tradition as far as possible. On the night, we set off fireworks on the harbour, float the Knarr out to sea under full sail, then the burning galley is sent to Valhalla. The founder of our group tosses in the first torch. It's tremendous fun.'

'Seems like a lot of work, just to set fire to it,' said Bugsy.

'Tell that to the people who make your cigarettes, Sergeant.'

'What exactly is a Knarr?' Jack was keen to know exactly how seaworthy this vessel was and its potential for transporting drugs or even illegal immigrants. This lady was smart so he decided to lead up to it obliquely, without putting her on her guard.

Valgerd put down her paintbrush and flicked back a wisp of grey hair tipped with bright red polyurethane paint. 'A Knarr, Inspector, is the Norse term for a cargo ship built for long voyages. In Viking times, they had hulls capable of carrying up to twenty-four tons and routinely crossed the North Atlantic at speeds of up to twelve knots. They were designed to be especially stable in the rough seas off Scandinavia. The Vikings weren't the first people to build ships but they built the best ships anyone had made up to that time.' She was warming to her favourite subject, as Dawes knew she would. 'They depended mostly on sail power and used oars only as auxiliaries if there was no wind. As you will have discovered, that doesn't happen often on Shetland so we plan to use sails for the Up Helly Aa.'

'What's the significance of the dragon's head?'

'Vikings were very superstitious. The heads on their dragon ships were intended to ward off sea monsters and spirits. The particular design and colour was symbolic of the leader of the group; in this case, we paint our Knarr red in honour of our founder, Ragnar Redbeard.'

'Would this model be capable of sailing as far as Scandinavia?' Jack asked. 'Bergen for example?'

She shrugged. 'Possibly. It would depend on the weather. But that wasn't our purpose in building it. It keeps us in touch with our Norse allegory and it's our contribution to celebrating the Up Helly Aa festival, that's all.'

I wonder if that really is all, thought Jack. 'Thank you for that, Valgerd, it was most interesting. Are all the commune members at home, do you know?'

'Yes, I think so. Do you want me to go and see? I believe Thora's in the kitchen preparing supper.'

'No, we won't interrupt you any longer, we can find our own way.'

They'd started to walk off when Bugsy turned back. 'Just one more thing, ma'am.' He couldn't see a pendant around her neck. 'The Viking necklace you all wear. Do you happen to have yours on you at the moment?'

'Oh yes, Sergeant.' She fished up Thor's Hammer on its leather thong from where it hung inside her tunic to protect it from the paint. 'It's an important symbol of our community. We never take them off.'

'Thank you, ma'am.' He winked at Jack who nodded back.

Maggie tapped on the back door and they walked straight in. Thora Sharptongue started violently. 'Goodness me, Inspector Dawes, you didn't half give me a turn. Were we expecting you?'

'No,' said Jack, 'and this isn't a social call. I'd like you to ask all the members of the commune to assemble here in the kitchen. I need to speak to everyone.' Oh God, he thought immediately afterwards, I've engineered another "Agatha" moment.

Thora became flustered. 'Well, I'm not sure everyone's free right now, what with it being Christmas Eve tomorrow. There's such a lot to do. Of course, I realize the Vikings weren't Christians but some of us like to—'

DS Malone cut her short with a curt, '*Now*, if you don't mind, ma'am.'

She scuttled off and soon they could hear loud voices complaining outside; then the commune members filed in, looking disgruntled. Valgerd was with them, wiping her hands on a rag, streaked with red paint.

'Look here, Inspector, this is bordering on police harassment.' It was Kettil Flatnose. 'I thought the business about Astrid jumping off Doomdochry tower was finished.'

Jack ignored him. 'Would you all please sit down. Normally, I would interview each of you individually down at the nearest police station, but since that is patently impractical, I'd be grateful if you would all co-operate. I promise we won't keep you any longer than is necessary.'

There was mumbling and grumbling but eventually they settled down, grudgingly. Jack counted rather more Viking men than he remembered from their first visit. One of them, loitering at the back, rubbed continually at a long scar on his cheek, partly hidden beneath his bushy beard. His companion had staring eyes that scanned the room, like a snake. He leaned casually against the door jamb, peeling an orange with a small, serrated fruit knife.

'Sergeant Malone, would you explain why we're here, please?' Jack sat where he could see everyone and study their faces for reactions.

Bugsy pulled no punches. 'We now believe Astrid was murdered. The post mortem showed that she was indeed pregnant, as you correctly guessed, Ms Sharptongue, and prior to being chucked off Doomdochry Tower, she had been injected with a lethal dose of heroin.'

There were gasps of disbelief. 'Well, she didn't get it here,' declared Kadlin, firmly. 'We told you before, Inspector, we don't tolerate the use of drugs or any other intoxicants at Laxdale. We are an eco-commune.'

'That's right,' said Valgerd. 'We get our "highs" by connecting with nature, growing vegetables, caring for our animals, confronting the tides and weather and exploring the rugged landscape as the Vikings did. Our lives are down to earth, challenging and inspiring; we don't need artificial stimulants.'

'What evidence do you have that Astrid was murdered?' Ketill asked.

Bugsy didn't answer this because, so far, they hadn't any; only a very strong motive by a bloke they suspected of having killed twice more. These brown-ricers were on another planet and needed bringing down to earth.

'Since Astrid's death, there have been two more murders at Doomdochry and we're examining the possibility that the same killer was responsible for all three.'

There were no gasps this time: just stunned silence.

'So why have you come *here?*' It was Flatnose again. 'What makes you think we can help you find this man?'

Malone turned on him. 'I haven't said it was a man, yet, sir.' It was time to find out which of them had lost their Thor's Hammer in Flora MacAlister's bedroom. It might not be evidence on its own, thought Bugsy, but it'll be a bloody good start and it'll speed things up. He looked across at DC Mellis who was scribbling frantically. She'd done well to find it.

'Constable Mellis will be taking statements from you all regarding your real identities and your whereabouts at the time of the murders.' Of course, there was always the possibility that one of them had legitimate business in the castle at some time and had lost their pendant then. It was unlikely, but he still needed to rule it out. 'Have any of you been inside Doomdochry Castle?'

Valgerd put up her hand. 'I have, Sergeant. It was open to the public when I arrived here last summer and I was interested in the subterranean dungeons and passages in the rocky foundations. There's documented evidence of a Norse settlement on the site, long before the castle was built by the first Earl. Viking maps show a possible tunnel connecting Doomdochry with Laxdale. It's believed to have been used as an escape route by Vikings fleeing compulsory conversion to Christianity. According to Snorri Sturluson's Saga of St Olaf written in 1225, those who didn't give up paganism had their hands and feet cut off and their eyes plucked out. Others were hanged or decapitated.'

'Yes, thank you, ma'am.' Bugsy cut her off swiftly before they were treated to another of her Viking lectures. In any case, he knew she still had her pendant, he'd already seen it.

'Did you explore the subterranean tunnel?' asked Jack. If Flora's killer was a member of Laxdale, he was curious as to how he had escaped back there in the middle of the afternoon without being seen and without a vehicle.

'No, I'm afraid not, Inspector. The dungeons were full of rats and raw sewage; impossible to penetrate without a significant health risk.'

'May I ask you all to show Constable Mellis your Thor's Hammer, please?' Although it was ostensibly a polite request, when it was barked out in Malone's interrogation voice, it was a request that you refused at your peril.

'Why?' asked Flatnose, predictably confrontational.

Malone eyeballed him. 'Just do it, please, sir. It'll save a lot of time if you don't argue.'

They fished under tunics and shirts and eventually every Viking held out the silver pendant.

'Where's your founder, today?' Jack had been scanning the faces and noticed that Ragnar Redbeard was conspicuous by his absence.

'He's away on business,' growled the man with the scar.

'I thought Laxdale *was* his business.'

'We're a small, self-supporting community, Inspector,' explained Valgerd. 'Our main income is from residents and guests who come to enjoy this wild and beautiful environment. It restores a spirit that is flagging from the stress and frustrations of the outside world. But in order to come here and enjoy the benefits, they need to know about us. Ragnar handles the commune's Internet advertising and promotes us with the Scottish Tourist Board and the National Trust. He's doing some local work today.'

'Would he have worn his pendant?' asked Bugsy.

Thora bit her lip. 'I don't think so. He was wearing a conventional suit with a collar and tie. A Viking necklace would have been out of place. I could show you where he keeps it, though. I'm sure he wouldn't mind.'

Thora took them across the yard to one of the cottages which she said was used by Ragnar. It seemed he slept badly so didn't live communally with the others for fear of disturbing them. Jack was struck by the high standard of furnishings and equipment which was far superior to the rest of the commune.

Bugsy hadn't liked Ragnar from the off. He was the kind of toffee-nosed git who could recite the Kyoto Protocol by heart. He put his mouth close to Maggie's ear. 'I bet you a tenner the pendant isn't there.'

'You're on, Sarge,' she whispered back.

Once inside, Thora went straight to an elegant cabinet, took out a velvet-lined case and opened it. She held it out for them to see.

Surreptitiously, Bugsy slipped a tenner into Maggie's outstretched hand.

'That's a bit of a bugger, isn't it, guv?' They had skidded and ploughed their way back to Doomdochry, having taken statements from all the commune members and having achieved nothing very much. Only Thora and Valgerd had proof of identity; the others claimed they'd relinquished their old lives including their names and any documents relating to them. Bugsy groaned. 'If they've all still got one, whose flamin' necklace was it under Flora's bed?'

'Maybe they keep some spares for guests,' offered Maggie.

'No. I asked,' said Bugsy. 'Old Mother Droopy Drawers said Thor's Hammers aren't particularly expensive, but they are considered very special. One is only requisitioned when someone is accepted as a full member of the commune. They present it at a celebratory meal and after that, it's specific to that person and it can't be passed on.'

'What happens when someone dies?' asked Jack.

'They burn them.'

Maggie's eyes widened. 'You mean, they perform their own cremations? Float the body out to sea on a boat and set fire to it, like the Vikings? Isn't that illegal, Sarge?'

'No, you dipstick. I mean they burn the silver charm. Melt it down in a kind of pseudo-Viking fire ceremony.'

'Who's the only other member of Laxdale whose pendant we haven't accounted for?' asked Jack.

Bugsy and Maggie thought and then chorused, 'Astrid!'

Jack nodded. 'Did they melt *hers* down after she was dead, I wonder?'

'They couldn't have, could they, sir?' said Maggie. 'She never took it off, not even in the bath, so she'd have been wearing it when she was killed. It would have been removed by the pathologist, and bagged up with her clothes.'

Jack phoned Doctor MacLeod and asked. No such necklace had been found on Astrid's body. Dawes put down the phone. 'So we work on the assumption that the Thor's Hammer we found under Flora MacAlister's bed was Astrid's even though Astrid had never been in Flora's bedroom. Added to which, it shows all the signs of having been tugged off during the struggle. That leaves us with two possibilities. Either the killer took it off Astrid before he threw her from the tower ...'

'Doubt it, guv,' interrupted Bugsy. 'If you're about to top someone, you don't nick their jewellery first. If it's valuable, you pinch it after they're dead.'

'... or,' continued Jack, 'When Grant found her body, he removed the pendant before he called the police.'

'Why would he do that?' asked Maggie.

'Gawd alone knows,' declared Bugsy. 'The geezer didn't have a full set of marbles on a good day. Maybe he wanted a keepsake if he was keen on Astrid, like Flora claimed. Maybe he wore it himself after-wards to remember her. It's the kind of poncey thing a bloke like that *would* do.'

'I don't think he was wearing it that first time we questioned him,' said Maggie. 'He was wearing one of those open-necked ghillie-shirts and I'm sure I'd have noticed something as distinctive as a Norse hammer.'

'No, I don't think he was wearing it, either.' said Jack. 'Of course, someone else could have taken it off Astrid's body before Grant found her, but you have to ask yourself who and why. I think a more likely scenario is that Grant took it then gave it to somebody else. Maybe his mysterious lady friend.'

'Well, he wouldn't give it to another bloke, would he?' Bugsy thought about it. '*Would* he?'

'I think we have to keep an open mind on that one,' said Jack. Occasionally, he liked to put the grit of doubt into the oyster of logic.

'Could we test the hammer for fingerprints? DNA?' asked Maggie.

'Waste of time,' said Bugsy. 'It'll have been handled by the world and his wife including you, Constable, and the silversmith who made it. Wouldn't prove a thing. We could test the leather thong for DNA to find out whose neck it'd been around besides Astrid's but unless their DNA's on file, we'd have to check everybody, always assuming they'd consent which most of 'em wouldn't. It'd take forever and we still might draw a blank. Meanwhile, the killer dies of old age.'

'I agree,' said Jack. 'And we don't want to burden the only young lady still standing in the forensics lab with a pointless exercise. So what are we left with? After Astrid's death, her pendant somehow ended up around our killer's neck where it was torn off by Flora while she was being smothered. The candidate with the best opportunity for acquiring the pendant is Grant, but we know he couldn't have been Flora's killer because he was already dead. It's the one certainty in a maze of imponderables. Any thoughts?'

'Aye,' said Maggie. 'Fraser Grant took the necklace off Astrid's body before he called the police and wore it for sentimental reasons. The shameless hussy he was fornicating with … that's Mrs Melissa MacAlister, sir … was jealous and made him give it to her. She was wearing it when she went into Flora's bedroom and murdered her.'

'Why would Melissa MacAlister want to kill Great Aunt Flora?' asked Jack, fascinated with Maggie's bile at the expense of Melissa MacAlister.

'It's obvious, sir. The wicked besom didn't want to live in the castle. She wanted the Earl to sell up to the American gentleman, but she knew that by the terms of Mack's grandfather's will, Flora had to agree. The old lady said it would be over her dead body, so Melissa saw to it.'

'So did Melissa kill Astrid and Grant, too?'

'She could have, sir. She'd no' much of an alibi for either of them.' Maggie thumbed her notebook. 'At the time of Astrid's death, she claimed she was in bed asleep with her husband. He says she often can't sleep in the castle and goes for a walk, so he wouldn't know if she'd gone missing that night, would he? And he's loyal enough to lie for her anyway.'

'And the heroin?'

'She stole it from Mack's medical bag. Then, when Grant was killed, she pretended she was taking a bath. For three hours? I don't think so. Who needs three hours for a good scrub down with soap and water?'

Jack smiled thinking Melissa MacAlister wasn't the kind of lady to have a 'good scrub down' and he doubted she'd let soap anywhere near her expensively moisturized skin. 'Motives, Constable?'

'Jealousy, sir. She didn't like Grant's friendship with Astrid so she got rid of her. Maybe she found out the lassie was pregnant and believed it was Grant's even though it wasn't.'

'And Grant? Why would she kill him if she was enjoying an affair with him and possessive enough to eliminate a rival? Isn't Mack, the deceived husband, a more likely suspect?'

DC Mellis frowned. 'Actually, I haven't worked out a motive for Melissa to kill Grant, yet. Maybe he *was* killed by the thugs Geordie saw because of his gambling debts.'

'Do you agree with any of that, Bugsy?'

'No, guv, but I do think the same killer did all three murders. It wasn't Melissa, though. The way Flora told it, it was Astrid's "rich and powerful" lover who killed her. She gets pregnant, he gets fed up with her and goes back to his wife. Turns out he's a major villain; Astrid knew it, turns bunny-boiler and threatens to shop him so he kills her. After he'd chucked her off the tower, he remembered the pendant belonging to some weirdo commune she lived in. He goes down and takes it off her body to hinder identification. If you remember, she had nothing on her when she was found, no handbag, no mobile phone not even a watch and nobody in Doomdochry admitted to knowing her. He thinks he's in the clear, then f-flippin' F-Fraser pops up and starts blackmailing him so he has to get rid of him, too. He had a sloppy attempt at making both murders look like suicide; Astrid's because she was a pregnant junkie and Grant's because of massive gambling debts. I agree with Maggie that the semen on the sheets was the result of a shag with Melissa, if only because I can't see it being anyone else, but I think she'd left Grant's cottage before the killer got there. After that, somebody mentions how close Grant was to Auntie Flora, and the killer knows that the police … that's you, Jack … are particularly keen to question her. Ergo, he has to do away with her as well.'

'So why was he wearing Astrid's pendant at the time?'

Bugsy scratched his head. 'That's the bit *I* haven't worked out, yet.'

'And have you a suspect in mind?'

'Yep. It's the Yank, Randall MacAlister. No doubt about it. It's like you said, he isn't here to trace his ancestors and turn Doomdochry into a tartan Disneyland. That's just a cover. He's running something big and crooked out of the most unlikely place anyone could imagine. His alibis for the killings are always that he was bladdered and out for the count. I don't believe it. He falls into bed apparently drunk and out of it, Nicole MacAlister takes a sleeping pill and gets in beside him, he waits until she's asleep then gets up again. She'd be none the wiser and that kicks his alibi right up the arse.' Bugsy paused, then: 'What about you, Jack? What's your theory?'

'My version of events isn't as well thought out as yours and Maggie's. I think a different person was responsible for each of the three murders. The MOs were different, the locations were different and the opportunities were different, but in the end, I believe the motive for all three was the same. I haven't a shred of evidence but at the same time, I'm sure I'm right. The worst part is, I've an uneasy feeling that something as big as the Titanic is going down here, and all we're doing is fiddling with the deckchairs.'

CHAPTER TWENTY

CHRISTMAS EVE

It was nine minutes past nine in the morning and the weak Shetland sun was just rising. At one minute to three in the afternoon, it would set again. A little under six hours of daylight in which to catch a killer.

Malone gyrated down the spiral steps and made his way to the library. The doors were partly ajar and he thought he saw Jack silhouetted against the window, mobile phone clamped to his ear. But when he heard the man's voice, he realized it wasn't the Inspector and lurked in the doorway, motionless and silent, hoping to hear something useful.

'Yeah, I can meet today's deadline, no sweat. How many? Sure I can handle the shipment at this end, but some London cops are sniffing around so I gotta be careful. What? Yeah, soon as they quit, we can speed up the consignments. I got the merchandise if you've got the bucks....'

Maggie burst in behind Malone, full of her customary enthusiasm.

'Morning, Sarge!'

Her voice was loud enough to crack glass and Malone winced. The man turned and immediately snapped his phone shut.

'Hi guys. How are ya?' Randall was his usual, bluff self, but for a brief second, Malone recognized the shifty look of a guilty man. The geezer was up to something a lot heavier than designing a naff Highland leisure park; he'd stake his pension on it. Randall made for the door, explaining ruefully as he made his escape. 'Gotta go find my old lady. I was pretty wasted last night and blacked out. She's gonna be real mad. See ya later.'

For a man who had allegedly drunk enough whisky the night before to have lost consciousness, Randall showed very little sign of a hangover. It could be, thought Bugsy, that the bloke's system was able to take it, but he still believed he was putting it on to fool everyone, including his wife. Malone turned on Maggie who was smiling at him, innocently.

'DC Mellis, never come blasting into a room where your sergeant is trying to earwig on a private conversation!'

'Sorry, Sarge, I didn't realize.'

'All right, but don't do it again. We're never going to crack this case without a bit of stealth and treachery. Have you got a pair of wellie boots?'

If Maggie was surprised at this complete *non sequitur*, she didn't show it. 'Yes, Sarge. I never go anywhere without them.'

'Good, because you're going to need them. The Inspector wants to take a look around the underground chambers and you heard what Valgerd said, they're full of shite and rats. You're not scared of rats, are you?'

'Och, no, Sarge. Why would I be? They'll only be the brown beasties. The black ones are reckoned to be extinct on Shetland.'

'I don't give a toss what colour they are, I hate the buggers.'

Maggie grinned wickedly. 'Will I tie some twine around your ankles to stop them running up your trews, Sarge?'

Bugsy shuddered.

Inspector Dawes strode down the third floor landing, his head a hive of buzzing clues, each of which insisted on precedence and none of which would fit together with any other to form a coherent hypothesis. Chief Superintendent Cameron was due to arrive at Doomdochry that day, presumably in Donnie's helicopter. Nobody sane would opt to spend Christmas Eve in a damp, depressing ruin of a castle unless it was imperative. What was scheduled to happen today that Charlie couldn't divulge, but that Jack's team were required to support? He still had deep reservations about the Laxdale commune. Yesterday, as they'd been leaving, they'd bumped into Kettil Flatnose. Jack had asked if he'd noticed anyone strange hanging around lately. The man's reply had been typical of his perpetually surly attitude, but not typical of the relaxed ethos of Laxdale's mission statement.

'Inspector, this is a commune. They all hang around and they're all strange.' Then he'd stomped off with his Wagnerian partner, Helga, striding beside him like a Valkyrie looking for her next corpse.

While Bugsy and Maggie had been checking out the pendants, Jack had been checking out the members. There were several he hadn't seen on their first visit, including two particularly ugly looking characters who skulked at the back, except for when they thrust their Thor's Hammer belligerently under Maggie's nose. Beneath the mandatory set of Viking whiskers, one of the men, muscular and bull-necked, had rubbed persistently at a long jagged scar which clearly wasn't the result of over-enthusiasm with a safety razor. His orange-peeling companion had snake eyes that darted around the room. Neither man seemed the type to till the soil and fiddle with chickens so what were they doing there? In fact, apart from the genuine acolytes like Thora, Valgerd and one or two of the others, Jack wondered what any of them were doing there.

He had reached the part where the corridor narrowed before opening onto the grand staircase when a sudden movement, just below the lofty ceiling, caught his attention. He glanced up and there she was. Lady Jean MacAlister. She was floating high above the ground, level with the ornate but crumbling cornice. The Green Lady was dressed just as Bugsy had described: a green bodice with billowing sleeves, and a long, emerald-coloured cloak with a hood. There was only her top half; nothing below the waist. As she materialized, a sickly stench of rotting flesh drifted down and filled the narrow space. Jack held his handkerchief over his nose, then stretched up to touch her. A firm hand on his arm restrained him and he turned to find Geordie, hiding in the shadows. The old ghillie put a finger to his lips and beckoned Dawes to follow him. They crept back along the corridor and round a few corners until Jack reckoned they were outside the room flanking the spot where Green Jean had appeared. Geordie quietly eased open the door and motioned to Jack to look inside.

Melissa MacAlister sat with her back to the door, tapping the keys of her laptop with elegantly manicured fingers. A step-ladder stood against the wall with a wireless PC projector balanced on it. She had removed the ventilation grid just below the picture rail, so she could project images through the gap and onto the wall of the corridor opposite. Jack coughed loudly and she swung round, shamefaced, like a little girl caught playing with her mother's make-up.

'Mrs MacAlister, would you please come down to the library for a little chat?' asked Jack, in the tone he normally reserved for tiresome children.

*

'I'm not going to talk to you if you're going to be aggressive.' Melissa sat in a chintzy armchair, arms folded defiantly across her small bosom. In every woman, thought Jack, there is a quality of apparent innocence, which conceals a diabolical cunning. Melissa had remained silent while Jack explained her antics to Bugsy and Maggie, but now she was stroppy and unrepentant.

'How long have you been projecting images of a ghost on the castle walls, Mrs MacAlister?' asked Jack.

'Only a week or so,' she answered, sulkily.

'It's wicked, so it is!' spat Maggie. 'Conjuring up a bogle just to frighten an old lady into believing someone was going to die.'

'That isn't why I did it!' Melissa retorted. 'And anyway, somebody did die. Two people, in fact. It wasn't my fault. Just an unfortunate co-incidence.'

'Why did you do it?' asked Jack.

'Because Mack told me we'd have to live here for ever if his father didn't sell to Randall. I knew the legend of Lady Jean haunting Doomdochry appealed to Randy and I thought it would encourage him to increase his offer if somebody who wasn't senile and potty claimed to have seen her.'

'Like three police officers, for example?'

She pouted. 'Well, yes. I needed a bit of gravitas. I suppose you're going to be very cross with me, Inspector.'

'Fortunately for you, Mrs MacAlister, my wife is a woman so irrational behaviour doesn't shock me. On the contrary, it was a most impressive performance. How did you do it?'

'It was easy. I use the projector in my interior design business. I show clients what curtain fabrics and wallpaper would look like by projecting the patterns directly onto their blank walls, so they can see the effect before they decide. In this case, I just pulled in a graphic of a fifteenth century lady, made her green and a bit hazy, then floated her about on the wall. I didn't ask people to believe it was a ghost. People see what they want to see.'

'What about the stench of rotting flesh?' asked Jack. It had been foul.

Melissa smiled. 'I put one of Moragh's rotting sheep's heads in the ventilation cavity. The Shetland gales waft the smell through very effectively.'

Sergeant Malone had stayed quiet while Jack questioned her. Now for his part in the good-cop bad-cop routine. He leaned forward and thrust his face into Melissa's. Time to take that smug little smile off her face.

'In case you haven't been paying attention lately, people have been dying here, love. It's not a bloody game. Did you push Astrid off the tower?'

She looked at him as if he'd said something deeply obscene. 'No, of course I didn't. Why would I? I didn't even know her.'

'Because you were jealous of her relationship with Grant.'

'Fraser?' She looked genuinely baffled. 'What relationship? I don't understand what you mean. Why would I be jealous?'

'Because you were having an affair with him.'

'No, I wasn't. He was a weak-willed idiot with the personality of a pea. I didn't even like him.'

'But you've already admitted you were prepared to do whatever it took to free up the sale of the estate to the Americans. Did that include smothering Great Aunt Flora with a pillow so she couldn't object?'

Melissa MacAlister panicked then. She looked from one to the other in horror. 'No! No! I didn't do that. I couldn't kill anyone. It was ghastly!'

'Maybe you planned it with Grant? He was going to claim a cut of the proceeds as the illegitimate heir. Had you arranged to run away together after the sale had gone through?'

'No! You're being ridiculous. I ...'

Bugsy became impatient. 'Come on, love, we know it was you because the old lady snatched the pendant Grant gave you. The one he took off Astrid's body. We found it under her bed.'

The colour drained from her face. 'What pendant? What are you talking about? I didn't kill Aunt Flora!'

'Who was it then?'

'I don't know! Someone broke in to rob her, she screamed and they shut her up with a pillow. You're the detectives, you work it out.'

Jack took over now. 'Did she have anything worth stealing?'

'Of course she did. The Landseer.'

'Landseer?' repeated Jack, parrot-like.

'Yes, The painting by Sir Edwin Landseer. He sculpted the lions in Trafalgar Square and ...'

'Yes, I know who Landseer was but we were given to understand that the paintings in the castle are fakes.'

'They are. Mack's parents sold all the real ones ages ago to pay for the upkeep of Doomdchry. All except for the Landseer on the wall in Flora's bedroom. She wouldn't part with it. It was the head of a deer-hound. She called it her "wee doggie", the senile old cow.'

'Did many people know about it?'

'I've no idea, but Fraser did, because he told me. He said it was worth a fortune.'

'And you believe someone broke in to steal it?'

'Well, they must have, mustn't they, because it isn't there now. Can I go? I think I'm going to be sick.'

The flaky doors burst open without warning and Mack erupted into the room, his face creased with rage and anxiety.

'Why are you detaining my wife? You have no right. I've already called our lawyer and he says you are to release her immediately.'

'We aren't detaining Mrs MacAlister, sir,' said Jack calmly. 'She was simply helping with our enquiries. She's free to go any time she chooses.'

'I think you'll find she has something interesting to tell you,' grinned Bugsy. 'Something about your ancestor, the Green Lady Jean.'

Melissa flashed Malone a poisonous look and flounced out of the room, followed by her husband. They could hear him in the corridor. 'What does he mean, Mellikins?'

'Mellikins! Huh!' mimicked Maggie, disgustedly. 'It was a wicked thing the brainless besom did!'

'Come on, Mags,' said Bugsy. 'It wasn't that bad. She only repro-duced the ghost of Doomdochry for the Yank's benefit to get him to up the ante.'

'I don't mean that! It was wicked pretending she'd didn't have a laptop when I asked to borrow one. It would have saved me hours of writing all those statements by hand.'

Jack smiled. 'All the same, DC Mellis, I think we can safely assume she isn't responsible for any of the murders. It was pretty obvious she knew nothing about the Thor's Hammer pendant and I believe her when she says she didn't care for Fraser Grant. So if it wasn't Melissa who was in bed with him on the night he was killed, who was it?'

'There's only one other woman it could have been,' said Malone. 'The same one who nicked the Landseer from Aunt Flora's bedroom to add to her art collection back home in Seattle. Nicole MacAlister.'

'I *knew* there was something missing from that room,' said Maggie.

'It was that wee painting. It left a white square on the wall. I don't know why I didn't spot it at the time.'

'We mustn't jump to conclusions,' said Jack. 'Nicole MacAlister may have nicked the painting but it doesn't prove she smothered Flora. She may have arrived after the murder, saw her chance, nipped in and grabbed it before Alice went up with the tea and found the body. She probably reckoned it wouldn't be missed in the hullabaloo and by the time it was, she'd be long gone, on her way back to the States on the Gainsborough.'

'And Randall MacAlister with her if we don't act quickly. I'm telling you, guv, Randall's our killer. I'm sure of it. They could even be in it together. It's like I said, he's the rich and powerful older man who got Astrid up the duff and had to get shot of her when she threatened to grass on him. He was in here this morning on his phone, talking about shipments and merchandise. It's gotta be drugs. What else could it be? Let me get him in here. Lean on him, hard …'

'Not yet, Sergeant.' Jack's voice was firm. 'We've spent the last week going round in ever decreasing circles with the predictable result. Now, at last, I believe we're close to the killer, but we need evidence; hard proof. First, I need to find the underground tunnel linking Doomdochry and Laxdale, the Viking escape route that Valgerd described. It could explain a great deal.'

CHAPTER TWENTY-ONE

Christmas Eve. In Inverness, there were two women with more urgent concerns than last minute Christmas presents. Charlie Cameron and Corrie Dawes were each preparing to travel north to Doomdochry. Two wives with different objectives but whose paths would ultimately converge in a terrifying way that neither could possibly anticipate.

It was ten in the morning and barely light. DCS Cameron looked down at the bleak, snow-covered terrain rising rapidly to meet them as Donnie landed the chopper as close as he dared to Doomdochry Castle. Charlie had telephoned ahead and DI Dawes had arranged to meet her with the station wagon.

'Why on earth do you need to be in this bloody wilderness on Christmas Eve?' Donnie Cameron helped his wife undo her safety belt.

Charlie sneezed volcanically. 'Sorry I couldn't give you more notice, darling, but I'm not supposed to tell anyone. It's a big, hush-hush operation.'

'What here? On Doomdochry? Is it to do with the murders? I thought Jack Dawes was handling that.'

'The murders are just part of it. We're after a massive consignment of Class A drugs and the gang responsible for bringing it into the UK. A courier brings the stuff up from London to Shetland, then somehow, it's being transported abroad via Scandinavia.'

Donnie swallowed hard. 'This gang you're after, they're dangerous, aren't they? They kill people.' It was more a statement than a question.

'About as dangerous as criminals get, and very well-connected. That's why it's taken so long for us to catch up with them. They have friends in high places: influential people on the take who are prepared to risk everything to protect their share of the huge profits. To them, killing's just a part of their trade and they do it without a qualm.'

'But why Unst? Why Doomdochry?'

'Because we're after the man at the top and we think that's where he's hiding out, waiting for the drop.'

'Do you know who he is?'

'No, not yet, but the SCDEA team do.'

'So why haven't they arrested him?'

'Because until now, they haven't been able to get sufficient evidence to nail him. This operation will flush him out. They've had officers working, undercover for months, setting it all up. Some time tonight, there'll be a series of synchronized raids spanning several countries and this time, we'll get them all, including the police mole who's been leaking classified information.'

'These raids,' said Donnie, 'do you know exactly where they're going to be? Who are the undercover officers?'

Charlie looked hard at him. 'I don't know and if I did, I couldn't tell you. I've told you too much about the operation already. The fewer people who know about it before the hit, the better. Why are you so interested?'

'I'm worried about you, sweetheart. This man, the head of the organization, he sounds ruthless. I don't want you caught in the cross-fire when they try to take him. How much backup will you have? Will they be armed?'

She sneezed again and pulled a handful of tissues from her pocket. 'Stop worrying. I'll be fine. Go home and mull some wine for when I get back. I'll ring you when it's over.' The Volvo was approaching and she grabbed her bag.

Donnie went to kiss her on the cheek and drew back. 'Charlie, you're burning up. You've caught the flu, haven't you? '

'Actually, I think I have. I ache all over and my head's throbbing.'

'Look, you're ill. Let me take you home before it all kicks off. You're not fit enough to get involved in a major strike. Tell them you're sick and let the serious crime officers handle it.'

'No, I'll be fine. I can't abandon Jack and his team. Until I brief them, they know nothing about this operation or the size of the coup we're planning. I'm the senior officer; I need to stay operational until it's over.' She climbed out, ready to wave him off. The rotor blades began to turn slowly but still he seemed reluctant to leave.

Silly old sod, she thought, affectionately. He's such a worrier.

Christ Almighty, he thought. What the bloody hell do I do now?

Corrie Dawes had lost count of the number of taxis, planes and trains she'd travelled on to get from London to Inverness. The weather and the looming Christmas holiday had completely disrupted the usual services and it had taken her the whole of the previous day to get this far. Last night, she'd fetched up at a comfortable hotel where she'd fallen into bed exhausted, then overslept and missed breakfast. Now it was late morning and she was stoking up on strong coffee and wondering how she was ever going to get across to Shetland. Since witnessing the cold-blooded and cynical elimination of the young prostitute, she had a chilling sensation of being hunted. Once the initial terror had subsided, she'd tried to convince herself that it might just have been a hit and run in a stolen car, like the traffic cops said. But intuition told her it was much more than that and her intuition was never wrong. Well, hardly ever.

She caught a glimpse of herself in the mirror behind the bar. Blimey, what a sight! The paramedics had taped a large dressing over the cut on her forehead where she'd head-butted the pawnshop security grill and her right elbow, heavily strapped, was throbbing like an old Bee Gees single. Underneath her trousers, both knees were bandaged and she had a huge bruise on her hip. They'd warned her to watch out for concussion and to stay at home in the warm. No chance of that. With a stab of conscience, she realized she had been lucky. By slamming her into that shop doorway, the girl had probably saved her life and now it was up to her, Corrie, to make sure the killer didn't get away with it. Somehow, she had to get to Jack. He'd know what to do.

It was as she poured her third coffee that she hit on the perfect solution to her problem. Dredged up from a half-forgotten gossip with Cynthia, Corrie recalled how the Garwoods went up to the Highlands for golf and salmon fishing with their friends, the Camerons, and it was the same Chief Superintendent Charlie Cameron that Jack had gone north to assist. Her husband, Donnie, ran a commercial helicopter business. Corrie pulled out her mobile and rang the Garwoods' number.

'Hello,' trilled a slightly tipsy Cynthia. 'Merry Christmas, whoever you are,' and she gave her tinkling, cut-glass laugh. In the background, Corrie could hear noisy conversation and corks popping. Of course, it was Christmas Eve. The Garwoods would be having their annual, preluncheon champagne party. Coriander's Cuisine had supplied the canapés and nibbles.

'Hello, Cynthia. It's Corrie.'

'Darling, how marvellous! You've changed your mind and you're coming over to help out.'

'No, I can't, I'm in Inverness.'

The tinkling laugh again. 'Just for a moment, I thought you said you were in Inverness. Silly me! It's Jack who's in Scotland, isn't it?'

'Yes and so am I, now. Listen, Cynthia, I need you to give me the phone number of Donnie Cameron.'

'Donnie? Why?' Cynthia sounded vague as well as tipsy.

'Because I need him to fly me to Shetland. I have to find Jack.'

Cynthia giggled. 'I get it, darling! You're going to surprise him as a Christmas present. What fun! Hang on a minute, I'll ask George.'

She was gone for several minutes during which Corrie could hear a muffled conversation and George's braying laughter then Cynthia returned with the number. Corrie wrote it on her napkin. Cynthia was still giggling.

'George wants to know what you were doing walking down Portsmouth Road at one o'clock in the morning dressed like a tart. He says aren't we paying you enough for the catering?'

Damn! The traffic police must have told him. 'I haven't time to explain now, Cynthia. Merry Christmas.' Corrie cut her off then called Donnie Cameron's number. He answered straight away as if the phone was already in his hand. Corrie thought he sounded stressed.

'Mr Cameron? My name's Coriander Dawes. We haven't met but we have mutual friends, George and Cynthia Garwood, and my husband's in Scotland, working with your wife on a murder case.'

'Is your husband Inspector Jack Dawes?'

'That's right. He's on Shetland, at a place called Doomdochry.'

'I know, I flew him there in my chopper last week.'

'That's brilliant,' said Corrie, relieved, 'so you'll know exactly where he is. Could you fly me there, too, please?'

'Not from London, I couldn't. Isn't there a plane or a—'

'No,' Corrie interrupted, impatiently. 'I'm not in London, I'm in Inverness. I must get to Jack as soon as possible, it's desperately important. It might even be ...' she paused for dramatic effect, '... a matter of life and death.' Mine, she thought grimly, if the driver of that Mercedes catches up with me.

Donnie was on edge. Events were spiralling out of control. He was about to refuse but then he hesitated. It was the connection between London and Doomdochry that worried him. More than that, it scared the bloody daylights out of him. Better to find out what Jack Dawes' wife wanted than leave her hanging around Inverness, a potential loose cannon.

'All right, Mrs Dawes.' He looked at his watch. 'I have some business to attend to first. Can you get to the heliport by six?' He gave her the location.

Corrie thanked him gratefully. She had time for a rest, some lunch and then she'd pay her bill, collect her gear and find a taxi.

Donnie punched a number into his phone and realized his hands were shaking. A calm voice answered.

'I hope this is urgent, Cameron. I don't have to remind you that I'm incommunicado for the next twenty-four hours and you should be, too.'

'I know, but you need to hear this. I've just flown my wife to Doomdochry. She says the police are about to launch heavy raids across the whole of your organization. She doesn't know when but it could be today.'

'What! Why didn't you tell me this before?'

'Because I didn't bloody well know before, that's why! Charlie's only just told me. The Serious Crime Agency has found out about the consignment of heroin and they're going to seize it.'

'How did they find out? Who grassed?'

'They've had agents working undercover, feeding them information, just like I've been feeding police information to you. They've got you this time; they know who you are and they're going to take you out. You and the whole of your filthy organization.'

'Which, I hasten to point out, includes you, Cameron. Now listen very carefully and stop panicking. We just need to change tactics, that's all. When the courier arrives in Inverness with the consignment, you pick it up as usual, but instead of bringing it to me, you fly it straight to our contact in Bergen. Then you collect the money and put it through the laundry. Meanwhile, I'll leave at top speed on the yacht with Nicole, heading for the States. The police are after me, not you, so they'll target all their resources on the Gainsborough and of course, they'll catch up with us. Only we won't have the stuff and by the time they've searched and realize they've been fooled, you'll be long gone.'

'There's something else. Dawes' wife has turned up in Inverness. She wants me to fly her to her husband in Doomdochry Castle. Says she has urgent information for him and it's a matter of life and death.'

The voice at the other end sounded pleased. 'So ... the bloody woman's turned up in Inverness, has she? Excellent. Pick her up like you've agreed then here's what you do ...'

Donnie Cameron listened and recoiled. 'Oh no. Definitely not. Are you mad? She's a policeman's wife; he's a Detective Inspector in the Met. Can't you see the danger it'll cause at the London end?'

The voice was still calm. 'It's because I can see the danger that you need to do as you're told.'

'No, I don't! Making drops and shifting merchandise was one thing but I'm not one of your thugs. I don't want anything more to do with it.'

'I think it's a little late for that, don't you? Have you forgotten the assistance my organization provided when you lost your pilot's licence? I assume you remember that unfortunate flying accident, when you were over the limit? What happens when the authorities find out you're flying on forged papers and running multiple off-shore bank accounts for the purposes of money laundering?' His tone was mocking. 'Dear me, and you the husband of a Chief Superintendent, which, of course, has been extremely useful to us.' The voice hardened. 'You've taken the money, Cameron; now get on with the job.'

'I don't care anymore.' Cameron's voice was edged with hysteria. 'Do what you like; I'm not killing for you. I'll go to prison for all the other things but not for murder.'

The voice was cold, threatening. 'In that case, I can promise you that when the raids kick off and my men start shooting their way out, DCS Cameron will get the first bullet.' The line went dead.

Constable Mellis drove the station wagon with Malone beside her and Jack and DCS Cameron in the back. Now they were in the car with no danger of being overheard, Charlie thought it safe to bring the police officers up to speed. Time was running out. She described at length the drug trafficking and money laundering organization that she'd previously hinted at, and the illegal immigrants used to facilitate it in London. She said how shocked she'd been when she learned that Shetland was involved and Unst had been identified as the point from which an imminent consignment would be smuggled to Norway.

'The reason I'm here, Jack, is because I've been asked to provide support for a big raid that's planned for tonight. I don't know the exact time, but we'll find out when the guys make the first hit. It'll be pretty spectacular.'

'What guys?' Malone wanted to know.

'Officers from the Scottish Crime and Drug Enforcement Agency. Two of them have been working undercover here for the last six months, planning this strike. It has to work. They won't get a second crack at it.'

'Do we know who they are?' asked Jack.

Charlie shook her head. 'SCDEA suspect a leak so even I haven't been told, but they'll make themselves known when the time's right. Our job is to provide backup if necessary and it'll be dangerous. The criminals we're dealing with are ruthless. They won't hesitate to kill in order to escape. The SCDEA team will be armed but we won't.'

'No change there then,' said Malone, dryly. 'Armed killers come at us with Uzis and we poke 'em in the eye with a police-issue biro. Count me in.'

'Me too,' called DC Mellis over her shoulder.

'Er … I don't think so, Maggie,' said Charlie. 'You've had no experience of this type of action and I'd rather …'

'Please, Super,' begged Maggie, bouncing with excitement. 'I can look after myself and I've always wanted to work with the Serious Crime team.'

'All right, but stay close and don't take risks. I don't want any dead heroes on my team.'

Too bloody right! Sergeant Malone made a mental note to put himself firmly between Maggie and any gunfire. It had happened before; a keen young constable had got himself shot whilst in his charge. The lad had recovered, but it had been a nightmare experience and he wasn't about to let it happen again.

The pieces of the puzzle were slowly coming together in Jack's mind. His initial hunch had been right. The three Doomdochry murders had been callous executions to prevent the victims from revealing the identity of the man at the head of this drugs organization. First Astrid, then Grant and finally, poor batty old Aunt Flora. Like Chinese whispers, information had been passed from one to another, but terminated before it reached the ears of the police; that meant Jack's ears. He could have kicked himself when he realized how close he'd come to finding out from Flora.

'So the murder victims all knew the identity of this man?'

Charlie nodded vigorously and then wished she hadn't. Her head was splitting and she hoped to hell she wasn't infecting the others with flu. 'Almost certainly, Jack. And my contact in SCDEA tells me there are to be simultaneous raids at the London end. Your Met officers have had a man working undercover there, too. They're hoping to collar the whole gang.'

Nice of Garwood to tell me, thought Jack, but then again, Garwood probably didn't know. If he had, he'd have been figuring out how to claim the credit from the safety of his plush office once the bad guys were securely behind bars and top brass were handing out commendations.

'Our main concern,' continued DCS Cameron, 'is that this man and his associates don't slip through our fingers like they have so many times before. The undercover agents believe he has an escape route. He can vanish and reappear at a moment's notice. They believe he'll use it for a fast getaway after the drug shipment arrives. So far, they haven't been able to find it.'

'I think we have,' said Jack. 'We need to plug it before the raids start.'

From Bugsy's description when they were first searching the castle, he had found the entrance to a cave-like tunnel with steps cut in the interior of the rock itself. In times of battle, it could be blocked with the utmost ease by the defenders or used as a means of escape. Privately, Jack was thinking that if Bugsy was right and Randall MacAlister was the man behind it all, he could nip down the underground tunnel to Laxdale and be away with Nicole on his high speed yacht before anyone realized he was gone.

When they reached the castle, Jack made for the Guard Chamber. Charlie followed, flushed and sneezing. It was clear she had finally succumbed to the flu and was willing herself to stay upright until the Christmas Eve raids had been brought to a successful conclusion. Bugsy was tempted to try and win his tenner back by betting Maggie that the Super would keel over within the next hour but decided it would be in poor taste, even for him.

When they tried the door to the underground castle dungeons, it opened with surprising ease considering few people ventured down there. According to the Earl, it hadn't been used for years. He couldn't understand, he said, why the police wanted to see it. It was unhealthy, the tunnel was unsafe and no one could remember where it led. In fact, he was pretty sure it didn't lead anywhere; just came to a dead end this side of the castle graveyard, so was it worth the risk? He couldn't take responsibility for any accidents. He wasn't insured for visitors tramping about underground. DI Dawes remained firm.

'All the same, sir, I'd like to take a look down there. If what I suspect turns out to be true, we'll be making some arrests.'

'If necessary,' added DCS Cameron, 'I'll obtain a warrant.'

The Earl and Lady Alice exchanged anxious glances. The Earl hadn't believed that what they'd been doing was so criminal as to justify the arrival of a Northern Constabulary Chief Superintendent, even a sick one who looked as if she should be away to her bed. The situation was obviously very serious and as the Earl, it was his duty to 'take the rap', as Randall would say. He was on the point of falling on his metaphorical sword when Geordie stumped forward.

'Let me go down first, Inspector Dawes. Just to make sure it's safe. I'm familiar with the castle layout and I'll no' come to harm. If the passage leads anywhere, you can come and see for yourself.'

Jack was doubtful. 'I don't think so. I can't put a member of the public at risk. What if you get lost or fall? There'll be no phone reception down there and we won't hear you shouting through these solid stone floors.'

Geordie thought about this one. 'The bagpipes,' he said. 'I'll play my pipes. You can hear them for miles. Just follow the sound o' the Black Bear.'

'Seems like a good idea to me, guv,' said Malone, who was disinclined to face the rats if it turned out to be a wild goose chase.

The entire Doomdochry contingent gathered around the entrance, only Randall and Nicole were missing. Randall had gone out into the snow to walk off yet another hangover and inspect the land he was planning to buy. Nicole had taken the speedboat to the Gainsborough, where she intended to stay until after Christmas. It could be seen, moored just off the coast, lights blazing.

Carefully, Geordie descended the slippery stone steps on his stout bow legs and disappeared into the darkness. Mack had fitted him with a fishing headlamp so he could see where he was going. There was a long pause and grating noises, as if something heavy was being dragged along the stone floor. Jack was beginning to worry that the old man had come to grief already. Then they heard the wail of the pipes as Geordie inflated the bag and began to play.

'What a ghastly stench,' complained Melissa, peering down the steps. 'I think I'm going to be sick.'

The old ghillie had been right about the carrying sound of the bagpipes. They could hear it clearly as they plodded after the lively skirl that meandered this way and that, beneath their feet. They'd reached the twin-tower gatehouse when the music suddenly stopped. No flourish or final wailing notes, just abrupt silence. They stood in the biting wind, snow settling on the Earl's whiskers, waiting for Geordie to start up again.

'Maybe he's run out of puff,' suggested Malone, eventually.

'No,' said Mack, clearly worried. 'I've known him play for hours without a break. Something's happened to him.' He turned to Jack, animosity suspended. 'I think we should go down after him, Inspector.'

'I agree,' said Jack, 'but not you, I'm afraid, sir. I'm not allowing another member of the public down there. Sergeant Malone and I will go, but I'd appreciate a powerful torchlight if you have one. The battery in mine's dead.' Grimly, he hoped Geordie hadn't joined it.

Five minutes later, they were back at the steps. Jack started down first, followed by Bugsy, string tied firmly around the cuffs of his sleeves and trouser bottoms. He sensed Maggie on his shoulder, preparing to follow.

'Where d'you think you're going, Constable?'

'I'm coming with you, Sarge.'

'No, you're not. Stay here and look after DCS Cameron.'

She grinned. 'But ye need me to scare away the wee brown beasties.'

'Come on then, but keep close.'

After trudging through raw sewage for some minutes and with Bugsy trying to ignore scuttling noises and small pairs of beady eyes, shining in the dark, Jack tripped over something. He shone the torch on the ground. It was Geordie's bagpipes. Malone picked them up and his sharp, detective's eyes spotted something else in the pool of light.

'That looks like blood, to me, guv.'

They called out and flashed the light, but there was no response.

'Shall we carry on to the end of the tunnel?' asked Malone.

'No, Sergeant, it's too dangerous and there aren't enough of us. In any case, I'm pretty certain Valgerd was right and eventually, it'll lead us to Laxdale. We need to report back to Chief Superintendent

Cameron so she can co-ordinate any further activity with the SCDEA officers. We don't know where they are or what they're planning and the last thing we need is to meet an armed raiding party coming the other way.'

CHAPTER TWENTY-TWO

Corrie's taxi skidded into the heliport at five minutes to six, which was something of a miracle given the appalling weather. They had slithered and slewed most of the way and very nearly ended up buried in a snow drift.

Corrie paid the driver and added a hefty tip, she was so relieved to have made it this far. Just a short trip in a chopper and she'd be safe with Jack. She wanted to ring and tell him she was coming but once again, decided against it. He'd only urge her to go back to Inverness and wait for him. Once she reached Doomdochry, it would be too late to send her back, although she'd get the usual lecture about the dangers of interfering in crimes that didn't concern her.

The powerful Robinson R44 helicopter was waiting on the helipad. She knew it was Donnie Cameron's because a floodlight illuminated the logo on its slim, dark blue flank: "Cameron Helicopter Services". She hurried over, grazed knees smarting as they rubbed against her trousers.

'Mrs Dawes?' He frowned at the dressing on her head. 'What on earth happened to you?'

'Hello, Mr Cameron. I walked into a door. Nothing serious.'

He shrugged. 'If you say so. Shall we climb aboard, out of the snow?'

Once inside, Corrie relaxed. 'Thank you so much for agreeing to take me. Especially in these conditions and on Christmas Eve.'

'No problem,' he said, belting her in. 'My wife's working tonight anyway.'

Corrie nodded. 'So is Jack. Crime doesn't stop for Christmas, does it?'

'Unfortunately not, Mrs Dawes.' He looked at her. Nice lady caught up in a lousy business, although she didn't know it yet. In her case, snooping had been her downfall. For him, it was stupidity, weakness and ultimately, greed.

Once they were airborne, Corrie began to chat and Donnie listened, unwilling to be too friendly, knowing what was to come.

'Please call me Corrie. I feel we know each other, if only through our spouses. You must be wondering why I had to dash up to Shetland at such short notice. I know I sounded panicky and melo-dramatic on the phone, but I really do think I might be in danger. You see ...' Corrie prattled on, telling him about the gruesome murders Jack had been working on in London before he was seconded to the Northern Constabulary and how he hadn't been convinced they'd caught the man responsible. She'd been doing a bit of sleuthing herself, she said, and a young woman had contacted her with infor-mation but she'd been run down just as she was about to give her the murderer's name.

'You still don't know who he is, then?' asked Donnie.

Corrie bit her lip. 'Well, actually, I rather think I do.'

'So, who is it?'

She hesitated. 'I know I can trust you, because you're the husband of a DCS and you must know heaps of things that you need to keep secret, but all the same, I think I'd rather talk to Jack about it first. After all, I might be on the wrong track altogether and it would be awful to slander an innocent man. Besides, he's in London. I don't suppose his name would mean anything to you up here in the Highlands, would it?'

'No,' agreed Cameron, grimly. 'I don't suppose it would.' He glanced sideways at her. 'Does Jack know you're coming?'

Corrie looked guilty. 'No, I didn't tell him. He'd only give me a lecture about being a nosy parker and how it can get you into trouble.'

And he'd be dead right, thought Cameron. They were over the Atlantic now and skilfully, he balanced the helicopter's controls until they were hovering. 'Does *anyone* know you're here, apart from me?'

'Only George and Cynthia and I don't think they were listening, really. They were in the middle of a Christmas Eve champagne party and a bit tiddly. I expect they'll have forgotten all about it. Why do you ask?'

'No reason.' Cameron looked hard at Corrie, then made a split second decision. He raised the collective, yawed to the right, and soon they were flying in over the lights of Shetland Mainland, heading north over Yell and up to Unst. Finally he began to descend over the bleak wilderness surrounding Laxdale. Corrie peered out of the cockpit as they approached.

'Is that Doomdochry?' she asked, as they flew low over the commune house. 'It doesn't look much like a castle. The way Jack described it, it was like something out of a Hammer Horror film with haunted towers and crumbling battlements. That building looks more like a bad barn conversion.'

Donnie didn't reply. He landed the helicopter in the field furthest from the main house, near the Laxdale outbuildings. Jumping down, he hurried round to the passenger seat, undid Corrie's safety harness and virtually dragged her out. The sleet stung their faces and a bitter wind straight from the Arctic tore at their clothes. Taking a firm grip of Corrie's arm, he steered her towards a ramshackle building. In the lights of the chopper, she could just make out a sign over the door that said "Dairy".

'Ow! Ow! That's my bad elbow, Mr Cameron.' Corrie tried to free her arm. 'Where are we going? I've left my bag in the helicopter.'

'You won't need your bag.' He slid out the length of timber that barricaded the double doors, bundled her inside and hung his torch on the wall. The shed clearly hadn't been used as a dairy for years; certainly not since the commune had acquired the property. Bales of mouldy straw and dusty, dented churns were piled up in one corner. Cameron shoved Corrie into one of the cow stalls. She struggled but she'd been taken completely by surprise.

'What's happening? Why are we in here? Where's Jack?'

Cameron grabbed a length of baler twine, swiftly bound Corrie's wrists together then tied her hands above her head to the steel restraint pole above the stall. 'I'm sorry, Mrs Dawes, believe me. It's nothing personal; you're just in the wrong place at the wrong time.'

Her temper flared then, overcoming the shock. 'You've got a bloody nerve, tying me up like this. Let me go at once. When Jack finds out, he'll throw the book at you. He'll ...'

'But Jack doesn't know you're here, does he? And by the time he finds you, it'll all be over. I'm really sorry.'

Corrie could feel her heart beating in her throat. She could barely breathe for panic. 'I don't understand. Why are you doing this? You're married to a police officer ...'

'I know, and don't think I wouldn't turn the clock back if I could. I wish to God I'd never got mixed up in this stinking business. But I'm not a complete bastard. I was supposed to chuck you out over the Atlantic.'

Corrie gulped, thinking how easy it would have been. 'Why?'

'I can't tell you. I just need you to stay in here and keep quiet until it's all over and I know Charlie's safe. He has to believe you're dead, you see?'

'Who does? Tell me! We'll find Jack, get him to ...'

Cameron pulled a roll of duct tape from his jacket pocket, tore off a strip and stuck it over Corrie's mouth. Then he collected his torch and left, closing the shed doors behind him, leaving her in total darkness. Corrie heard the barricade being shoved back in place.

Dawes, Malone and Mellis crawled up the slimy stone steps of the underground Guard Chamber looking and smelling like three sewer rats. They emerged into the light, blinking at a group of anxious faces.

'Where's Geordie?' croaked Mack, hoarse with anxiety.

'We're not sure yet, sir.' Malone handed over Geordie's dripping bagpipes. Seeing Moragh's leathery old face, creased with anxiety, he didn't mention the blood. 'But don't worry, we'll find him.'

'I need to know what instructions Chief Superintendent Cameron has been given by the SCDEA. Where is she?' Jack couldn't see her.

'She was here beside me a minute ago ...' Mack turned and there was Charlie, flat on her back on the cold stone floor.

I'd have won the bet after all, thought Malone.

Maggie half-carried the Chief Superintendent to bed, still protesting deliriously that she was fine. Five minutes later, when Jack went in to ask how and when he should liaise with the SCDEA, she was out for the count, having been sedated by Mack.

'What now, guv?' asked Sergeant Malone. They were back in the library. It was getting late and very dark outside. The planned raids must be imminent if they were to take place before Christmas Day dawned, but they had received no orders and had no clear idea what form the first strike would take. Briefly, Dawes considered ringing Garwood but knew he'd be worse than useless. At this time on Christmas Eve, he'd be handing out cognac and cigars to the senior officers he wanted to impress at the New Year promotion board.

'Have we got Chief Superintendent Cameron's phone?' asked Jack.

'Yes, sir.' Maggie handed it to him. 'But I've already checked her contacts and I couldn't find anyone who might be SCDEA. I think she had to wait for them to contact her for security reasons then deleted the number. I tried ringing her husband to let him know she was poorly, but it went straight to voicemail. He isn't answering his mobile or their home phone.'

'Right,' said Jack, with a confidence he didn't feel. 'The SCDEA know we're here in the castle because Charlie told them. For the time being, we don't do anything that might jeopardize their operation. We wait for them to contact us then act on their orders. Please God, we'll find Geordie in the process.'

Corrie was now more outraged than scared. Who did this jumped-up, self-styled, two-bit gangster think he was? First he'd tried to have her run over, then he wanted her thrown out of a helicopter into the sea. Now she was tied up in the dark like a side of beef in an abattoir freezer, and very nearly as cold. She could take a joke as well as the next woman, but this time, he'd gone too far. At one point, she'd believed she knew who he was, but her intuition had let her down because she was obviously wrong. The danger in London had followed her to the Shetlands, where she should have been safe.

Her efforts to loosen the thick, hairy twine had made her wrists sore. Donnie Cameron had pulled the knots very tight. When she got back to London, she'd tell Cynthia she didn't think much of her choice of friends. She certainly wouldn't fancy a round of golf with Cameron. He was perfectly capable of bashing you over the head with his four-iron and leaving you to die in a bunker, like Hitler. She'd been trying to make some sense of what Donnie said about keeping quiet until he knew his wife was safe. It seemed this Mr Big, whoever he was, had made Donnie obey orders by threatening Charlie.

The tape over Corrie's mouth was starting to smart. She wished she could reach it but her hands were tied above her head and her fingers were starting to get numb. If she were Lara Croft or Beth Tweddle, she'd simply do a couple of pull-ups until her face was level with her fingers and rip it off, but since she probably weighed as much as both of them put together and her elbow was knackered, it wasn't really an option. Not that there was anyone to talk to if she did get her mouth free. Out here in this abandoned shed, she could scream herself hoarse and no one would hear.

As her eyes became accustomed to the gloom, she made out the basics of an ancient milking parlour. It must have been built in the days when farmers milked by hand because a mechanized parlour would have needed electricity. The stalls were constructed of tubular steel poles that slotted into each other so that they could be lengthened to accommodate any number of cows. Corrie grasped the one she was tied to with her deadened fingers and tried to wriggle it loose. It was jammed solid with years of built-up muck and straw. Gripping it firmly, she began a rhythmic forward and back motion, like an exercise in her Pilates class. If this doesn't work and I die anyway, she thought, I'll have the best toned abs in the mortuary.

Eventually, the pole moved half a smidgeon, making a metallic grinding noise. Now, if she could just work it free, she could slide it out of the bracket and … done it! She slid the twine off the end, lowered her arms and rubbed the life back into her fingers. Her wrists were still bound together but at least she could move about to keep warm and now she could pull off the tape. She yelped as it ripped a layer of skin from her lips.

The next challenge was to find a way out. The barricaded wooden doors were old but stout and her feeble attempts to kick them open resulted only in a painful toe. Mind you, she wasn't sure what she'd do if she did get out. It was cold enough in the shed but outside, there was freezing snow. Her coat and bag were still in the helicopter and by now, Donnie had probably dumped them in the Atlantic. She remembered with a pang that her brand new phone, an early Christmas present, was still in her bag. She had no idea where she was, probably miles from Doomdochry Castle, and it was pitch dark outside. Was it sensible to wander about, get lost and risk dying of hypothermia or should she sit tight and wait for someone to find her? But that could take months and only Cameron knew she was here. She began to hop about while she thought and it was then that she heard the groan. At first, she thought it was the wind moaning through the slats in the roof. She stood still and waited. There it was again. It was definitely human and it was coming from the far side of the shed, behind some bales of musty hay. There was somebody else in the shed with her.

'Hello?' She waited … then called again. The groan answered this time, louder and more insistent. 'Keep groaning, I'll find you.'

Something was glowing dimly behind the haystack. Corrie made her way to it. In the rapidly diminishing light of his fishing headlamp, an old man in a kilt lay among the straw. Blood was oozing from a nasty gash on his head and had run down into his matted beard. Like Corrie, his hands were tied but behind his back, with a cable tie around his thumbs. Duct tape covered his mouth. Corrie grasped the edge and eased it off very carefully. Even so, it took some of his whiskers with it, but he was too weak to cry out.

'Who are you?' asked Corrie, gently.

'Geordie.' His mouth was dry and his voice, feeble. Corrie could see he needed medical attention, urgently. She wished she had her bag with the bottle of mineral water; she could at least have given him a drink. If she'd had the foresight to put her phone in her pocket instead of her bag, she could have called an ambulance but she'd have no idea where to tell them to come.

'Do you know who did this to you, Geordie?'

The old man shook his head. 'Hit me from behind. Two o' them.'

What on earth's going on, here? Corrie wondered. What kind of thugs would attack an old man and why? 'Don't worry, I'll get help.' She held out her wrists. 'If I kneel down behind you, do you think you could manage to untie my hands?' She said it more in hope than expectation as the poor old soul was barely conscious and the light was too dim to untie knots behind his back.

'Skean dhu.' The old man lifted his head painfully and nodded towards the ceremonial dagger sticking out of the top of his sock. Corrie silently gave three hearty cheers for the judicious serendipity of the Scottish Highland dress. She pulled out the knife with two hands and using her teeth, removed the sheath. The blade was twin-edged and razor sharp. She helped Geordie to sit up, then carefully cut through the cable tie that secured his thumbs. Shaking, he took the dagger from her and cut free her bound wrists. She massaged the red pressure marks, gratefully.

'Geordie, do you know where we are?'

'Aye, this is Laxdale.'

The name immediately rang bells. Laxdale was the commune that Jack had told her about on the phone. A dozen or so eco-warriors struggling against global degeneration and social warming, or should that be the other way around? Anyway, they aimed to be self-sufficient and leave non-existent footprints on the planet. Jack had gone to speak to them, it couldn't be very far.

'Are we anywhere near Doomdochry Castle? Only my husband's there. I'm Coriander Dawes. My husband's Inspector Jack Dawes. He's a policeman and he'll help us if I can reach him.'

A spark of recognition lit up in the old man's watery eyes. 'Aye, your man's there in the castle.'

'How do I get there? Can I walk to it?'

Geordie shook his head. 'Too far. Too cold.' He swallowed hard. 'There's a tunnel. It leads to Doomdochry. I was down there playin' my pipes when they hit me. Knocked me out but I remember being dragged up through a trap door.'

'Where is it? Where's the trap door, Geordie?'

'Dragon,' he wheezed. 'It's under a red dragon.'

He passed out then, exhausted with the effort, and Corrie couldn't revive him. The poor old chap needed a hospital, urgently. She had to get help. She took the lamp off his head and put it on her own, smarting as it pressed on the dressing over her cut forehead. The light was dim, but better than nothing.

'Don't worry, Geordie,' she said to his motionless body. 'I'll get us out of here.' But where the bloody hell do I find a red dragon? What could the old man have seen? Corrie racked her brains, trying to remember what else Jack had told her about Laxdale apart from it being inhabited by a load of barmy eccentrics done up like Vikings. Of course! Viking long-ships had dragons' heads on the bows, didn't they? There must be a galley here, somewhere, and the entrance to the tunnel was under the dragon. That's what Geordie saw briefly as they pulled him out.

Now she had some light, she crept round the shed looking for a possible exit. She found a spot where the roof leaked and water had run down, rotting the wood beneath it. She picked up an old pick-axe handle and bashed at it. Eventually, the decayed wood disintegrated and a cutting wind screamed in, hurling flurries of snow through the hole she'd made. She found a couple of smelly sacks covered in silage and dried cow manure and gritting her teeth, she wrapped them around her for protection. Then she crawled through the hole and out into the stormy Shetland wilderness.

Through sheer luck, Corrie found the Viking ship quite quickly. The Galley Shed was right next door to the Dairy and the gales had fetched the sign down so that Corrie almost tripped over it. Violent gusts had wrenched one of the doors from its hinges and now it was banging to and fro in the wind. Corrie crept in, wary now. In the last couple of days, she'd been attacked by people she trusted in places she thought were safe so she was taking no chances. In the dim light from her headlamp, the impressive Viking ship rose up some twelve feet, with a fearsome dragon's head at the bow. It was up on supporting blocks and if Geordie was right, there was a trap door underneath leading to a tunnel that would take her to Doomdochry Castle and Jack. On the other hand, Geordie might well be concussed by the bang on his head. The common sense approach would be to wait for morning and hope someone would come. But what if the 'someone' who came was that same someone who ordered Donnie Cameron to chuck her in the Atlantic? On balance, she decided she'd take a chance on descending into the bowels of Shetland earth, never to be seen again.

Discarding the stinking sacks, she crawled on her stomach under the hull of the ship. It was a snug fit for a lady of Corrie's ample proportions, but if two thugs could manage it, dragging an unconscious Geordie, so could she. The floor beneath the ship was covered in tarpaulin. With knees smarting and elbow throbbing, she yanked it away and there, some three feet square, was the trap door. It was then that she smelt it. Wet paint. Someone had recently painted the ship's hull and she was smothered in it; polyurethane, bright red and sticky, all over her hands and down the front of her new cashmere sweater. It would, she observed wryly, be a bugger to get off. But compared to being flattened by a Mercedes, swimming with the fishes in the Atlantic and being manacled to the headlock of a bovine mating pen, it seemed a small inconvenience.

The trap door slid smoothly sideways as if it was regularly in use. The steps, carved into rock, were worn and slippery and disappeared into a dark void. Gingerly, Corrie lowered herself in, feet first, and started to descend, wondering if this would be the last anyone would see of her.

CHAPTER TWENTY-THREE

t was half past eleven. Only thirty more minutes and Christmas Eve would be over with neither sight nor sound of the promised raids. Sergeant Malone went out into the vaulted entrance hall and lit another roll-up made with the pipe tobacco that he'd bummed off Geordie before the poor old sod had disappeared. He didn't want another fag, it tasted hot and bitter. The ones he'd already smoked had coated his mouth with thick, acrid nicotine, but he had to do something to pass the time. He poked his fag through an arrow-slit window and puffed smoke rings into the snow. How much longer? It's like waiting for bloody Christmas, he thought, and smiled at the irony.

'Quick, Sarge, you'd better come.' Maggie darted out into the hall and grabbed his arm. 'The Inspector's on the phone. It's Valgerd from the commune. I think it's started.' They sprinted back down the passage to the library. Jack put Valgerd on speaker so the others could hear. Her normally calm, academic voice was edged with panic.

'The police have surrounded us, Inspector Dawes. They've erected floodlights and I can see policemen with dogs and guns. There's even a police helicopter flying low over the main house. We haven't done anything criminal, we were all fast asleep in our beds. What on earth's going on?'

So the SCDEA have targeted Laxdale rather than Doomdochry, thought Jack. He knew how these hits worked. They would have set up an armed perimeter around the Laxdale estate with officers positioned every few hundred metres on the roads and land surrounding the property. They needed to make sure their man didn't slip through the cordon.

'Just stay where you are, Valgerd, and tell everyone else at Laxdale to do the same. Don't go outside unless you're told. Are any members missing?'

'I don't know. Do you want me to go and check? Thora's here, she could ...' Jack heard gunfire then the sound of doors being kicked in and men shouting. 'Get down! Lie on the floor! Do it now!' Valgerd and Thora screamed, then the line went dead.

'Let's get over there, Jack,' said Bugsy, who found masterly inactivity nerve-racking. 'I bet my pension Randall MacAlister's holed up there with a stash of drugs and dirty money. He'd be expecting the police to hit Doomdochry Castle first, so his plan would be for Nicole to nip across to Laxdale in the speedboat, collect him and the consignment, then back to the Gainsborough and away, while the SCDEA are still searching for him in this bloody great mausoleum of a castle. Piece of piss! Say bye-bye to Randall and a few million quid's worth of cocaine.'

'But how would he know there was going to be raid in the first place, Sarge?' asked Maggie.

'You heard what the Chief Superintendent said. There's a mole. Randall's been paying someone on the inside to feed him information.' Bugsy scowled. 'If there's one form of pond life I can't stand, it's a copper on the take.'

'That's a reasonable hypothesis, Sergeant,' said Dawes, thoughtfully. 'So, if we accept that Randall is trapped inside the Laxdale commune, what means of escape could he use to slip through the police cordon and meet up with Nicole in the speedboat further down the coast at Doomdochry?'

'The tunnel!' chorused Malone and Mellis.

'Right. The same means of escape employed by the nasty Vikings when the nice Christians tried to convince them that Jesus wanted them for sunbeams by burning out their eyes,' said Jack. 'Come on, we'll get back down there and cut him off.'

'Do we need to go right *inside* the tunnel, guv?' ventured Malone. 'Couldn't we lie in wait by the entrance and grab him when he comes out?'

'Nice try, Sergeant, but while we were down there, I saw possible openings to other access tunnels. I expect the Vikings made sure they could scatter and get away in different directions if pursued. I shouldn't want our man nipping down the bypass and getting away and I don't think he'll hang about, trying to make up his mind. Let's go.'

Mack tapped on the door and poked his head round. 'May we come in, Inspector?' Since Geordie's disappearance, Mack's aggressive attitude had mellowed. He was clearly more anxious than angry. Melissa followed him in. 'We're worried about Randy. He went out to get some air; needed to walk off his hangover, he said.'

'He told Mack he'd only be gone half an hour,' said Melissa, 'and that was simply ages ago.'

'I know you have weightier issues on your mind than Randall wandering off into the snow, but I'm afraid he may have passed out somewhere. In these temperatures, hypothermia would set in very quickly, especially if he had a high level of alcohol in his blood. Shouldn't we call out the emergency services to search for him, Inspector? I realize it's virtually Christmas Day, but that's two men who have gone missing now.'

'I think we know where to look for Randall MacAlister, sir, and I shouldn't be at all surprised if we find Geordie at the same time. We're going back down to the Guard Chamber.'

The battery in Corrie's headlamp died just as she finished negotiating the steep stone steps down into the tunnel. As she trudged along in the dark, her nose told her it wasn't just mud and water she was squelching through, and the pattering of tiny feet meant rats. She shuddered. She had no idea how far she was from Doomdochry Castle; the tunnel seemed to go on for ever and without the proverbial light at the end of it, but turning back was no longer an option.

After ten minutes, she reckoned it must be nearly Christmas Day, so she started to sing carols, to keep up her spirits. She finished the second verse of "Ding Dong Merrily on High" and took a deep breath to do justice to the "Glo … or … or … ia" when she was suddenly grabbed from behind and a hand was clamped over her mouth. For a split-second, she wondered whether it was the gangster who wanted her dead or a disoriented potholer with perfect pitch. Caught completely off guard, she stumbled clumsily backwards, nearly sitting down in the sewage. Strong arms held her upright, but she struggled, gamely, making a muffled but passable attempt at a scream.

'Shut up and keep still, you interfering bitch, or I'll cut you!'

Not a potholer, then. The man's voice was a hoarse, insistent whisper. She was about to kick backwards at his shins when she felt the blade of a knife pricking her throat. After everything that had happened, Corrie was almost resigned to her fate. Whether by accident or design, the man who'd been trying to have her killed had finally caught her. But why, she wondered, did he insist she kept quiet? Who was likely to hear her in this endless underground tunnel? Why didn't he just finish her off with the knife and have done with it? Nobody would find her until something went wrong with the drains and they sent the Dyno-Rod man down. Then she saw them; three powerful torches jiggling towards them from the direction of the castle. She struggled desperately and tried to make a noise but when the point of the knife pierced her skin and she felt blood trickling down her neck, she froze. Her captor manhandled her roughly backwards into a dank recess, hollowed out of the rocky tunnel. He held her close, pressing them both so tightly against the cave wall that Corrie could smell his aftershave. It was a pleasant change from sewage but odd, because he had a beard. She could feel it, rough and hairy against her cheek. He was wearing some kind of miner's helmet and possibly a bullet-proof vest which felt hard and metallic against her back. Out of the corner of her eye, she saw a rat scurry along a rocky ledge and pause, its beady eyes level with hers.

This time, Jack, Bugsy and Maggie carried a powerful torch apiece as they jogged down the tunnel which they were now certain would exit at Laxdale. They were roughly half-way when they saw the lights coming towards them.

'It's him, Jack; it's Randall,' panted Malone, squinting into the blinding glare. 'He's trying to get away. Leave him to me. I'll get the bastard.'

There were two of them. Malone roared 'Stop! Police!', threw away his lamp and ran at the first one, shoulder-charging him and bringing him down hard. The man hit the ground with a grunt, dropping his light and fighting like a wild animal. Before Jack could stop her, DC Mellis rugby-tackled the second man. For some moments, four bodies rolled and wrestled in the excrement. The tunnel echoed with shouts of, 'I've got him. sir!', 'Let go, you bugger!' and 'Oh, no you don't, sunshine!' Jack leapt from one writhing skirmish to the other trying to find a suitable point to intervene and clobber someone.

Finally, Malone sat down hard on his man, immobilising him. He grabbed the front of the bloke's jacket, prior to bashing his head on the ground a few times, and his hand closed around something squashy and female.

'Bring that light over 'ere, Jack.' The beam shone full on the face of his furious antagonist who was still kicking and struggling. 'Well, I'm blowed!' panted Bugsy. 'It's Helga. What the bloody hell are you doing down here?'

Hearing this, Maggie stopped grinding her opponent's face into the effluent and he took the opportunity to open his mouth and shout: 'Constable Mellis, will you please get off me!' She released him, reluctantly, and he scrambled to his feet. Jack held up his torch.

'And Kettle Flat-face,' said Bugsy. 'The other half of the dynamic duo.'

Jack hadn't time for confrontations with eco-numpties, traipsing about in the bowels of the earth, looking for the meaning of life. 'You two have no business down here,' he snapped. 'You're obstructing a very serious police operation for which you can be arrested. And ...' he added as an afterthought, '... you may be putting yourselves and others in danger.'

'That's right, hop it, the pair of you!' said Malone, heaving his bulk upright. He pulled Helga to her feet and she responded by kicking him smartly in the shins.

'That's for groping me, you dirty old sod.'

'What exactly *are* you doing down here?' asked Jack, suddenly wary.

The man they knew as Kettil Flatnose was almost speechless with rage. When he could finally trust himself, his voice was cold and contemptuous. 'What we are doing here, Inspector Dawes, is working undercover to tackle, disrupt and dismantle serious organized crime with an emphasis on the trafficking of Class A drugs and money laundering. What we're *not* here to do is get two bungling Metropolitan Police officers OUT OF THE SHITE!' He took a deep breath to calm himself. 'I'm DI Graeme Carter from SCDEA and this ...' he indicated his glowering sidekick, '... is DS Judy Cook.'

'You got any ID on you?' asked Malone, still suspicious.

DS Cook replied in a withering "watch my lips" voice. 'You don't carry ID when you're undercover, Sergeant, because you don't want anyone to know who you are.'

'Yeah, right. I knew that,' said Malone, meekly.

'So, where is he?' asked DI Carter.

'Where's who?' asked Dawes, suitably chastened.

'The man we're after. He escaped down here before we could grab him. He must have passed you. Why didn't you stop him?'

'We didn't pass anybody,' said Malone, puzzled. 'You sure he's in the tunnel?'

Carter snorted with disgust. 'Of course, I'm flaming well sure, Sergeant. We saw him disappear through the trap door. We were only seconds behind him. He must have sneaked past you lot without your seeing him. We're dealing with an outstanding criminal intellect here, not one of your petty Metropolitan pot-peddlers. He'd have no trouble fooling you three.' He turned to DS Cook. 'Come on, Judy, we have to catch him before he legs it from the castle and onto that boat.' They sprinted off without a backward glance, leaving Jack wishing he'd had the wits to confirm they were all chasing the same bloke. A pretty basic prerequisite, but it might save some embarrassing confusion later, when the handcuffs came out.

'What do we do now, sir?' asked Maggie.

'We go after them, Constable Mellis.'

'Right, sir!' DC Mellis, bruised, breathless and mucky, went off like a two-bob rocket, keen not to miss any of the action. Malone, acutely reminded of his duty of care to an inexperienced officer, was hard on her heels. Then he stumbled on a rock and fell headlong. Instantly, Maggie sprinted back to help and as she hauled him to his feet, she caught sight of her huge luminous watch. 'Hey, Sarge! It's midnight. Merry Christmas!'

Bugsy was cold, aching, covered in unspeakable filth and quite sure he had just felt a rat sink its teeth into his ankle. Wearily, he lifted his face from the muck. 'And a merry bleedin' Christmas to you too, Constable Mellis.'

Corrie was faint from the twin effects of desperation and suffocation. Jack had been so close. When she heard his voice, she almost wept. If only she'd had the breath and courage to create some kind of fuss, he'd have heard her and come to the rescue. But by then, she'd probably have had her throat cut and she didn't want Jack to find her in that condition. As a considerate wife, she owed it to him not to end up a gruesome murder case laid out on a mortuary slab.

Minutes later, when it was quiet again and the lights had vanished into the far reaches of the tunnel, Corrie's captor relaxed his hand on her mouth and eased the knife slightly away from her throat. She took a deep, shuddering breath to try to restore oxygen to her numb brain so she could think straight.

'Who are you? Let me go at once!' To her mortification, her voice came out weak and wobbly instead of firm and authoritative as she'd intended.

'Belt up!' The man obviously didn't intend to engage in any chippy repartee. He pricked her throat again to remind her he had a knife and shoved her ahead of him, down a tunnel leading off the main one.

Corrie stumbled on, wondering what to do. Clearly he wasn't intending to kill her straight away or he'd have already done it. So why did he want her alive? Then logic kicked in. From the conversation she'd overheard between Jack and the other police officers, this villain, whoever he was, was on the run. The police were closing in, cutting off all his escape routes. Soon, they'd have him cornered and what then? He'd need a hostage, that's what then! Something to bargain with, so that they'd have to let him go. And, she realized grimly, he was holding the perfect candidate; the wife of the Detective Inspector who was hunting him. But of course, he had no way of knowing that, had he? He'd simply pounced upon the first carol-singing loony who came strolling past. But hang on a minute. The young prostitute they'd run down had known she was Jack's wife. So had Donnie Cameron. This thug had called her an interfering bitch; so he knew, too. They were climbing narrow stone steps, now, spiralling endlessly upwards.

'Who are you?' Corrie yelped again. 'Where are you taking me? You won't get away with this, you know!' A small voice in her head said, "Don't be a twerp, of course he'll get away with it. He's the one with the knife and you're the one with it stuck in your throat". The steps seemed to go on forever, then suddenly they were at the top and he bundled her through a narrow door. Immediately, the bitter Shetland gale and stinging sleet pounded her face. They were out in the open, high up, beneath the stars. She gulped down the fresh air, gratefully. It was pitch black night and she could make out very little. She knew they'd climbed a long way but she had no way of judging how high up they were. Then, straight ahead, two bursts of white light bounced off a distant body of water. A few seconds later, the flashes came again. A lighthouse, thought Corrie. In the brief flashes of light, she made out black crenellations in front of her and a thick stone wall beneath her. Oh my God, I'm on the parapet of a tower, a mile up in the sky, with a lunatic holding a knife to my throat. What a way to spend Christmas.

By the time Inspector Dawes and his team reached Doomdochry, DI Carter and DS Cook had already burst out of the Guard Room, shouting, 'Nobody move!' Then they kicked in a few doors and generally put the wind up everyone without any sign of the man they were seeking.

In the vast Red Drawing Room, DI Carter was hunched in a corner, radio clamped to one ear, hand over the other, to block out the racket in the background. He was speaking urgently to his team who had rapidly relocated the armed perimeter up the coast from Laxdale to Doomdochry. Out in the bay, marine police had boarded the Gainsborough. Nicole MacAlister, handcuffed and screeching like a fishwife, had been bundled onto a police launch, scratching, biting and kicking every high-heeled step of the way.

Outside the castle, floodlights blazed, dogs barked constantly and police officers roared orders to each other. Inside, SCDEA men were stationed at various points, guarding the exits, while a dozen more swarmed all over the castle with big hairy Alsatians, searching for their quarry. DS Judy Cook had herded the MacAlister family onto a sofa in one corner of the room and was standing guard over them like a Rottweiler, barking questions. As soon as Jack appeared, Mack leaped to his feet and began protesting.

'What in heaven's name is going on here, Inspector Dawes? Who are these people and why have they invaded my parents' home? It's indefensible the way we're being treated. My wife's in tears as you can see.' He indicated Melissa who was snivelling, prettily, into a tissue. 'Why are they interrogating us like common criminals?' The rest of the family added their voices to the complaint until it was bedlam.

Jack held up placatory hands to calm the situation. 'An operation of this magnitude inevitably throws up a lot of innocent people, Mr MacAlister. People who haven't done anything wrong but who know things; things that could either put the villains behind bars or enable them to get away. We need to ask questions because time is running out and the man we want is hiding here.'

'Who is it you think we're protecting?' asked Mack, genuinely nonplussed.

'Randall MacAlister,' shouted Malone, above the din.

'Did someone mention my name?' The room fell suddenly silent as all eyes swivelled towards the dishevelled figure who had somehow wandered in via a side door and was standing, whisky glass in hand, blinking vaguely. 'Has something happened?'

'Quick, there he is!' yelled Malone. 'Grab him, Constable!' Jack, still unsure, held out a restraining hand as Maggie was about to dive at

Randall's already buckling legs. The man was making no attempt to escape, nor did he look capable of having just sprinted down a long tunnel. His shoes and socks, Jack observed, were completely clean.

'For God's sake, Randall,' exploded Mack, 'where the hell have you been? We've been looking everywhere for you.'

Randall smiled guiltily. 'Sorry, guys. Guess I had a drop too much of the MacAlister Malt. Must've passed out. I woke up in the gunroom, under the musket table.' He peered around. 'Has anyone seen Nicole?' He consulted the huge Rolex on his wrist, 'it's Christmas Day and I've got her a great gift.'

'Yeah, we know,' snapped Malone. 'A few million dollars' worth of stuff to snort up her nose.'

'What?' Randall looked at him, blearily. 'No, it isn't perfume, Officer; it's a pair of diamond earrings. Real big ones. Coupla carats each.' He suddenly became aware of the strangers in the room and the racket going on outside. 'Have I missed something? Are we having a party? Who are all these guys?'

Malone turned to a scowling DI Carter who had snapped his radio off. 'Aren't you going to arrest this man, sir?'

Carter looked Randall up and down. 'Why? What's he done?'

Now Bugsy was confused. 'But isn't he the bloke you're after? The head of the drugs cartel; the mastermind behind the trafficking and the murders?'

The Chief Inspector snorted, derisively. 'No, of course he isn't, Sergeant! You know very well who we're looking for; you've interviewed the bastard. Up here, he calls himself Ragnar Redbeard.'

Before he could explain, one of his men rushed in, breathless and insistent. 'You'd better come outside quick, sir. Our man's up on the parapet of the tower and he has a female hostage.' He lowered his voice. 'She's covered in blood, sir.'

CHAPTER TWENTY-FOUR

Doomdochry Castle was ablaze with light. The Death Tower, criss-crossed by a barrage of beams from the police floodlights, soared into the night sky like a gaunt, yellowing fang. Etched in sharp relief against its wall, two figures were locked together on the parapet, high above the waves of the restless, indigo ocean. Down below, a hushed group of onlookers had gathered in the curtain-walled courtyard, risking a crick in the neck to gaze upwards at the battle of wits that was about to ensue.

The wind howled around the battlements, bringing with it the compounded smells of the Shetlands; sea, earth, fish, gulls, and specific only to Corrie's nostrils, her captor's mingled odours of sweaty fear and expensive aftershave. Both scents were overpowered by the cloying fumes from the red polyurethane paint that was down her front, in her hair and all over her hands and arms. Now there was light, she squirmed around to look at her attacker. If she survived, Jack was bound to want a detailed description. She snatched a quick glimpse before he yanked her round and held her firmly with her back to him; a human shield with a knife against her throat.

He was a fit, muscular man, probably in his early forties, she guessed. Fair skinned under the full set of bushy red whiskers and eyebrows. Bizarrely, he was wearing fancy dress. What she had taken to be a miner's hard hat was a Viking helmet, and the metallic, bullet-proof vest was actually a chain-mail jerkin. It was impossible to get a clear view of his features because of the prolific face-hair and the helmet's nose-guard. This was the man who wanted her dead yet she would have sworn she'd never met him before, until he spoke.

In the time it took for Dawes, Malone and Maggie to elbow their way through the cordon of police holding back the onlookers, DI Carter had positioned police marksmen on every available site. They

197

crouched on rocky-ridged outcrops and squatted behind crumbling turrets; anywhere they might get a clear shot at the target. Carter shouted through a megaphone to the man eighty feet above their heads.

'Come on, Ragnar, give it up. You're surrounded by armed police. Throw down the knife and let the lady go. Don't make things any worse for yourself.' He lowered the megaphone and muttered angrily to DS Cook. 'What a sodding cock-up! How the buggery did he slip through the net after months of careful planning? And where the hell did that bloody woman come from?'

'Bloody's the word, sir,' said Cook. 'She needs medical attention and fast. The bastard's butchered her. It's a miracle she's still standing after losing all that blood. She's smothered in it.'

'Is the ambulance on its way?'

'Yes, sir.' DS Cook's radio crackled and she spoke into it briefly. 'That was B-Team. The old housekeeper has shown them the steps that lead to the tower. They want to know if they should try and surprise him, take him from behind, while his attention's on us.'

It was almost as if he'd heard them. Ragnar shoved Corrie forward until she was teetering on the very edge of the parapet, the blade of the knife close to her jugular. The crowd down below gasped in unison and the police marksmen took aim, waiting for a clear shot.

'If anyone tries to come up, I'll cut her throat and chuck her off, so I will! Do you hear me?'

DS Malone squinted at the hostage, now clearly visible in the flood-lights. He blinked hard, not believing his eyes. Beside him, DI Dawes was busy, wiping snowflakes off his specs. Bugsy nudged his arm, hardly daring to break the news.

'Er … Jack. That woman up there. Is it who I think it is?'

Dawes replaced his glasses and stared up. 'Oh my God, it's Corrie!' He staggered a little and Bugsy grabbed his arm to steady him. Jack gulped hard and looked again, telling himself it wasn't possible. 'But it can't be Corrie. She's safe at home in London. It's someone who looks like her, isn't it?' He appealed desperately to Malone for confirmation, knowing he wouldn't get it.

'Sorry, guv, it's definitely your missus. How did she get up there?'

'Oh Christ, Bugsy, she's covered in blood. What has the bastard done to her? I'll kill him … I'll choke the life out of him with my bare hands …' He shrugged off Malone's restraining arm. 'I'm going up there …'

A worried DC Mellis had overheard the conversation and spoke urgently to DI Carter. He strode over. 'Constable Mellis says the hostage is your wife, Dawes. How the blazes did Ragnar get hold of her?'

Jack could hardly speak for the fear that constricted his throat. 'I don't know.' His face was ashen. 'For God's sake, Carter, don't provoke him. Don't make him kill her. Let me go up there. I'll talk to him … I'll …'

'Sorry, Inspector. You know I can't let you do that.' DI Carter raised the megaphone again. 'Take it easy. No one's coming up.' He nodded to DS Cook who hastily radioed B-Team to back off and do nothing to spook the target. Carter shouted again. 'Let's talk. We can sort this out without any more bloodshed.'

'Never moind the craic,' Ragnar hollered back, the Belfast accent of his violent youth coming through strongly now he was cornered. 'I want a helicopter. Get Cameron to lift me off and I'll let the woman go.'

'OK. Give us time. We'll get you a helicopter.' DI Carter lowered the megaphone and frowned. 'That's DCS Cameron's husband he's asking for. This is turning into a bloody police outing! How many more husbands and wives are going to get in on the act, for Christ's sake?' He turned to DS Cook. 'Why would he ask for Cameron personally? Why not just any old chopper?'

'I think maybe we just found our leak, sir,' said Judy Cook.

'Yeah and the sooner we plug it, the better.' He looked around. 'Where is DCS Cameron?'

'She's away to her bed with the swine flu, sir,' answered Maggie.

'No, she isn't.' Charlie's voice behind them was grim and angry. Her face was flushed and she was sweating profusely, the flu symptoms at their worst. She turned on Carter. 'I heard what you said about Donnie. Just what are you implying, Inspector?'

Carter replied, respectful but firm. 'Chief Superintendent, you shouldn't be out here in this weather, you'll catch pneumonia. Go back to bed and leave this to me.'

'I'll do no such thing. I'm the senior officer here and I'm staying.' She swayed slightly and leaned on Maggie who put an arm around her. 'My husband runs a successful commercial aviation service. He's well known all over the Highlands. Just because this "Ragnar" person asks for him by name does not mean Donnie's involved in anything criminal.'

'Maybe not, ma'am,' replied Carter, 'but someone has been selling classified information that could only have come from a police source. Until we know for certain, I'd like to play safe. And with respect, I'm the senior officer in charge of this operation.'

'For pity's sake, that's my wife up there!' yelled Jack. 'While you two are arguing about who's in charge, she could be bleeding to death. Can we cut the crap and get Donnie Cameron here?'

Charlie Cameron pulled out her phone and speed dialled the number. When it started to ring, DI Carter snatched it from her. 'If you don't mind, ma'am.' Graeme Carter hadn't been recruited to the Serious Crime mob because of his nice manners; he was there because he understood vicious criminals and the hold they had over the people who worked for them. DCS Cameron might be his superior in rank, but he had no intention of giving her the opportunity to warn her husband.

Donnie Cameron flipped open his phone and saw his wife's name. 'Charlie? Are you all right?'

'Mr Cameron? This isn't your wife, sir, it's DI Carter of the SCDEA. We need your help.' He explained the situation and a stunned Cameron agreed to come straight away.

After Carter had rung off, Donnie Cameron tried to ring Charlie's number again but her phone had been switched off. He took out a hip flask and knocked back a stiff dram to steady his shaking hands. He'd known something was wrong when the courier hadn't turned up in Inverness with the consignment of drugs. Now he knew why. The police had been tipped off and they'd intercepted the stuff at London Docks as soon as it arrived from Holland. Worried about the raids and Charlie, he'd flown back to Laxdale only to find it surrounded by armed police and a gun battle going on. He'd landed close by and switched off his lights so he couldn't be seen. Not knowing what else to do, he waited. Then he'd spotted the police launch just off the coast. They'd boarded the Gainsborough which was lit up like a Christmas tree. They'd have arrested Nicole by now. Gradually, they were picking off the whole organization, one by one.

And now the police wanted him to fly to Doomdochry. That copper had told him he was needed to lift a man from the top of the castle tower and fly him to Norway. He knew exactly who that man would be. He also knew enough about police procedure to realize they were just stalling for time; they weren't going to let him get away, no matter what they'd promised. That meant he'd land Donnie in it, too. He took another slug from his hip flask. How the bloody hell was he going to get out of this one? The short answer was that he wasn't, unless he could think of a last-ditch escape plan. He opened the throttle and the engine roared into life. The great blades slowly revolved, spun into a blur, then became invisible. The helicopter lifted and lurched into the night sky.

Corrie's teeth were chattering. Her panicky breaths emerged as little puffs of white smoke in the freezing air. If Jack doesn't get me down soon, I shan't have to worry about this man cutting my throat, I'll have died from exposure. I'm a living ice-sculpture, with the 'living' part rapidly diminishing. She was still desperately racking her brains, trying to remember what it was about her captor's voice and smell that was familiar. After all, he'd hardly spoken except to give her curt orders, in a hoarse whisper. But when he'd shouted to the policeman in charge, it suddenly came to her. She could scarcely believe it. It wasn't possible. Was it? Her nose was close to his neck and she took a deep sniff. Definitely the same aftershave, seductive and expensive. She challenged him. Probably not smart in her position, but then what did she have to lose?

'We've met before, haven't we?'

'No! Will yez shut the fuck up!' The Falls Road nuance was even more pronounced now he was agitated.

'Why are you wearing that ridiculous false beard,' jeered Corrie.

'Didn't I tell yez to belt up?' he retorted, angrily.

Corrie ploughed on, undaunted. 'When we last met in your club, three days ago, Mr Hadleigh, you were clean-shaven and wearing a smart blue dinner jacket. You haven't had time to grow a beard and it doesn't fool me for a moment.' Taking him by surprise, she wrenched an arm free and grabbed at his face. Half the beard came away in her numb fingers and he yelled with pain and rage. Twisting her arm brutally up her back, he forced her forward until she was leaning dangerously over the edge of the ramparts. She screamed and down below, the crowd gasped even louder. For a heart-stopping moment, Corrie thought she was done for. Then she saw lights in the sky and heard the unmistakable sound of an approaching chopper.

The helicopter seemed to hover interminably before setting down precisely in the middle of the cross that the police had marked out with lights. There was another wait until the blades finally stopped spinning.

'Where's my wife?' Donnie demanded, as two policemen frog-marched him from his helicopter to where DI Carter was waiting, in the sinister darkness of the MacAlister graveyard. 'I want to speak to Detective Chief Superintendent Cameron.'

'Take off your jacket, Cameron.' Carter's tone brooked no argument.

'What? Why should I?' Donnie still clung to a vague hope that he could get away. They had no proof he was mixed up in this. He'd pretend to co-operate with the police, pick up Hadleigh and then fly them both to Norway. All right, they'd lost the last consignment of heroin and it had been a big one, but the man had contacts all over the world. Hadleigh would soon be back in business but this time, without his accomplice because the police had already taken Nicole off the Gainsborough. It was then that the reality of his situation finally dawned on Donnie. Nicole wouldn't have thought twice about grassing up all Hadleigh's people if it meant a lighter sentence. She was completely without scruples, she'd made it clear that day on the cliffs. By now, the police would know he was in this shitty business right up to his neck. It was all over for him and Charlie. Police procedure was unequivocal. Discussing the details of a case with anyone, even a husband, was strictly against the rules. Charlie would be suspended while they carried out an enquiry. He wondered if they'd told her yet.

Carter was getting impatient. 'Don't piss me about, Cameron. Gimme the jacket!'

Donnie took off his distinctive 'Biggles' flying jacket and handed it over. Carter passed it to the waiting police helicopter pilot who shrugged it on and strode away towards Cameron's chopper. Two uniformed police took Donnie away in handcuffs to charge and caution him.

Minutes later, the sleek, powerful chopper with "Cameron Helicopter Services" on its dark blue flank thundered overhead. It hovered above the Death Tower and soon a rope ladder appeared with a harness attached. The pilot began to lower it to the two people waiting on the edge of the parapet.

Charlie Cameron clutched Dawes' arm. She was flushed and delirious with an astronomical temperature. 'Don't worry, Jack. It'll soon be over now and your wife will be safe. Donnie's an expert pilot. He'll wait until the bastard's dangling from the ladder then lower him to where Carter's men can grab him. If he jumps for it and tries to run, the marksmen will pick him off.'

'But Ragnar's no fool. He'll be expecting a trap.' Jack was far from confident that this tricky double-cross was going to work. 'What if he hangs on to Corrie, tries to take her with him? If they shoot him, he'll drop her.'

This possibility was exactly what was going through Ray Hadleigh's mind as he waited for the harness to descend. The police wouldn't risk a shot at him while he was holding Dawes's wife. He grasped Corrie tight around the waist. She tried to struggle, but he stuck her again with the point of the knife. She squealed. 'Stop it! They've sent the helicopter you asked for. Let me go.'

He snorted. 'And wait for them to shoot me like a fish in a barrel? I don't think so. You're coming with me.'

Corrie thought she would faint. She was terrified of heights. It had been bad enough just standing up here on this blooming great tower. The thought of being suspended from a helicopter like a spider on a thread was too awful to contemplate. Hadleigh would be safe enough; he'd be wearing the harness. She tried another tack, pathetic but all she could think of. She tried to sound confident but her lips were numb and her voice came out a querulous soprano.

'You made a mistake asking for Cameron's helicopter,' she piped, with unconvincing bravado. 'You think he's still working for you, but his wife's a senior police officer. She's down there now, giving him orders on the radio. Now you're trapped, he'll listen to her. He'll give you up to save his own skin.'

Hadleigh sneered unpleasantly in her ear. 'You're right. Cameron ignored my orders. I told him to chuck you in the sea but he didn't have the guts. Good thing he didn't because you're going to get me out of here.'

DI Carter didn't like what he was about to do. Detective Chief Superintendent Cameron was a good officer but she'd been foolish enough to share confidential police intelligence with a husband who'd betrayed her and Carter had no choice. His boss had just made that clear. With the helicopter about to whisk the suspect off the tower, there was no time to discuss it. He approached Charlie, flanked by two female constables, hoping he wouldn't need them.

'Chief Superintendent Cameron, I'm afraid I must ask you to accompany these two officers away from the scene.'

She turned angrily. 'What are you talking about, Inspector Carter? I've no intention of leaving while my husband's up there risking his life to help capture a dangerous criminal. I'll leave when I'm ready.' She turned back to where she was watching the dramatic airborne operation unfold, between Jack and Maggie. Carter nodded and the two officers insinuated themselves either side of her, each gently taking an arm. 'Get off me!' She tried to shake herself free. 'How dare you. I'm not leaving until my husband's safe.'

'That isn't Mr Cameron up there in the helicopter, ma'am,' said Carter. 'It's a police pilot. We've taken your husband into custody.'

'On what charge?' demanded Charlie.

'Among other offences, assisting in the trafficking of Class A drugs. And he's already admitted to selling classified police information. I'm obliged to inform you that you are suspended with immediate effect, pending an enquiry into how Mr Cameron obtained access to such information.'

DCS Cameron's mouth opened to protest, but nothing came out. Head down, she walked away between the two constables without a backward glance at Jack or Maggie.

The harness was just feet away now. Hadleigh wasn't feeling as cock-sure as he pretended. This was as close as he'd come to being caught in a long career of very lucrative crime and the extravagant lifestyle that went with it. He peered through the driving snow into the cockpit and was relieved to see Cameron's familiar flying jacket. Only Nicole and this gobshite of a copper's wife knew that Cameron was bent. The man was weak, a gutless lackey, he'd never have told his wife he was on the take. It was going to be all right. He'd get away, he always did, and he'd have that last big drug shipment that Cameron would have collected from the courier. Pity about Nicole. She had bottle and a nice sense of evil for a woman, but she wasn't getting any younger and he had no qualms about leaving her behind to face prison. There'd be plenty more women, younger and sexier, when Cameron dropped him in Scandinavia. He'd change his identity and start up again in Holland. Plenty of contacts and opportunities there and he had ample funds stashed away in off-shore accounts. He gripped Corrie tighter and shuffled them both closer to the edge, ready to reach out for the rope ladder.

Corrie had no illusions about his intentions. As soon as he was winched up and safe, he'd drop her. She shut her eyes tight, wishing with all her might that someone – anyone – would come and save her. If she could just survive this, she promised never to interfere in Jack's police work again as long as she lived, which at the moment could be about five minutes. Suddenly, she felt Hadleigh's grip slacken and tentatively, she opened one eye. He was backing away. His face, with the beard ripped away, was white and contorted with fear.

'Go away.' His voice was a terrified whisper. 'Leave me alone.'

Corrie couldn't understand what had got into him. Surely he wasn't letting her go? He'd just said he needed her to make his escape. Then she realized he wasn't speaking to her. His terrified gaze was fixed on a point further down the wall-walk. She looked but there was nobody there. Hadleigh flailed his arms, as if trying to shove something away from him.

'No! Get away!' he shrieked. 'Don't come near me.' Frantic with fear, he looked wildly about him for some means of escape and spotted the nylon rope ladder, still hanging some ten feet clear of the parapet. Desperately, he backed up, took a run and jumped for it. His fingertips, numb with cold, brushed the bottom rung. He clawed at it desperately, before it slipped from his grasp and he plummeted into the darkness, thrashing and screaming. Corrie covered her face with her hands and collapsed in a heap on the stone parapet.

When she opened her eyes, she was sitting on the battlements with a blanket around her. The Shetland snowflakes, once so harsh and hostile, seemed suddenly festive and Christmassy because Jack was there, cradling her in his arms.

'It's paint,' he kept crooning into her hair. 'It's only bloody paint, you daft bat. Thank you, God. Oh, thank you, God.'

Corrie looked around warily. 'Is Hadleigh dead?'

'Well, what do you think?' asked Jack, still holding her tight. 'Even international crime lords don't bounce back after falling eighty-odd feet. Corrie, what the hell are you doing here? You nearly gave me a heart attack.'

Her brain began to clear then, and she remembered the old man called Geordie that she'd left behind in the cowshed at Laxdale. 'Jack, I'll tell you everything but first, you have to get an ambulance. There's an old man with his head bashed in and he ...'

'It's all right, sweetheart. Carter's men found Geordie when they raided the place. He'll have been airlifted to hospital by now. Come on, let's get you down off this blasted death tower.'

'Death tower's right,' she agreed, shuddering. 'Oh, Jack, why on earth did Hadleigh jump like that? It was so weird. I'd just prayed for someone to come and save me, like you do when you're about to die horribly, and suddenly it happened. One minute he was the callous killer, planning to get away in Donnie's helicopter after dumping me, like unwanted ballast. Next thing, he was backing away, rolling his eyes. He saw something that terrified him and started screaming, "Annie! Karen! Leave me alone!". I looked where he was pointing but I didn't see anyone. Then he leapt over the edge and I passed out. What did he see that I couldn't?'

The ever vigilant Sergeant Malone who had been hovering, tactfully, now came forward with more blankets. 'At a guess, I'd say he saw the two women he murdered; Karen Baxter and her daughter, Annie, known to us as Astrid.' He coughed discreetly. 'I'd get up off that cold stone floor if I were you, Mrs D. It'll give you terrible "farmers".'

CHAPTER TWENTY-FIVE

CHRISTMAS DAY

By six o'clock that evening, everything was relatively calm. The shattered remains of Ray Hadleigh alias Ragnar Redbeard, had been taken to the mortuary where, in a macabre twist of fate, he was placed in a freezer drawer between Fraser Grant and Flora MacAlister. Back at Inverness Police HQ, DI Carter and DS Cook were questioning Nicole MacAlister who was singing like the proverbial canary. Far from mourning the death of her lover, she'd been furious when she found out Hadleigh hadn't waited for her to fetch him in the speedboat but attempted to escape by helicopter, leaving her behind. Now all she cared about was persuading Randall to get her the best defence lawyers that his considerable fortune could buy. Randall didn't want to know, and despite her pleas, refused even to speak to her. He'd tolerated her lovers and her selfish extravagance for most of their married life, but when the police told him they were charging Nicole with murder and accessory to murder in respect of Flora MacAlister, Karen Baxter and Fraser Grant, it was the end of the line.

He told DI Carter, 'I'm a billionaire and you don't make that kind of loot by being Snow White. But I've never dealt drugs and I've never made money out of other folks' misery, like those poor illegals that Hadleigh has been exploiting. As far as I'm concerned, the guy got what was coming to him, and Nicole is guilty as hell.' He hadn't even wanted to apply for her extradition, so she could be tried in the States. Her crimes had been committed in the UK, he said, and it was only right that she should face justice there.

After all that had happened, Randall P. MacAlister no longer had the stomach for developing a Highland Theme Park on the site of his Scottish ancestors. A sad and disillusioned man, he had been cleared of any knowledge or involvement in Nicole's crimes and had returned to the Gainsborough with instructions to the crew to take him home to Seattle as fast as they could.

In the library incident room of Doomdochry Castle, Dawes and Malone were packing up their files, ready to be flown home to London, courtesy of the SCDEA. It was a special concession as public transport on Christmas Day at such short notice would be nigh on impossible, especially in bad weather.

DC Maggie Mellis had been given some well-earned leave and since she was already near to her family home at Baltasound, she planned to spend Christmas there. She hovered, now, reluctantly waiting for the Met officers to formally release her. It had been a shock seeing DCS Cameron led away under suspension and an even bigger shock when Maggie learned that she had immediately offered her resignation which had been accepted. Charlie had been her mentor since she joined the Northern Constabulary. Maggie looked up to her and now she felt let down and sad for her boss. She wondered what the New Year would bring. After the excitement of working with a Metropolitan Murder Investigation Team, the idea of going back to uniform was dispiriting.

Corrie was in the kitchen being looked after by Moragh. They had struck up an immediate friendship after Moragh learned that it was Corrie who helped Geordie when he lay near to death in the cowshed. Between them, they'd sponged off the worst of the paint and re-bandaged her elbow and head so she looked less like the walking wounded from Scutari. Privately, Jack hoped they weren't exchanging mutton recipes.

Bugsy's phone rang and he chatted cheerfully for some time before ending the conversation with: 'And a very merry Christmas to you, too, Julie, love.' He turned to Jack. 'Good news, guv. That was DC Molesworth with the guff on what's been going on back at the factory. While it was all kicking off up here, the Serious Crime lads launched simultaneous raids on Hadleigh's Blue Ray Clubs. They've all been closed down and a number of arrests made, including the gangs involved in the illegal immigrant trafficking. And they've seized a whacking great shipment of cocaine and collared the courier who was supposed to bring it to Inverness and pass it to Donnie Cameron. But here's the *really* good news. They've nicked Ducky Drake.'

'Don't tell me the "idle wanker" police have caught up with him at last,' said Corrie. She brushed off the flakes of paint that had showered her when she shoved open the ailing library doors. Paint suddenly seemed to have an affinity for her that she could well do without.

'No, Mrs D. Turns out he was the leak at the London end. Ducky was being paid by Hadleigh to tip him off when the police got too close.'

'Blimey, Garwood isn't going to like that,' said Jack. 'Donald Drake was his blue-eyed boy. It was Garwood who recommended him for promotion to DI. Mind you, it explains why Drake was so keen to close the case on Karen Baxter. By claiming that Lenny Lennox murdered her and then committed suicide out of remorse, he cleared it all up nicely and prevented any further investigation. No doubt he got a nice drink from Hadleigh in return. Garwood's going to have to duck pretty smartly when this one hits the fan.'

'Serves him right, guv,' growled Bugsy. 'If you remember, we were on our way to give the Blue Ray Club a tug when bloody Garwood reassigned us.'

Jack nodded. 'The irony is that Garwood had no idea he was sending us to investigate a murder on Shetland that was connected to the ones we'd left behind in London. He just wanted to get rid of us until after the DAC's visit.'

'If we'd interviewed Hadleigh first, there was a good chance that when we met Ragnar Redbeard, we'd have sussed that he and Hadleigh were one and the same, like your missus did. The bloke certainly had the luck of the devil.'

'Until the De'il himself took it back again, ' said Maggie.

'If Hadleigh's gone where he deserves to go, he'll be able to complain in person,' said Corrie, with feeling.

'The SCDEA lads got the thugs who killed Lenny, poor little sod,' said Bugsy. 'Couple of Hadleigh's hard men. The same gorillas he brought with him to Laxdale to put the frighteners on Grant. They were the blokes Geordie saw kicking in his front door and he assumed they'd come to collect his gambling debts.'

'I noticed them the last time we went to Laxdale to find out whose Thor's Hammer was missing. They were lurking at the back, dressed very unconvincingly as Vikings, presumably so they could report back about how much we knew. One of them had a long scar down his cheek and the other was peeling an orange with a fruit knife. Probably the same one he used to cut out Lenny's tongue. Very nasty customers.

Not the sort you'd expect to find in a gentle Shetland commune. But then, neither was Hadleigh. Ragnar Redbeard was an inspired disguise. It was the Edgar Allen Poe theory, the best place to hide something is among a lot of similar things where it won't be conspicuous. After all, apart from Valgerd, who can tell one Viking from another?'

'Remember Thora Droopy-Drawers saying Ragnar often brought "lost souls" to the commune for short stays? I reckon they were either villains, lying low when the heat was on, or illegal immigrants, waiting to be smuggled into Scandinavia. Nice little earner, Laxdale.'

Jack's phone rang. It was George Garwood and he wasn't full of Christmas cheer. At least, not where Jack was concerned.

'What the bloody hell have you been playing at, Inspector Dawes?'

'And a merry Christmas to you and Mrs Garwood, too, sir,' said Jack, ignoring his furious tone. He could hear Bing Crosby's "White Christmas" and plummy laughter in the background, so it was one of Cynthia's political parties aimed at impressing the right people.

'Never mind all that!' barked Garwood. 'I sent you to investigate a simple suspicious death. A mission of mercy, to help out a hard-pressed fellow officer, and what do you do…?'

Jack took a breath to tell him but Garwood blustered on. 'No, don't bother to argue, I'll tell you what you did. You blundered in and trampled all over an undercover operation that had taken months to set up. You destroyed the chance of an injection of much-needed US dollars to the Shetland economy by accusing a billionaire's wife of murder. And not only were you responsible for the resignation of a very good Chief Superintendent, but you had her husband arrested in the process.' His voice rose to shrill and accusing incredulity. 'The Camerons were good friends of my wife and me; we were all members of St Andrews and the Speyside Angling Association, the enjoyment of which you have effectively wrecked for ever.' He paused to take a deep breath and keep his rising blood pressure in check. 'I suspect you also had a hand in the arrest of Detective Inspector Drake, another excellent officer lost to the service. Can't I trust you to do anything properly?'

'But, sir, DI Drake had been taking bribes. He was …'

'Don't try to deflect the blame, Dawes. It's total chaos down here. The Anti-Corruption brigade's all over us, demanding information and impounding files. My office looks like a bomb's hit it. Just get yourself and Malone back here immediately and sort it out! Do you hear me?'

'Yes, sir,' said Jack, 'but the operation actually went rather well. The

SCDEA got their man and all his international contacts, and Customs recovered a consignment of cocaine valued at …' But he was wasting his breath. Garwood had rung off.

While Jack was having his ear chewed off, Corrie was trying to disentangle all the facts in her bemused mind. London and Laxdale seemed too far apart for any criminal network to span effectively, but of course, that was the very thing that made it successful. Hadleigh had never been arrested so he wasn't on the police computer and he didn't reckon on any London cops coming that far north and recognizing him. Law of probabilities said he should have been safe. While the Met tried to trace drug shipments coming into London Docks, Hadleigh's men retrieved them from the illegal immigrants and couriers whisked them to Inverness. There, Donnie Cameron flew the stuff to Shetland and handed it over to Hadleigh, who was posing as an eco-eccentric and dismissed as harmless. It was a brilliant set up and would have gone on working if it hadn't been for undercover police infiltrating the organization.

'How did they find out about Donald Drake?' Corrie wanted to know.

'Hadleigh's driver in London. He was an undercover copper.' said Malone. 'He drove Hadleigh to a meet with Ducky in a country pub, out of town. Saw money exchange hands and took pics.'

'I met the chauffeur at the Blue Ray Club when I was doing some sleuthing for Jack,' said Corrie. 'He wasn't particularly helpful. Quite brusque, in fact. I wondered why at the time.'

'Yeah, he told Julie you'd had a chat,' said Bugsy, diplomatically. 'He was worried you didn't realize the danger of asking too many questions and he tried to discourage you.'

'Oh, nothing discourages Miss Marple, here, once she's got up a head of steam,' retorted Jack. 'One of these days, Corrie …' He didn't finish the threat because there was a tap on the door and the MacAlister family trooped in.

Mack was diffident. 'I wonder if we might have a word, before you leave, Inspector Dawes. My father has something to tell you.' He didn't exactly shove the old Earl forward but it was close.

'Whisky,' muttered the Earl.

'No thank you, sir,' said Jack, 'it's a bit early even for Christmas Day.'

'I think what Father is trying to say is that he and Mother have been running an illicit whisky still at Doomdochry Castle. It was originally set up in the tower bedroom. You may have noticed the lingering smell, Sergeant.'

Bugsy grinned. 'Well, I didn't think the "spirit" I could smell up there was Green Jean.' He realized now why the stuff tasted so fiery; it was probably ninety per cent proof. The sort of booze that sends you blind.

Mack continued. 'They concealed all the equipment in the Guard Chamber before you arrived, and when you said you wanted to explore the tunnel, Geordie volunteered to go down first in order to move it.'

'Really?' said Jack, deadpan. 'Well, I'm not sure what to say ...'

'At first, the MacAlister Malt was only for personal consumption,' explained Mack, 'but when Randall arrived and expressed such a liking for it, they increased production so that he could ship it back home. Soon, the orders were coming in thick and fast. Randall must have intoxicated the whole of Washington with it and he paid extremely well.'

So that's what he was up to when I overheard him on the phone yesterday morning, thought Bugsy. He wasn't smuggling drugs, he was flogging cases of dodgy MacAlister Malt to his buddies back in the States.

'We knew it was against the law, but we needed the money badly,' said Lady Alice, forgetting she was only supposed to speak Shetland. 'The castle's falling down and Alistair wanted to preserve it for when Mack inherited the title. Shall we be sent to prison, Mr Dawes?'

Jack reckoned that manufacturing whisky without a licence might cause the lads in HM Revenue and Customs to wet themselves, but as far as he was concerned, it paled into insignificance compared to the huge drugs network that they'd put out of business.

'If you destroy the still and promise faithfully never to do it again, I think we might overlook it just this once, don't you, Sergeant Malone?'

'Reckon we might stretch a point, guv. Of course, if you've got a couple of bottles lying around that you'd like us to seize ...'

'Oh, we shan't be making any more, Sergeant, because we shan't be here,' said Lady Alice.

'Now that Randall won't be buying Doomdochry for development, and Mel and I definitely don't want to live here,' said Mack, 'Father has finally agreed to put the castle in the care of Historic Scotland. Geordie and Moragh are to take over Fraser's cottage and my parents are coming home with us to Surrey. The police found Aunt Flora's stolen Landseer when they searched the Gainsborough, so the money from the sale will buy them a cosy cottage with central heating and proper sanitation. They want to be near us, and ...' he patted Melissa's flat tummy affectionately, '... their grandson.'

Rats! cursed Maggie, uncharitably. No wonder the silly cow kept throwing up. Some women get all the luck and it's always the skinny, glamorous, witless ones.

Dawes and Malone offered their congratulations and Melissa blushed. 'The scan showed that our baby's a boy so, of course, we'll call him Alistair, in the family tradition. I suppose he'll become the 22nd Earl of Doomdochry.'

'Over my dead body,' said Mack, oblivious of the satire. 'And we'll call him John or James, anything but Alistair. With Flora gone and Fraser dead, there can be no further speculation about inheritance and I have no desire to pass on to my son a lineage that's inherently ill-fated. The misfortune was brought upon us in 1490 when the first Earl, mad with jealousy and greed, murdered poor Lady Jean. In the last fortnight alone, four more people have died on Doomdochry soil. The MacAlister dynasty ends here. Right, Father?'

The old Earl's smile was a fusion of relief and regret. 'Right, Son.'

The police helicopter lifted and made a final circuit of Doomdochry. The waving figure of Constable Maggie Mellis became a midget and she gradually turned away, back inside the comparative shelter of the castle to collect her belongings and make her way home. Jack smiled to himself. She didn't know it yet, but Maggie was to be offered a job with the SCDEA. DI Carter had been very impressed with the way she'd piled in and beaten him up in the tunnel. He said she was the kind of officer that he preferred to have on his side in a fight. DC Mellis would, Jack knew, be overjoyed.

Malone tightened his safety harness. 'Back to civilization, eh folks?'

'I don't know about civilization,' said Corrie. 'One in five Londoners thinks a haggis is a wild animal. But I shall be glad to get home.'

'Didn't you like the Shetlands?' asked Jack, watching the islands beneath them slip quickly away to be replaced by the ocean.

'Don't get me wrong,' said Corrie. 'I liked the majesty and grandeur of the Doomdochry landscape but I wasn't keen on the sanitation. They're obviously complete strangers to Harpic.'

'Well, I'll be glad to get some decent grub inside me,' said Malone. 'Reckon I've lost half a stone while I've been up here.'

'Tell you what. If you don't have any other plans, why not come to dinner tomorrow night, with Jack and me? There's loads of Christmas food going begging, including a ruddy great turkey and all the trimmings. And I need someone who won't be witheringly patronizing …' she stared pointedly at Jack, '… to explain things to me. What d'you say, Bugsy?'

Bugsy's stomach rumbled in anticipation. 'Lead me to it, Mrs D.'

CHAPTER TWENTY-SIX

BOXING DAY

On Boxing Day evening, the deplorable events of Christmas Day at Doomdochry seemed hundreds of miles away, which of course, they were. Seated at the Dawes' dinner-table, Jack and Bugsy had started on the bread rolls while they waited for the turkey to finish browning. Corrie drifted in from the kitchen together with appetizing cooking smells. She was still trying to make some sense out of the last two weeks.

'So Astrid was Karen Baxter's daughter, Annie,' said Corrie.

'That's right,' said Jack. 'Dr Hardacre's autopsy report showed that Karen had given birth some years ago. She was only seventeen and the baby went into care, but Karen kept in touch with the care home, although we never found any photos of a daughter among the things in her flat. When little Annie reached sixteen, full of the usual lofty ideals for world peace and saving the planet, she left the children's home and joined up with a convoy of travellers.'

Bugsy took up the story. 'Annie Baxter drifted for a couple of years, unsettled and in need of family roots. When she was eighteen, she traced her mum through the local authority who only held Karen's address as the Blue Ray Club. Karen cared about her daughter, but didn't want her to visit because she was working as a tom by then and didn't want her kid to end up on the game or get into drugs, like she had. At the post-mortem, Big Ron had found old needle tracks on her arms. Annie came to London anyway and made straight for the Blue Ray Club, looking for her mother. Although Hadleigh said in his statement that he only knew Karen by sight, she was, in fact, working for him as "Angel", giving him a freebie when he felt like roughing it, with a bit of dealing and laundering on the side to supplement her income,'

215

added Bugsy. 'Hence the five grand in euros we found, hidden in her freezer.'

'Karen Baxter also performed another valuable service for Hadleigh,' said Jack. 'The Jobcentre told us that Karen once had a proper job, something in the theatre. But then she left and dropped off their national insurance radar. The job was wardrobe assistant and make-up artist.'

'I get it,' said Corrie. 'She did the Viking outfit and the beard for when Hadleigh was hiding out at Laxdale as Ragnar, and the fake tan when he was being Ray, swanking it up in his Blue Ray Clubs. It was very clever and utterly convincing; no one would have guessed it was the same man.'

'You did,' said Jack.

'Yes, but that's because I'm amazingly observant, which is why I make such an excellent sleuth and the perfect foil for a non-intuitive Detective Inspector in the MIT.'

Jack dismissed this blatant piece of self-praise by chucking a bread roll at her. 'Anyhow, Karen was worried about her little Annie on the loose in the big city, and was foolish enough to mention it to Hadleigh. By this time, things were hotting up for him in London and he'd set up his Laxdale commune on Shetland as a place to lie low when he needed it and a safer route for exporting drugs and dirty money out of the UK. He needed to keep Karen sweet because she was useful to him, so six months ago, he offered to give Annie a home at Laxdale where she'd be looked after by the women. Hadleigh turned on the charm and of course, the poor kid fell for him. That's when she became Astrid.'

'It was about that time that Randall and Nicole MacAlister arrived in Doomdochry to trace his family tree. Nicole says she had a chance meet with Hadleigh when he was being Ragnar and discovered they were kindred souls. And they certainly were; evil, ruthless and greedy. She flew down to London and spent weekends with him at his flat, telling Randall she was shopping at Harrods and bringing stuff back in their carrier bags. And when she took herself off to the Gainsborough, to pamper her ravaged body, Ray went along to help.' Bugsy scratched his head. 'I don't understand women. Why do they never see through blokes like Hadleigh?'

'Because they're blinded by superficial, inconsequential things, like devastating good looks, a Ferrari and the size of his … er, wallet, I expect,' said Corrie. 'How come you're not married, Bugsy?'.

'Me? Well, it's always the same, Mrs D. I meet someone; they ask what I do for a living. I say, "I'm a copper, d'you wanna leave now?" and they go.' Bugsy's stomach growled and Corrie pushed a plate of mince pies towards him.

'Tell me why Hadleigh murdered Annie and Karen.' Corrie felt a deep sadness that mother and daughter had both met their deaths at the hands of Ray alias Ragnar. In a weird way, it was thanks to them that Hadleigh hadn't killed her too. She'd been on the very brink of death, praying for someone to save her, and suddenly he saw them, Karen and Annie. Corrie reckoned it didn't much matter what your views were about restless spirits and retribution, the fact remained that whatever it was Hadleigh saw had saved her life.

'Annie or Astrid, as she preferred to be called, became deeply infatuated with Hadleigh.' Jack thought he'd better explain, seeing that Bugsy had just put a whole mince pie in his mouth. 'He derived some kind of perverted pleasure from sleeping with both mother and daughter, safely apart at opposite ends of the UK. Then, as Flora MacAlister told us, Astrid got pregnant. She became a nuisance then, nagging Hadleigh to marry her. He told her to get rid of the baby and go home to her mother. She knew about his dual identity and she'd learned from Karen how he made his money, but it was only when she found out about Nicole, his rich, classy mistress, that jealousy made her vindictive and she threatened to shop him to the police. That effectively signed her death warrant. Hadleigh lured her up the Death Tower, injected her with heroin, and chucked her off, hoping the police would think it was suicide. And we did, initially. What Hadleigh didn't know, was that Astrid had become friends with Fraser Grant and told him everything.'

Bugsy swallowed the last of his mince pie and helped himself to another. 'When Ray told Karen her daughter had taken an overdose and killed herself, she didn't believe him. As a reformed drug user, she'd been sure that Annie never touched the stuff. Lenny Lennox overheard her on the phone in the Blue Ray Club saying, "I'll get you for this, you bastard. I know you did it and I can prove it". Hadleigh went straight round to her flat to shut her up. Took off his clothes, pretending he'd come for a shag, and attacked her. She grabbed a knife to defend herself; he wrestled it off her and slit her throat with it. Then he wiped it clean, washed off the blood, put his clothes back on, and calmly dialled 999 from the phone box outside, reported finding a body, and hung up. He disguised his voice so the emergency switchboard operator couldn't be sure if it was male or female.'

Corrie frowned. 'How do we know all this? I mean, the people involved are all dead; Hadleigh, Astrid, Karen, Fraser Grant and Aunt Flora.'

'Nicole MacAlister isn't,' said Jack, 'and she learned the whole story from Hadleigh and Grant. According to DC Molesworth, she's getting it all off her silicone chest as fast as she can, hoping it will impress the judge and get her a lighter sentence.'

'After he killed her, Hadleigh nicked Karen's phone so we wouldn't trace the calls he made to her. Then, being in something of a hurry, he used it to contact Nicole MacAlister at Doomdochry Castle and ask for her help. It was Nicole who phoned Honest Harry, the bookie, pretending to be Angel and putting Lenny Lennox in the frame. SIM cards, don't you love 'em? Boil 'em, bake 'em, bash 'em, they still tell tales. Harry said the caller was definitely a woman and the accent might have been Irish but of course, it was Yankee. She's a real nasty piece of work, that Nicole. She didn't give a sod about Hadleigh killing people or forcing young girls into prostitution. She'd even been shagging Fraser Grant, hoping he'd steal Flora's Landseer for her, because he was one of the few people the old girl would let into her room. Astrid told Fraser all about Hadleigh's criminal activities, but instead of coming to us, the stupid bugger, up to his neck in debt, tried to blackmail him. He was even daft enough to tell Nicole that he knew who'd killed Astrid. Of course, she tipped off Hadleigh, and together, they planned to shut him up. She went to Fraser's cottage that night to snort a few lines of the old devil's dandruff, shagged him a couple of times and got him drunk. Hadleigh turned up later, and between them, they forced more whisky down Grant's throat and tied a freezer bag over his head. It was only afterwards, they realized Fraser had told everything to Aunt Flora, so she had to be silenced, too. Hadleigh couldn't do it without being seen, so Nicole sneaked in, put a pillow over Flora's face, then pinched the painting on her way out, along with the post-its. Flora had jotted down everything Fraser told her in case she forgot.'

Corrie sighed. 'Dear God, Bugsy, what a truly dreadful couple. Like Bonny and Clyde; Thelma and Louise; Barbie and Ken.'

'George and Cynthia,' muttered Jack.

'DC Molesworth said Nicole denied having anything to do with the

murders at first. Said they were all down to Hadleigh and although she
admitted nicking the painting, she swore Flora was sleeping peacefully
when she left. She hadn't touched her. Then they told her they'd
matched her DNA with samples extracted from the Thor's Hammer
under the bed. Hadleigh had taken it off Astrid's body when he went
down to check she was dead.'

'Why was Nicole wearing it? It's a bit macabre, isn't it?'

'She was a macabre woman. She made Hadleigh give it to her, got
some kind of ghoulish thrill from wearing it. She said it didn't prove
she'd killed the old lady. Then they said they'd taken DNA from her
condensed breath on the back of the pillow she used to smother the old
lady.'

Corrie was fascinated. 'Can Forensics actually do that, Bugsy?'

'Doubt it. Did the trick though, she coughed to the lot.'

'Isn't that a bit ... well, unethical?'

'Not at all,' declared Jack. 'It's called giving the wheels of justice a
little squirt of oil.' His mobile rang. He pulled it out and looked at it.
'Speaking of little squirts, it's Garwood.' He answered it, grinning.
'Good evening, sir. I trust you and Mrs Garwood had a pleasant
Christmas Day.'

At the other end, Garwood was almost dancing with excitement.
'Have you seen the BBC news, Jack?'

Jack raised his eyebrows in mock wonderment. So it's 'Jack' now, is
it? Yesterday, it was 'Dawes' or 'Inspector'. He tried to sound
respectful. 'Er ... not yet, sir. Anything interesting?'

'I should say so,' enthused Garwood. 'We made the headlines. I've
had the DAC on, offering his congratulations. It's another triumph for
my MIT and a tremendous boost for our Home Office statistics.'

And, thought Jack, a glowing success in the nick of time before
Garwood's New Year promotion board.

George was still ranting, happily. 'We got him, Jack, an international
drugs baron. The Serious Crime boys have been after him for years and
we can all take the credit. A chance piece of luck on your part, scien-
tific skill and expertise from Forensics, a bit of undercover stuff from
the Scots lads plus solid, devoted team work under my supervision.
Glad they exposed Drake, at last. Surprised *you* didn't spot what he
was up to, Jack; I've had my eye on him for some time. Not the sort of
officer we want in the police service, very bad type. Switch on your TV,
old man. The news is on again in five minutes. Oh, and best wishes to

the wife. Tell her the party food was excellent as usual.' The phone went dead, no doubt so that Garwood could brag to the next person on his list. Jack switched on the TV just in time for the BBC's main headlines.

English and Scottish police launched simultaneous raids during the early hours of Christmas Day in a co-ordinated hit aimed at smashing a major drugs and illegal immigrants empire. They arrested more than 50 people across several countries, including 11 in Scotland and 10 in Norway. Scotland's Crime and Drug Enforcement Agency said in a statement:

'The target was a criminal network suspected of trafficking huge quantities of drugs and illegal immigrants and of laundering hundreds of millions of pounds, dollars, and euros in criminal profits. The gang's crime lord, Ray Hadleigh, a 43-year-old Irish-born club-owner living in Knightsbridge, was traced to Laxdale, an eco-commune on the Shetland Island of Unst where he had been hiding. He died from a fall whilst attempting to evade arrest. Police officers detained commune members, a commercial helicopter pilot, several city mobsters and four London lawyers.'

Metropolitan Police officer, Detective Chief Superintendent George Garwood, called it 'a hugely successful strike against well-established gangsters operating out of England, Scotland, Scandinavia and beyond. The scale of this joint initiative by law enforcement agencies from different countries is an indication of how prolific we think this network was. Today's arrests will have dealt a major blow to an organized criminal industry suspected of supplying drugs and illegal immigrant sex workers to gangs in cities across the UK and elsewhere in Europe. We also believe this network has been offering a global investment service, ploughing hundreds of millions of pounds of dirty cash into offshore accounts, companies, and property on behalf of criminals. A financial investigation is already under way.'

A Metropolitan Police Inspector who sold classified information has also been arrested. Donald Drake, a married father of two, supplied Hadleigh with details of police inquiries, including the investigations of two murders, and in return for his services, received large sums of money. He has admitted to misconduct in a public office and perverting the course of justice. Chief

Superintendent George Garwood said the disgraced officer had damaged the morale of the police and undermined public confidence. 'The message must go out that this sort of behaviour cannot be tolerated and will be severely punished'.

There was a photo of a smiling Garwood in his best uniform, gleaming with insignia and looking smug. Jack switched him off.

'No mention of the poor bloody infantry, then, guv?' said Bugsy.

'Or the poor bloody infantry's wife who got stabbed in the neck and drenched in blood,' added Corrie.

'You fibber, it was paint,' protested Jack.

'There was a bit of blood. Look. Just there.' Corrie pointed to a small square of sticking plaster on her throat where Hadleigh had stuck her with the tip of his blade. 'And don't forget my head wound and my bad elbow, all in the line of duty. I should get compensation!' She made for the kitchen, calling out, 'Don't go anywhere, you guys. I'm about to dish up.'

Malone chuckled to himself. 'Tell you what, guv, that Melissa was a bit of a lark. She was still taking the piss right to the end, even though she knew we'd sussed her little game with the projector.'

Jack was puzzled. 'How d'you mean, Bugsy?'

'When we were leaving in the helicopter and it circled Doomdochry Castle, I happened to glance down at the Death Tower. And there she was.'

'What? Melissa?'

'No, Green Jean. All of her, this time. She was in one piece, not just the top half. And she didn't have that morbid face on her, she actually smiled and waved. Clever, eh? I wonder how Melissa did it, out in the open like that.'

'Melissa didn't do it,' said Corrie, poking her head round the kitchen door. 'She couldn't have. Mack and Melissa were standing in the castle courtyard with Maggie, waving goodbye.'

'Well, what did I see on the tower, then?'

'The real ghost of Lady Jean MacAlister, of course,' replied Corrie.

'You can't have a "real ghost",' carped Jack. 'It's an oxymoron.'

Corrie ignored him. 'Green Jean's at rest now, because her dastardly murder has been properly avenged.'

'How d'you work that one out?' asked Bugsy. He'd never understood women's thought processes.

221

'It's obvious, isn't it? Astrid was a passionate young woman in love with an older man, who was using her for his own selfish ends, just as the Earl of Doomdochry had used Lady Jean. Subsequently, both women were murdered by their callous, evil lovers. Then the Earl fell from the parapet one dark, winter's night and smashed his brains out on the rocks below. Before he fell, he was heard screaming in terror and begging to be left alone although there was no one up there with him. When Hadleigh leapt off the tower, after the same terrified performance, it kind of evened up the score, so Green Jean doesn't have to haunt any longer.'

Malone was still mulling over this obscure logic when his mobile rang. 'Hello, Julie. Make it quick, love, I'm just about to eat me dinner. What?' He listened for a few moments, then swore. 'Bum-holes! What kind of miserable, selfish, inconsiderate, heathen piss-head gets himself murdered at Christmas?' There was a pause. 'Ah. A vicar.' Bugsy's stomach was rumbling, begging for food. 'It never rains but it flippin' buckets down.' He took the address. 'Yes, the Inspector's here, he's putting on his coat. We're on our way....'

EXTRACT FROM "A HISTORY OF HAUNTED SCOTTISH CASTLES"
DOOMDOCHRY CASTLE – SHETLAND

Doomdochry Castle, on the Shetland island of Unst, was once an imposing fortress set in a wild, desolate landscape. Even today, it is an impressive ruin. It was built in 1469 by Alistair MacAlister, Earl of Doomdochry, and held by the MacAlister family for over five centuries. The castle has one of the most intriguing ghost stories of its time and certainly one of the most gruesome.

The first Earl was well into his fifties when he married Lady Jean, an attractive young woman of eighteen from a rich family. Although he had no proof of infidelity, one fateful day, he strangled her in a jealous rage. When he realized what he had done, he panicked. In order to conceal the poor woman's body, he hacked it in two with his sword and hid her top half under the floor boards of the tower bedroom. Her bottom half, still clad in her green, blood-spattered skirts, is believed to have been buried in the family cemetery.

From then on, strange happenings plagued Doomdochry. The castle was persistently haunted by the phantom of Lady Jean's upper half, her lovely face contorted by despair and sorrow. The tower bedroom, where most manifestations occurred, had to be abandoned. Locals reported seeing her lower half walking in the family burial ground and refused to go near it after dark. Manifestations were said to presage misfortune or the death of a MacAlister. The apparition, wearing an emerald-coloured velvet cloak, became known as Green Jean and green became regarded as the colour of death.

In more recent times, a spate of murders occurred in and around Doomdochry Castle, following several reported sightings of Green Jean. Eerily, one of the victims was a young woman of similar age and appearance to Lady Jean. She was thrown from the top of the castle's massive keep by her lover. Before he could be brought to justice, the killer also met his death by jumping from the same lofty tower. Witnesses allege he was escaping the demonic green eyes of his victim whose phantom bore down on him, pointing an accusing finger. Since his death, no further sightings of either ghost have been reported.

However, on crisp winter nights, when the moon shows papery white against a deep cobalt sky and the Shetland wind moans in and out of the castle turrets, the figure of a handsome man in a blue dinner jacket appears on the parapet of the Death Tower. Witnesses say he is smoking a cigarette and looking wistfully out to sea. It seems that the colour of death has changed from green to blue.